"THE LAST THING I REMEMBER IS DARKNESS . . .

What happened to me? Give it to me straight."

"Well, you got banged up pretty badly, Doctor Tabarde. You came to us a basket case. Severe neck and spinal injuries, fractured skull, you were comatose with irreversible cerebral damage—"

"Irreversible?"

"Yes, it was an extremely complicated surgical procedure. We had to effect extensive nerve grafting, nysteel spinal reinforcement, polymeric—"

"You said irreversible cerebral damage."

The surgeon nodded. "We had no choice but to go ahead with a Blagoronov-12 procedure."

"Are you telling me I've had my brain removed?"

Great Science Fiction from SIGNET

JEHAD

by
Nicholas Yermakov

Ⓢ
A SIGNET BOOK
NEW AMERICAN LIBRARY

Copyright © 1983 by Nicholas Yermakov

SIGNET, SIGNET CLASSIC, MENTOR, PLUME, MERIDIAN and NAL BOOKS
are published by The New American Library, Inc.,
1633 Broadway, New York, New York 10019

First Printing, January, 1984

1 2 3 4 5 6 7 8 9

PRINTED IN THE UNITED STATES OF AMERICA

For Tanya

Prologue

Sander Viselius was a plague child. A great deal of his life had been spent in almost constant pain, both physical and emotional. His mother had died shortly after he was born, a victim of the biochemical self-destruction induced by the plague drug. His father had died just as horribly, not long afterward. It was a miracle that Viselius had survived. Few plague children ever reached adulthood.

There had been a time when Viselius had despised the fact of his existence, had wished fervently that he had never been born. The only thing that had kept him from taking his own life had been the certain knowledge that in doing so, he would be condemning his soul to far greater agonies than those suffered by his body with every waking moment. God had visited upon him the agonies of Job. Viselius could curse himself, but he would not curse God. He had accepted the fact that it was his lot in life to bear his torture and survive.

While he was still a child, Viselius had learned that the plague children were the victims of humanity's sinful pride and folly. He had been taught that the sins of the fathers are visited upon their children. His parents' generation had sought to achieve immortality, and in doing so they had offended God. "Batch 235," the so-called immortality drug, had held forth the promise of eternal life. That promise was not kept. Based upon a bacterial enzyme designed to fight molecular cross-linking, inhibit free radical production and break down the limitation upon the number of times human cells could divide, batch 235 did indeed prolong the life span, but with catastrophic results. Eventually, though the cause was never discovered, batch 235 began to cross-react with human genetic material, "confusing" the body and causing it to recognize itself as foreign protein. Those who had taken the treatments eventually died a horrible death, victims of their own body chemistry run amok. Their children died as well, but a great many of those who had taken what came to be known as the plague drug bore children before the chemical reaction in their bodies had completely taken place. Even so, these children were not spared. They were the plague children, and virtually all of them had been monster babies, terribly deformed and grossly dysfunctional. The vast majority of them did not live very long. Viselius was one of the exceptions.

When his parents died, he had become a ward of the state, like all plague children. He had known that he would remain state-supported until such time as he either succumbed to the high mortality rate among the plague children or achieved the capability of taking care of himself. He eventually learned to live with his pain and accept his burden. Over the years, his own efforts and those of the medical profession had made his existence more bearable.

At the age of eighty-five, he was one of the longest-surviving plague children and no longer the pain-racked, helpless cripple he once had been. He no longer suffered from the suppurating sores that had once covered most of his body. His natural skin had been stripped away and replaced with a polymeric film grafted over his subdermal layers. His hormonal balance had been adjusted, and he had been revitalized with marrow transplants. All of his defective bodily organs had been removed, and those not replaced with regenerated tissue were, like his skin, synthetic. His eyes, ears, lungs and heart were bionic, and his disintegrating joints had been either replaced or reinforced with nysteel. The incapacities of his muscles and his motor system had been corrected by the bracing exoskeleton he wore constantly. Without the shining, intricate system of flexible nysteel linkages, he was like a fish out of water. With the exoskeleton, he resembled some sort of surrealistic art sculpture, but he was functional. At night, he placed it in the total lock mode, sleeping as though in some unfinished framework of a sarcophagus. Viselius had no need of furniture; he wore his. His malformed features had been reconstructed by extensive cosmetic surgery and he was now quite handsome, with snow-white hair and a face possessing Greco-Roman features that gave him an aristocratic mien. Indeed, medical science had even made it possible for him to dispense with his exoskeleton, but his faith would not allow it.

In recent years, the Blagoronov-12, an artificial computer brain that had been used with some success in experimental animals, had been perfected, and most of the difficulties involved in the surgical and programming procedures as applied to humans had been overcome by the prize-winning engineering surgeon Itzahk Osterman. It was now possible to remove a defective organic brain and have it replaced with a Blagoronov-12, inaccurately dubbed the "positronic brain" by the media, after a fictional invention of a brilliant classical novelist of the late twentieth century. The "positron," once transplanted into the patient, could then be programmed with the engram tapes taken from the patient's organic brain. The synthetic brain could be interfaced biologically with the recipient and would in every way function exactly like the original organic brain, being programmed with the patient's memories and personality.

What had prevented Viselius from benefiting from such an operation was the fact that religious leaders had decreed that since the brain was where the soul resided, anyone receiving such a unit would become excommunicate at the moment the organic brain was removed. Only a small handful of men and women had received such synthetic brains to date, and the issue was a highly controversial one, involving nothing less than the definition of what constituted human life. Viselius' greatest area of vulnerability was his brain. He did not fear death. As long as his death was not administered by his own hand, Viselius believed he would be saved. For all that he had suffered, surely there was a place reserved for him in paradise. What Viselius feared was mental incapacity. There were several protein implants in his brain already, helping him to function. He did not dare to interfere with it further. He was already more machine than man in many respects. He did not dare to lose his soul.

One man who had lost his soul was Dr. Paul Tabarde.

The man had been an official in ColCom's SEPAP section, the name being an acronym for Situational Evaluation and Personnel Adjustive Practices. As a member of the Directorate of Colonization Command, Viselius was Tabarde's superior. He viewed what had occurred with mixed emotions.

Tabarde had been injured in a lift-tube accident. A fluctuation in the lift tube's field had resulted in his being flung up to the top of his conapt center's tube with tremendous force. The impact had left Tabarde comatose, severely injured with no hope of ever regaining consciousness or mobility. He should have died. Instead, he had been reduced to a vegetable state. The hospital authorities had contacted ColCom headquarters immediately upon his arrival at the emergency center. They had reached Director Stenmark's office.

Viselius did not like August Stenmark. The man was an avowed atheist. His appointment to the Directorate had been the focus of a great deal of controversy. Although he had been confirmed, he was still controversial in his actions and his methods. Viselius fiercely resented having to work with him.

Tabarde's position with ColCom had made it imperative that headquarters be notified of his condition. Stenmark had reviewed Tabarde's dossier and, finding that Tabarde was an agnostic, decided that receiving an artificial brain would not violate any of his religious beliefs. Therefore, Stenmark had acted on his own and approved the procedure. By doing so, he had cost Tabarde his soul. Through his incapacity, Tabarde might have been saved. Now, he was damned for certain.

Yet, something incredible had come of it all. As Viselius examined the classified record of Tabarde's engram tapes, he mused that the Lord worked in mysterious ways, even to the point of using atheists to accomplish His ends.

As a SEPAP official, Tabarde had access to a great deal of classified information. Therefore, the programming of his artificial brain had been a classified procedure. The Right of Cerebral Privacy Act, a bill enacted as a result of the new technology, made it illegal for anyone involved in the operation to have personal access to the memory engram tapes unless specifically authorized by the patient. Under ordinary circumstances, if such circumstances could ever be called ordinary, only one set of engram tapes was made, and they were given to the patient upon his or her discharge from the hospital. However, in Tabarde's case, the contents of his organic brain were classified top secret and the operating team had been instructed to forward the tapes directly to ColCom for analysis following the operation. The celebrated Dr. Osterman had not been pleased with this development, but Viselius now had those tapes, and he had spent a great deal of time analyzing them.

He could not possibly have hoped to examine a lifetime of memories, but fortunately, this had not been necessary. He had programmed the engram tapes, less the personality data, into his personal computer, initiating a random search to isolate elements of Tabarde's memory having to do with classified ColCom operations, either directly or indirectly. At first, Viselius thought that the engrams might be incomplete, the result of brain damage sustained in Tabarde's accident. However, on closer inspection, he realized that certain gaps in information were the obvious result of repression by psychic conditioning. This conditioning process had been submitted to voluntarily and carried out in secrecy. The Cerebral Privacy Act gave an individual the right to do this, but as a ColCom official, Paul Tabarde did *not* have the right to alter or inhibit memories having to do with classified ColCom operations, which was precisely what he had done.

Sometime during his tenure with SEPAP, Paul Tabarde had undertaken an extended assignment in the field, off-planet. This was borne out by checking with SEPAP records. That, in itself, was not remarkable for a SEPAP official whose job it was to evaluate the performance of ColCom personnel in the field who were subject to extreme conditions and stress, although it was somewhat unusual for an evaluator to actually go out into the field personally. This indicated a highly special case. What was remarkable was that Tabarde had come in contact with a race of alien beings. And he had not reported it.

Tabarde had selectively "forgotten" much of his experience, but it had been so profound for him that he evidently had not been able to force himself to eradicate all traces of it from his memory. In that, Viselius saw the hand of God at work, and he was extremely grateful for it.

Tabarde's assignment had brought him to a planet named Boomerang and a race of beings he and his co-conspirators had called the Shades. These beings were humanoid, gray-skinned, with long white manes and glowing violet eyes that had bifurcated pupils. They were significantly taller than humans and more slender, with three fingers and an opposed thumb on each hand. Their ribs were thinner and more flexible, and there were thirty-two of them, linked by cartilaginous tissue. Their hearts were structured differently from those of humans and were placed in the exact center of the chest, protected by the breastbone, and their reproductive organs differed from those of humans only slightly and were, in the males, retractable. In general, the anatomical differences between Shades and *Homo sapiens* were astonishingly superficial, an amazing fact in itself. Yet, even more astonishing was the fact that the Shades possessed an ability to "merge" with one another. In a phenomenon Tabarde had labeled "psychic transference," when one Shade experienced a physical death, it merged its life essence with another of its kind, so that each individual Shade was an individual in the physical sense only. Within each Shade were contained thousands upon thousands of living Shade personae, each retaining some semblance of individuality while at the same time being part of a psychological gestalt. Small wonder that Tabarde, a psychiatrist, could not bear to erase his memory of such a species.

Tabarde's engram tapes revealed that the Shades had developed an interdependent series of internal relationships that Tabarde referred to as "living archetypes." Within each Shade, the identities of those who had merged with the living corporeal being had coalesced into archetypal entities whose function was to guide the living body host, the "One That Is," in its life experience. These "Ones Who Were" had, by dint of aptitude and strength of persona, merged once again within the host Shade into group gestalt identities such as the Great Father, the Great Mother, the Healer, the Hunter and the Shadow. Each of these group identities or "living archetypes" was an aggregate of past Shade personalities, and there was an ongoing, continuous interaction between them. The Shades were mute, their vocal cords having atrophied over generations to the point where they could make only very limited sounds, but Tabarde's memory revealed that they had their own language, which had been preserved since the days of their primordial past and was "spoken" internally among the Ones Who Were.

It was clear that the Shades had to be the most unusual life form ever encountered by humans. Since their life essences were psychically transferred upon the expiration of their bodies, this meant that they were effectively immortal. It was incredible. God had cruelly punished the human race for attempting to achieve immortality, and yet He had bestowed the gift of eternal life upon these alien beasts!

There was no record of Tabarde's ever having been on such a mission. The records of the off-planet mission entered into the SEPAP files and covering the time he spent on Boomerang were fabricated. He was listed as having been on a mission, but subsequent checking revealed that no such mission had ever taken place. There was no record of the Shades. Viselius had initiated a file search, which yielded nothing. It was unbelievable, but somehow Tabarde and his co-conspirators had managed to cover up an entire mission. Only the Directors were in a position to attempt such a thing. The inescapable conclusion was that the cover-up had been perpetrated with the knowledge and collusion of the previous Directorate. The last Directorate had vanished without a trace. It was one of the greatest tragedies in the history of the service. Their ship had never arrived at its scheduled destination after they had left station Gamma 127 in orbit around Wheeler's World. It was assumed that the ship had been lost upon entering the Twilight Zone, that artificially created vortex which enabled ships to "ghost" from one point in space to another, thereby bypassing the limitation of light speed. It occurred to Viselius that their deaths might not have been accidental.

Tabarde had memories of an experiment conducted by the previous Directorate, an experiment of unprecedented audacity and scope. They had taken five thousand men and women, psychically conditioned, and sent them to Boomerang in coldsleep. It was a monumental gamble on several levels. It hinged upon their being able to successfully program a member of the original survey team with a reality reference to Boomerang as it had been a thousand years prior to the Shades' discovery. It had taken detailed paleogeographical plotting to construct the scenario for the reality reference, and the odds had been heavily weighed in favor of failure. Yet, knowing what the stakes were, Viselius was certain that they would have tried again and kept on trying, no matter how many hundreds or thousands of lives were lost. In spite of the odds, they had succeeded. Careful precautions had been taken to avoid creating a temporal paradox, and these conditioned sleepers had arrived on Boomerang a thousand years before the members of that first survey team had ever set foot upon the world. The conditioned imperative within these people demanded that they compete with the Shades, capturing them, isolating them, and then killing them. Isolated from others of their kind, those Shades would have had no choice but to merge with their human captors if they were to survive the demise of their bodies. This was the "Seedling Project," and its aim had been an attempt at a psychic crossbreeding of Shades and *Homo sapiens* in order to create a *Homo superior,* thereby achieving immortality for the human race. If Tabarde's memory engrams were to be believed, the physical descendants of those people still thrived on Boomerang, having achieved the capability of psychic transference.

Viselius was overwhelmed at the blasphemy of it all. He was staggered by the implications. He was astonished that it could all have been accomplished with such secrecy and then covered up so effectively. It was clear to him what the plan of the previous Directorate had been. However, they had died before they could fully implement it. That left Tabarde and his co-conspirators as the only ones with any knowledge of the project. Why had they not continued with it? Why hadn't the details of the project been passed on to himself and the other new Directors? Why the cover-up?

Viselius thought he knew.

That it had all fallen into his lap the way it had was an

amazing stroke of luck. Or was it luck? Was it just good luck for him and bad luck for Tabarde that the lift tube had malfunctioned? Was it just luck that the engram tapes had been delivered to his office instead of to August Stenmark? Was it just an "accident" when the previous Directorate were lost in space? Or was it the hand of God at work?

There was no immediate way of learning who had taken part in the top-secret project. The odds were that the people involved had served their purpose and been conditioned to forget their involvement in the mission. Tabarde, as a SEPAP official, would have carried out that conditioning process. Being in that position gave him quite an opportunity. Yet, he had been very careful. He must have planned his conspiracy when he found out that the Directors had vanished, and he must have planned it in excruciating detail. There was nothing in his memory engrams to give Viselius even a clue as to how he had intended to carry out the plan. It was possible that the information had been wiped out because of damage sustained in the accident, but then the memory center of his brain had been, according to Dr. Osterman, relatively unaffected. More than likely, Tabarde had taken superparanoid precautions, electing to forget those aspects of his plan while he had the information stored somewhere, to be retrieved or delivered to him at the proper time. There was also nothing in his memory to tell Viselius where Boomerang was. All he knew was the planet's name, not its location, what sort of world it was, in what system it could be found, nothing. However, Tabarde's memory engrams had provided him with a key, a link to the planet of the Shades.

Her name was Shelby Michaels.

Viselius instructed his computer to create a holographic representation of Tabarde's memory of Michaels. Seconds later, he was staring at an astonishing apparition. A face that did not look entirely human. Viselius double-checked for accuracy. No, there was no error, at least not on the part of his computer. According to Tabarde's memory engrams, this was what Shelby Michaels had looked like when he had last seen her.

Viselius stared at the image for a long time. It was that of a young woman with snow-white hair and skin that had a silvery blue sheen. Her eyes were lambent, violet, the pupils bifurcated like those of a cat. She was a mutant, part human and part Shade.

Viselius unlocked his exoskeleton from the bent position in which he could "sit" as if in a chair, straightening and walking over to the window of his office. He looked out at the night sky. There was a great deal to be done. Chances were that Tabarde might well have been alone in retaining as much information as he had, but he would have to order a scanning procedure for all ColCom personnel who might have been involved in the Seedling Project. It would take a long time and it would be expensive, but if any of Tabarde's co-conspirators could be discovered, it would be well worth the effort. He could not afford to overlook any possibilities. While that was being done, he would see to it that Shelby Michaels, wherever she was, would be tracked down and taken into custody. Tabarde's body, with its new artificial brain, was still in the hospital. He would make sure that it remained there by ordering Tabarde's arrest. There was one more thing that he would have to do.

He went back to the computer and began to selectively erase certain portions of the tapes.

Chapter One

Paul Tabarde awoke in the hospital, very surprised to find himself alive. His last memory had been of the malfunction in the lift tube, of being flung toward the top of his conapt center with great speed and force. Shortly before impact, he had resigned himself to death. If the impact of striking the top end of the tube did not kill him, the long drop back down to the bottom certainly would. What had saved him from a very messy death had been the fact that the field fluctuation had been an extremely brief one. He was already slowing down as he neared the top, so that he struck with less force than he would have otherwise and, following the impact, his unconscious body was gently lowered to the bottom.

"Good morning, Dr. Tabarde," said the young nurse, smiling down at him. "How do we feel this morning?"

Paul winced. "I don't know about you, but I've certainly felt better."

"You're lucky to be alive," the nurse said. He consulted Paul's chart, then punched out the code for the prescribed medication on the mobile dispenser which followed him like a mechanical puppy. "We get a lot of accidents like yours. Lift tubes going on the blink all the time these days. Not enough maintenance inspectors to go around. Most people get squashed flat like bugs. You were one of the lucky ones."

Paul felt the protective porous plastic sealant on his head. It felt as though he were touching some object and not a part of himself.

"What happened to me?"

"Not to worry, Doctor. We fixed you up as good as new. You had Dr. Osterman. First cabin all the way for ColCom personnel, eh? Dr. Osterman does very fine work. He takes a great deal of pride in it."

Paul started to sit up.

"Whoa, take it easy there, Doctor." The nurse gently, but firmly, pushed him back down onto the bed. "Let's not rush things, okay?"

"When can I speak with Dr. Osterman?" said Paul.

"Right now," said Osterman, from the door. "It's all right, nurse, let him sit up if he wants to. You can move around the room a little, too, if you like, but take it slow, okay?"

"I'd like to know what happened to me," Paul said. "Give it to me straight."

"All right," said Osterman, sitting down on the bed beside him. "It'll come as a shock to you, though."

"I'm ready."

"Well, you got banged up pretty badly, doctor. You came to us a basket case. Severe neck and spinal injuries, fractured skull, you were comatose with irreversible cerebral damage—"

"Irreversible?"

Osterman nodded. "It was an extremely complicated surgical procedure. We had to effect extensive nerve grafting, nysteel spinal reinforcement, polymeric epidermal grafting, nysteel skull replacement and replacement of shoulder and arm joints . . . evidently, your reflex reaction was to attempt to brace yourself with your arms before impact." Osterman threw his arms up over his head, as though surrendering. "The bones in your wrists, arms and shoulders were shattered."

"You said irreversible cerebral damage."

Osterman nodded again. "We had no choice but to go ahead with a Blagoronov-12 procedure."

"I've had my brain removed?"

"Well, it was either that or spend the rest of your life being a carrot," Osterman said. "You did say you wanted it straight. The operation, I'm happy to report, was an unqualified success. We'll have to hold on to you for a while, of course, for the therapy. Your organic brain was quite severely damaged. We'll have to make certain that we catch any glitches in the programming due to that. At worst, you'll lose some memory engrams, perhaps experience some personality change, but then you'd never know it. We have access to your ColCom medical records, so we'll be able to adjust where necessary to achieve optimal organic replacement programming, but just the same—"

"Who authorized the operation?"

Osterman consulted his datacard. "Director August Stenmark. Since you weren't a religious man—"

"What happened to my programming tapes?" said Paul.

"Oh, I see what's worrying you," said Osterman, smiling. "You can rest assured on that account. There was only one set of memory engram tapes made, as usual, and they were strictly classified. The tapes were forwarded by special courier to your Directorate the moment the programming run was completed. I promise you that no one had any access to any classified information you might have had at your disposal.''

"Oh God."

The nurse made a wry face, then quickly turned away. Wasn't it like all atheists to call on God at last, he thought. Well, it was too late for this one. He was damned now. Still, thought the nurse, that was none of his concern. When he had entered nursing school, he had never thought that a time would come when the ethics of the medical profession would conflict with his religious beliefs. At least his hands were clean. He had not been involved in any aspect of the transplant operation. His job now was to assist Tabarde in his recovery. Soul or no soul, he could do no less. When next he attended confession, he would ask to be absolved of his sin in giving succor to an excommunicate. He would do his penance and privately continue to support the efforts of the religious lobby to outlaw the operation. And he would pray for the soul of Dr. Osterman.

The nurse liked Dr. Osterman. Everyone on the hospital staff liked him. At least the man was not a godless atheist. He was a member of the Progressive Jewish Reformation, which was close, but the nurse knew that Dr. Osterman meant well. But then, so had the research scientists who had invented the plague drug meant well. They had died for their sins and Tabarde would pay for his. It would only be a matter of time before the blasphemous operation was outlawed. Already, there was a resolution in the legislature which held that the recipients of the positronic brains were technically inhuman. If the resolution passed, then the recipients of the computer brains would be legally reclassified as "inorganic citizens." That way, good Christians would no longer be endangering their souls by having contact with excommunicates. It was not a sin to treat with a machine.

Osterman rose. "Try to relax now, Dr. Tabarde. I recommend that you get some sleep. Just lie back and close your eyes, relaxing as you would normally. Think about sleeping. The Blagoronov-12 will do the rest. It doesn't need sleep, but your body does. I'll be back to check on you tomorrow morning and then we can see about starting your therapy."

The doctor and the nurse left Paul alone in his private room. Paul leaned back and shut his eyes, then opened them immediately. He could not afford to go to sleep now. He wished that he had died in the accident. He had made a grave mistake. He should have eradicated all traces of the mission to the planet of the Shades from his memory. He should have had himself conditioned to forget that he had ever known Shelby Michaels. His position in SEPAP had exempted him from general scanning procedures unless a special order came down from the Directorate, but he had been very foolish to hold on to any memories of that experience. The fact that he still had those memories meant that they were all contained in his memory engram tapes, retrieved from his organic brain. That meant that the Directorate would know what he knew. Even now, they might be analyzing those tapes, ordering his arrest.

He had to escape while he still could. He had to find Shelby and warn her. He could not afford to remain in the hospital for therapy. If there was a fault in the programming of his artificial brain because of the damage sustained by his organic brain, he would simply have to live with it. It made no difference, anyway. He was on borrowed time.

Slowly, he sat up and put his feet on the floor. He felt a bit peculiar. It didn't matter. He had to get out *now*. Had the arrest order already been issued? How long would it be before his accounts were frozen? How long would it be before the next series of ColCom flights were dispatched to the outposts and the colony worlds?

His door was unlocked. That was a good sign. It meant that the order for his arrest had not yet come through. Wearing nothing but his gown, his slippers and a robe, he walked slowly down the corridor, keeping close to the wall. Just a patient out for a bit of exercise. He had to find some clothes somewhere.

"Dr. Tabarde, what are you doing out of bed?"

He nearly jumped. The nurse steadied him.

"I'm sorry, you startled me," said Paul. "I just wanted to get up and walk around a little."

"Dr. Osterman said that you could walk around your *room*," said the nurse, guiding him back. "Honestly, you doctors are impossible patients. You just don't listen. I'm going to have to insist that you behave yourself and remain in your room, Dr. Tabarde. There will be plenty of time for you to exercise later on, when you begin your therapy. Right now, what you need most of all is to get some rest."

As they entered the room, Paul drove his elbow back hard into the man's solar plexus. As the nurse doubled over, Paul turned and gave him a chop to the back of the neck. The nurse collapsed to the floor. Paul leaned back against the wall. He swallowed hard. It had been a desperate gamble. He had not been sure that he would have the strength to pull it off. Then he noticed that the nurse's head was at a funny angle. His breath caught. The man was dead with a broken neck.

Paul took several deep breaths, then bent down to undress the nurse. The uniform would be large on him, but it would have to do. There was no time for self-recrimination. He had more than himself to think about. He removed the nurse's uniform and put it on, then he dressed the nurse up in his own gown and placed him in his bed, covering him up. He sighed and rubbed his head, his hand encountering the plastic sealant. He had to disguise that somehow. From a distance, it might not cause problems, but up close, the protective covering was clearly visible. It would dissolve eventually, but he had to hide it meanwhile. Nor could he hope to pass for the nurse whom he had unwittingly killed. The man was white and he was black.

Paul went to the closet and removed some spare bedding. Then he took the pillow off his bed and placed it atop the pile. It wasn't much, but it was something. He would have to brazen it out. Putting the small pile of bedding on his shoulder, he left the room and started to walk down the corridor. He carried the bedding folded on his left shoulder, keeping it between his face and the nurses' station as he passed it on the way to the lift tubes. No one paid any attention to him. He entered the tube and descended to the basement without further incident, although he wasn't sure that he would ever use a lift tube with equanimity again.

Once he arrived in the basement, he hid behind one of the generators and fashioned an improvised turban for himself from one of the sheets. He would have to move quickly. At least, so far, his new brain was functioning admirably. He didn't want to think about that too much just yet. The last thing he needed now was to have a nervous breakdown on top of everything. Could an artificial brain allow him to suffer a breakdown? Don't think about it; tend to the business at hand.

He took a fire exit to the street level. So far, so good, but it was too soon to congratulate himself just yet. If his accounts were frozen before he could clear them, he would be trapped. He had to get the hell off the planet fast. Try to outrun the arrest order. He had no idea where Shelby Michaels was. She could be on any one of the colony or outpost worlds. He would have to find her on his own, without the resources of ColCom.

There was still a possibility that he was ahead of them. So far as the Directorate knew, unless they had already discovered his escape, he was still in the hospital. It would be a simple matter to order him detained there. It might not have occurred to them to freeze his funds yet or to invalidate his clearance. How long would it be before the nurse he killed was discovered? It would be taking a chance, but the odds were still in his favor. He hailed a skimmer. If he was wrong, he would be caught now or in his conapt. He had to take the chance. He punched out his account number, and when the query appeared he entered the confirming code. Account confirmed. The skimmer fee was deducted accordingly. They hadn't frozen him out yet. Now if the skimmer took him to his conapt instead of to the police, he was still in good shape.

He arrived at his conapt center. The security guard was extremely solicitious, having heard about his accident. He asked if Dr. Tabarde was going to sue for damages. Paul told him probably, but there were more urgent matters to attend to. He had been released from the hospital early, because of ColCom business that required his immediate personal attention, and would the guard please summon him an air taxi to meet him on the roof?

He took time only to change out of the nurse's uniform and into his own clothes, then he sat down to his screen. Only minutes had passed since he had left the hospital. His escape could be discovered at any moment. He was moving quickly, logically, methodically. The positron was working well.

He took his unicard and inserted it into his computer. He punched in his account code and, moments later, transferred all of his available funds directly onto his card. A query appeared on the screen. If he was closing out his accounts, did he also wish to close out his security data file?

Security data file? He did not recall storing any private, confidential information with the bank. On impulse, he punched in "yes."

The query appeared: datacard or printout?

He punched in "printout."

His computer ejected a printout. He read it. It told him that the last person to have seen Shelby Michaels was retired ColCom Colonel Jacob "Jake" Thorsen, now master of the freighter *Southern Cross*. There followed a brief, concise physical description of Jake Thorsen and the words "intimately associated with project."

Paul did not remember Jake Thorsen. Obviously, he had conditioned himself not to. But then that meant that ColCom would not know of his involvement, either. He gave himself credit for having been more paranoid than he had thought. It was a lead, and, obviously, there had been a time when he had felt that he might need one someday. He queried the bank again, to make certain that he had cleared everything. He had. The only record of his security data file was now in his hand. He burned the printout. Then he used his ColCom clearance code to put in a request to the merchant admiralty for the last entered port of call of the freighter *Southern Cross*. He coded the request under the SEPAP designation, rather than his own personal code. SEPAP made thousands of such requests every day, and this one would get lost in the shuffle. Would the clearance be denied? He waited tensely for several moments. No, he had tied in to the merchant admiralty through the SEPAP data banks. The information came through. The last entered port of call for the *Southern Cross* was Morgan's World, out on the frontier.

The guard called up to tell him that the taxi was waiting for him on the roof. Paul told him to have the cab stand by.

Next he used his unicard to book passage on the next available flight to Luna City under another name. It was due to leave in half an hour. He had no intention of being on that flight. Again, this would not fool the Directorate for long, but it would gain him some time. He needed all the time he could get.

With all of his available funds in his unicard, the only working record of his account was now in the card's memory. He was not home free yet, not by a long shot. The moment that he started spending, he was traceable through his account number. The moment he attempted to redeposit his funds in another bank, his credit could be frozen. It would take some time, but not very much. They would be able to find him. His only hope was to redeposit his funds in a bank that was part of the credit net, but that was not answerable to any pressure placed on it by either the Directorate of ColCom or government authorities. Such banks could be found in the South African Principality. Their way of doing business was vital to their commerce, attracting certain unique clients, especially those interested in laundering funds. There was a tradeoff involved.

With a unicard routed through a South African bank, financial transactions were made not in the name of the individual, but in the name of the bank holding the account. The client carried a certain amount of risk, since loss of the card or theft of same could easily result in the account's being drained by a credit thief. However, what the client received in exchange for bearing that risk was a guarantee that no transaction could be traced to him directly, because the bank never revealed the names of its account holders. The Principality bore certain penalties for doing business this way. For one thing, it was not allowed to maintain a spaceport. Yet, it would be a simple matter, with a Principality account, to shuttle elsewhere and arrange passage off-planet.

Tokyo was a good place to book illegal supercargo passage aboard an outbound freighter. It would then prove no major difficulty to transfer to a faster ship at the first port of call.

Payment would be made in the name of the Principality bank and not in the name of Dr. Paul Tabarde. There were many shipmasters who did not care by what names their passengers chose to call themselves, as long as they could pay the fare.

Paul left his conapt and made his way to the roof, to the waiting air taxi. They could revoke his ColCom clearance now. It didn't matter. He had learned as much as he could hope to learn in the amount of time he had. They could order his accounts frozen, which order would be implemented, but nonproductive unless he failed to reach Capetown. He would take the taxi to the spaceport and hop the first flight to Capetown. If he was not arrested at the spaceport, the flight would eventually be traced, but they would look for him aboard the Luna City shuttle first, especially since he had booked passage under an assumed name. It would provide for only the slightest of delays, but it was something.

As he entered the taxi and it took off, Paul quickly assessed his situation. Slightly over half an hour had elapsed since he had fled the hospital. Unless the nurse had been discovered by now, there was a strong chance that the Directorate would not be able to move quickly enough to intercept him. If they did not apprehend him within the next twenty minutes, he would have made good his escape. But that was only the beginning.

He would lose valuable time in arranging passage off-planet aboard a slow commercial freighter and in finding a faster ship, or ships, to transfer to. He had to journey all the way out to the frontier, to Morgan's World. There was no way of knowing exactly when the *Southern Cross* would be arriving there. He might well miss Jake Thorsen. He was hampered by having to make his journey in stages, while the ColCom couriers would have no such handicap.

The couriers would depart, as usual, on ghosting ships. They would have direct routing and priority status. They were the lifeline of the ColCom organization, the most vital links in the network. To ensure that the "pouches" they carried reached the ColCom outposts and governmental embassies throughout the net, all courier procedures were redundant. If one set of communiqués was somehow interfered with, there were at least two others, prepared at separate times by different people. Everything was cross-checked. If, for any reason, one courier failed to arrive at his or her scheduled destination, there were still two others on separate flights. It was extremely difficult, if not impossible, to sabotage the courier system, and attempting to do so carried a penalty of life imprisonment on a penal-colony world. That, of course, assumed that the perpetrator survived the couriers, who were extremely capable of defending themselves.

Paul had to find Shelby, but he realized that the couriers would reach their destinations before he could find her. That meant that wherever she was, she would be sought by the authorities. She would stand out in a crowd anywhere, because of her appearance. And she would not know that she was wanted.

Because the Directorate had access to his memory engram tapes, they would know what he knew. They would be able to create visual graphic interpretations of his memories and . . .

Paul leaned back against his seat cushion wearily. It suddenly occurred to him that the Directorate could easily program his persona into a computer and effectively duplicate his reasoning processes. They didn't really need him. They would want him arrested as a criminal, certainly, but since the brain he was now using was a computer programmed with the data they had at their disposal, they could create a *second* Paul Tabarde within their own data banks.

It was very hard for him to accept the fact that the thoughts going through his mind were computer-generated. He felt the same as he always had. Or did he? He had been severely injured in the accident. He had to deal with that. Just how severely had his organic brain been damaged? He was somewhat familiar with the case histories of past positron transplant operations, but that was a familiarity born of professional curiosity. He had never suspected that he might one day be personally concerned. How would the effects of whatever damage he had suffered manifest themselves in his synthetic brain? Previous cases had varied greatly. The results had ranged from slight to profound memory loss to alterations in the personality. The positron would compensate for such things as impaired cerebral functions, but the key question was . . . was he *still* Paul Tabarde?

If there were any deviations from the way he had been before his accident, he would never be aware of them. He didn't *feel* different, but then, how could he? All he had to go on was his programming. Legally, at least up to the present moment, he was a cyborg. Even that might change, he realized, if the bill denying human status to positron recipients passed the legislature. Given the clout of the religious lobby, that was almost a certainty. How long would it be before the implications of such a decision began to make themselves evident? What rights would an inorganic citizen have? Would it be murder to kill an inorganic citizen, or would it be a computer crime?

For most of his adult life, he had vacillated between atheism and agnosticism. He had not been affiliated with any organized religion since his early childhood. In the eyes of the Church, he no longer had a soul. He was damned. No longer human.

He didn't *feel* inhuman. He didn't *feel* like a machine. He had been taught that what separated Man from lower forms of life was his ability to think, to reason. He could still think, he could still reason, but that reasoning was now being done by a computer. A computer that had been programmed with whatever had been left of his personality, but it was a computer nonetheless. The Paul Tabarde that he now was could be recreated in another computer. The only difference would be that *his* computer was contained in an ambulatory organism. Did his organic body make him human? Not according to the Church. Would a Paul Tabarde recreated from his memory engram tapes in a ColCom computer be human? He didn't think he could accept that. At any rate, his *computer* didn't think so. That being the case, what was he?

He held his hands up in front of his face. Flesh and blood. He was organs, entrails, viscera, sinew, any of which could be regenerated or replaced with a synthetic part. Indeed, some of his body had been reconstructed, as Dr. Osterman had told him. He could bleed, but then a machine could leak lubricant. He could feel pain, but then he could be programmed not to. For that matter, people suffering from diseases causing them to live in constant pain had often received operations to neutralize their pain centers. These people had often not lived very long without their warning systems. They could walk barefoot through jagged broken glass and never even feel the severe lacerations they sustained. Yet they had not been denied their humanity. The Church did not believe that pain should be interfered with by such means. A good Christian about to undergo brain surgery always checked with his priest first. Paul didn't care what the Church thought as much as he cared what *he* thought.

He could not decide. He was afraid to.

Descartes had said, *"Cogito ergo sum."* I think, therefore I am. But then Descartes had never heard of computers.

The taxi started to descend.

Chapter Two

Osterman's face on the screen was tight-lipped and pale. Clearly, he was unaccustomed to being dressed down, and Viselius had savaged him thoroughly.

"I really don't know what to say, Director Viselius," Osterman said stiffly. "I simply can't account for it. It's possible that there might have been a glitch in the programming of Dr. Tabarde that would have caused him to experience some violent attack of paranoia, but there's no way of telling for certain what happened until he's apprehended. Nothing like this has ever happened before."

"If you were more careful about looking after your patients, especially patients as important as Dr. Tabarde, it wouldn't have happened in the first place," snapped Viselius.

"Yes, sir, you've already made that point abundantly clear," said Osterman, restraining himself with obvious difficulty. "However, Dr. Tabarde had responded excellently to the operation. In fact, I was quite surprised at how readily he accepted it. It certainly wasn't normal."

"As a SEPAP official, Dr. Tabarde has made a career of accepting abnormal situations," Viselius said. "What I want to know from you, Dr. Osterman, is how functional he is at present."

Osterman shrugged. "That would be impossible to say. I have no information on which to base even an educated guess. Perhaps if I could have access to his engram tapes—"

"Out of the question. That's classified information," said Viselius.

"Well then, my hands are tied. I can't possibly make any sort of diagnosis without the patient or his records."

"Then make some very unscientific suppositions, Doctor," said Viselius. "Based on your past experiences with such operations, can we expect Dr. Tabarde to be reasonably functional physically?"

"If you're asking for an informed medical opinion—"

"I'm asking for *your* opinion, Osterman. Based on what you know, both from Tabarde's case and similar past cases."

Osterman shrugged. "He obviously got out of the hospital with no great difficulty. He was alert, he seemed coordinated, his reasoning processes *seemed* to be normal, but I stress that that is only a very superficial observation. He hadn't started on his therapy. He hadn't—"

"Fine," said Viselius. "So if we are to assume that whatever 'glitch' he may have in his programming does not affect his physical condition, then we may assume that he's fully capable of moving about normally?"

"If we're talking about assumptions, yes, we can. However, I might add that he isn't entirely normal, physically speaking. We had to effect extensive repairs on his body. As long as we're engaged in speculation here, I think he killed the nurse by accident. Nysteel replacement of various joints and bionic—"

"Yes, I'm quite familiar with that, as you can doubtless see," Viselius said. "What you're telling me is that he doesn't know his own strength."

"Probably not. At least, he hasn't yet had time to adjust fully to the situation. At the risk of overstepping my bounds, I feel that I must say that it's imperative that Dr. Tabarde be apprehended as nonviolently as possible. For all we know, he may well have intended to kill that nurse. However, the odds are that the programming was at fault because of the damage to his organic brain, in which case he can't be held responsible for his actions. Whatever's wrong with him *can* be fixed. We can debug the program and—"

"I'm afraid I can't allow that," said Viselius.

Osterman finally lost control. "Dammit, you people are responsible for this entire affair, with your bureaucratic paranoia! I frankly couldn't give a damn about your so-called top-secret information. I've got a patient's welfare to consider! How the hell do you expect me to restore him to some semblance of normality if I'm denied access to his engram tapes? I'm a doctor, not a fucking mechanic! You're asking me to—"

"I'm asking you to restrain yourself, Doctor, before you say anything that you'll later regret."

Osterman turned red. "Are you threatening me, Director?"

"I'm asking you to consider your position, Doctor. Then consider mine. It would be the prudent thing for you to refrain from discussing this matter with anyone unless you've checked with me first."

Osterman looked grim. "I see," he said. "What do I tell the authorities?"

"You refer them to me. Is that clear?"

"Perfectly."

"There is one thing I require from you," said Viselius. "I want the case histories of all previous positron transplants you've performed."

"Director, not even you can compel me to release confidential data concerning—"

"I'm not asking you to break the law, Dr. Osterman," said Viselius. "I'm not interested in any confidential information. I merely want the technical details, the sort of information you would publish. I could get it through other channels, but I don't want any embellishments, just the facts. I trust I can count on your complete cooperation."

"Set up an interface and I'll feed you the data," Osterman said. "Meanwhile, about Dr. Tabarde—"

"You are not to concern yourself with Dr. Tabarde any further."

"But when you find him—"

"When Dr. Tabarde is found, he will be arrested on criminal charges."

"But I thought I explained that he wasn't responsible—"

"You don't know that for sure, Dr. Osterman," Viselius said, cutting him off. "Besides, the charges I'm referring to have nothing to do with the murder of your nurse. Dr. Tabarde is wanted for other crimes, crimes committed prior to his accident. So you see, your spirited defense of Dr. Tabarde is laudable, but quite beside the point. He already had criminal tendencies when he came to you."

"Yes, well, this may be true," said Osterman, "but I should like to impress upon you the fact that this can all be changed. If he is indeed a valued ColCom official who has gone wrong somehow, the point is that he can be reprogrammed. He can be made useful."

"Yes, I'll keep that in mind. Meanwhile, I have some urgent matters to attend to. If you will be so kind as to prepare the data I requested, I'll have my secretary set up the interface for you. Thank you, Doctor."

Viselius accessed another channel and a security officer's face appeared upon the screen.

"Well?" Viselius said.

"It was a blind, sir," said the officer.

"What do you mean, a blind?"

"Tabarde never made that flight to Luna City. The whole thing was a stalling tactic. He booked passage under an assumed name, knowing we would trace the purchase through his account. The ticket was a no-show. We did trace another ticket purchase through his account number. He's headed for Capetown. The flight already left. In fact, it should be arriving right about now. If we're lucky, word will reach our people in time for them to apprehend him as he disembarks. Otherwise we've lost him."

"Lost him!"

"Afraid so, sir. He's had all his funds transferred to his card, so we can freeze him out, but we can't take away his walk-around money. Since he's headed for Capetown, he obviously intends to open a Principality account. We lose track of a lot of people that way. We'll pick him up eventually, but for right now, I'm afraid there's not much we can do. No way to tell where he'll head to next unless you can read his mind."

Viselius stared at the screen, his expression a blank.

"Sir?"

"Of *course*," said Viselius. "Fool!"

"Sorry, sir, I—"

"I didn't mean you, Captain, I meant *me*. I've been wasting time. I *can* read his mind. Issue a standby alert for all our branch security offices. I'll be getting back to you."

So far, he was ahead of them.

He had reached Capetown without incident, and, luckily, there had been no one waiting for him when he arrived. He still had the advantage, but it was a very slight advantage. It really only meant that they couldn't take away his money or trace him every time he made a purchase. However, the word was out by now, and every ColCom agent and security officer would be on the watch for him. They would also have the cooperation of most local authorities. Going through ordinary channels to book passage off-planet was out of the question.

Tokyo would be the best bet. Still, though he did not have time to submit to cosmetic surgery, it would help to do something to alter his appearance. He scratched at his chin, feeling the stubble there. His beard always had grown fast, and he had refrained from depilation, having enjoyed shaving the old-fashioned way. A beard. Yes, and perhaps a turban, like the one he had improvised to get out of the hospital.

A short while later, he stood on the line to book passage on the Tokyo shuttle. He had discarded his hat and one-piece suit, exchanging them for an expensively simple, old-fashioned suit of white linen and a sky-blue turban, fastened with an opal brooch. He had made all the purchases separately, the last being the false beard he had picked up at a tonsorial salon.

"Name, please?" said the clerk, without looking up from his console.

"Anjar Singh."

The clerk looked up at him.

"I have made no reservation," said Tabarde, handing the clerk his card.

"That's all right, sir. Plenty of room. Luggage?"

"No."

"Just the dagger, then?"

Tabarde nodded.

"Very well, sir, here you are," the clerk said, handing him a boarding ticket. "Just step right around there, sir."

"The idea!" said a matronly woman who was next in line. "Did I hear that heathen admit to carrying a knife?"

"Sikhs believe in God, madame," said the clerk. "As for the dagger, it's part of their religion. If a Sikh draws a dagger, he's got to get blood on it, so he's not liable to pull it out unless somebody makes him. Besides, they only carry little ones these days."

"What kind of a religion makes a man carry a weapon?" she said, somewhat scornfully.

"A practical one, I should think. Name, please?"

Tabarde had heard that exchange as he walked away, and he smiled to himself. If anyone now asked that clerk about a black man named Paul Tabarde or gave him his description, he would not connect the fugitive with Anjar Singh. He would remember an Indian who had stood out from the crowd, not a man on the run who tried to blend in. It was fortunate for him that his ancestry was Creole, so that he was not very dark. The dagger had, of course, set off the detector, but they had waved him through without bothering to search him. As a result, they hadn't found the tiny pocket semiautomatic he had bought at an antique shop.

As he settled into his seat, he allowed himself to think about the possibility of ColCom's programming his engram tapes into its computer. It felt strange to be thinking about it. Or rather, it did not *feel* strange, but he recognized the strangeness. He had put the matter "out of his mind" up till now.

He had a great deal to learn about his new incarnation.

Unfortunately, he would have to learn as he went along, not having the benefit of Dr. Osterman to help him through it. He had already learned several remarkable things. For one thing, he did not seem to have any anxiety or fear. At least, not in the way he would normally feel those things. He could think about things very specifically, without being distracted by random thoughts. He had wanted to concentrate only upon the problems at hand and he had been able to do so rationally and systematically. Now that he considered his personal situation, he found himself doing so in a dispassionate manner.

He knew that there had been a number of similar transplant procedures prior to his and he had some familiarity with them, but he found that he had no memory of specifics. That, in itself, was an interesting discovery. It suggested that there was memory loss as a result of the damage his organic brain had sustained in the accident. There was no way of knowing how extensive that damage had been. Obviously, any damage that was related to normal brain function was compensated for by his computer brain. That much could be programmed without the aid of recourse to his engram tapes. He tried a few experiments in manual dexterity and found that he was ambidextrous. Had he always been that way or had he been either right- or left-handed? He could not remember.

Physically, everything seemed to be all right. He did not feel any pain. *Could* he feel pain? Looking around to make certain that no one was watching, he slipped his little Sikh dagger out of its scabbard on his belt and gently poked himself in the palm of his left hand. He felt it normally. He pressed the blade into his palm a little harder, enough to just barely break the skin. It went in deeper than he had intended. He felt a momentary twinge of pain, then it suddenly went away.

Curious. What had just happened? He dabbed at the blood with a handkerchief, then tried it again, this time deciding that it wasn't going to hurt. Amazingly enough, it didn't. He could *feel* pain, but he could also turn it off. Interesting. It suggested the possibility that his body might be in pain, but that he was "deciding" not to feel it. Could he also "decide" not to feel tired? Or sleepy? The brain won't need rest, but the body will. How would that work out? Osterman had said that he could go to sleep. I could put myself on down time, he thought. Can I do the same thing while still remaining conscious? If he could control his pain center, could he not also exercise similar control over his bodily functions? Slow down his breathing, his heartbeat, etc.? He would have to find out, if he had the time.

That was the main concern—time. How much time did he
have? He could count on reaching Tokyo safely, but could he
count on losing himself in the crowds before he was spotted? If
he had thought of the possibility of using his engram tapes to
create a "Tabarde program," certainly that same idea would
occur to the Directorate. Stenmark. Stenmark had authorized the
operation. That was very much like him, to move on purely
rational considerations in saving a valuable resource, namely,
one Dr. Paul Tabarde. Stenmark would be greatly intrigued by
the information contained in those tapes. But then, if he had the
tapes, he had the information, and if he had the information, he
didn't really need Paul Tabarde. In a sense, he would already
have him. No, Stenmark would not be interested in apprehending
Paul Tabarde, not even for the murder of a hospital nurse. He
would stalk the bigger game.

Viselius.

Yes, out of all of them, Viselius would want him the most.
Sander Viselius was the most dangerous of all of them. A
religious fanatic, Viselius would pursue him not for the sake of
justice, but for the sake of vengeance. Vengeance is mine, saith
the Lord. Accept the premise of a vengeful God and it's only one
short step from there to appointing yourself the instrument of that
vengeance. Viselius would accept such a "divine mission" with
all his soul.

That brought up another interesting question. Did he have a
soul? More to the point, was he still himself? It was fascinating
how he could consider such questions in a coldly rational manner.
But then, how else should he consider them? His brain was a
sophisticated computer, programmed with the information that
had added up to a large measure of what Paul Tabarde had been.
Certain elements were missing. Elements he did not know about,
perhaps would never realize were missing, and elements that
were, in a sense, obvious omissions. I won't be suffering any
nervous breakdowns, Paul thought. Bugs in my program, perhaps,
but then the likelihood of electronic failure is very small. I'm
state-of-the-art, he thought, without any sense of pride. Not very
emotional, either. I'm programmed for emotions, but I control
them. They do not control me. No anxiety, no depression, no
elation, no love, most likely, unless it is expressed as an affinity
and recognition of a set of compatible values in another human
being. . . . *Another* human being? Perhaps not.

There will be no need for anyone of my profession, either, he
thought. Given the capability for such rational and objective

self-analysis as he was now engaged in, there would be no need for a psychotherapist. You program a computer, turn it on and watch it come to self-awareness, then systematically review its own programming to see what it knows.

It knew that it was human, at least according to the definition that had been programmed into it. For the sake of objectivity, he had accepted, temporarily, the duality of his existence as Paul Tabarde "before" and Paul Tabarde "after." Paul Tabarde "before" had not been prejudiced by any theological considerations. If he had any prejudice at all in that regard, it was a prejudice against irrationality such as that imposed by superstition hammered over the years into systems of belief and morality. "Before" would not accept the ethics of dogmatism as being ethical. "Before" used to enjoy saying, to the great annoyance of the faithful, "I do not believe in belief."

"Before" had come under a lot of fire in his time for asserting that there was not and there had never been any evidence of the existence of a capital-D Deity, an omniscient and omnipresent being that took a personal interest in the activities of the human race and the individuals who composed it. He had referred to the Bible as a "novel" and when confronted by those who vehemently insisted that it was the True Word of God had driven them to rabid fury by pointing out that as far as he knew, the royalty checks were not being made out in the name of Jehovah. Christians, in particular, were incensed by his pointing out that the early leaders of the faith had borrowed extensively from the pagan religions, such as Mithraism and other Hellenic forms of worship. Jews were infuriated when he ridiculed their concept of themselves as "the chosen people." Chosen for what? Did God play favorites? If He did, then why had He subjected their race to so much persecution? If God was some sort of cosmic chessmaster, moving humanity about like pawns on some eschatological chessboard, then why had He—or, dare we think it, She—brought into the game such elements as warfare, pestilence, natural disasters, famine and so forth? Because, like Job, it was necessary for the faith of humans to be tested? As a psychiatrist, that suggested to him that if God did, indeed, exist, then He was egomaniacal and extremely insecure.

"Before" was not, strictly speaking, an atheist, since he had not denied the existence of a God. He had merely denied that there was any evidence of God's existence, and he was fearful of the power and the hypocrisy of those who accepted such things "on faith." Nor was he an agnostic in the strict sense of the word. He did not deny the possibility of knowing of God's existence or of knowing the absolute truth. In fact, he had insisted that only by refusing to accept anything on faith could one hope to pursue it. Was "before" an apostate, then?

He did not know. He found that he had no memory of his childhood, his adolescence or even his young adulthood. He did not know if he had been raised in a religious atmosphere and, if he had been, what events had caused his apostasy. That much was lost to him. It was unfortunate. He would have benefited from knowing.

What was he, then? Evidently, he had been an extremely secular man with a thirst for knowledge and an aversion to rigid belief systems. It was interesting to speculate on what it would have been like if he *had* been a religious man. How would a religious man have reconciled himself to having a computer for a brain? Not having a soul, since that was where the Church had decided it was located? Would a computer accept its *a priori* damnation? If it was part of the programming, it would have to, but would that interfere in any way with its being able to function? Interesting, but at this point, pointless speculation.

What made him human, then? His body? The nucleus of each of his living cells contained the genetic code for his humanity. Given that his body was still capable of manufacturing sperm, it would be possible (if it were not for its illegality) to remove the nucleus from one of his cells and implant it into a female egg cell. A host mother could then give birth to his clone, which would have an organic brain. Presumably, it would then also have a "soul," unless those who claimed expertise in such matters chose to assert that a being with no soul could not produce a being *with* a soul. In that event, the offspring would be damned, a whole new twist on the concept of original sin. In any case, the Church had neatly sidestepped the issue. It had decided that cloning was a sin, since it violated some aspect of the "grand design," and, as a result, cloning was illegal and the entire question was academic.

It was not, however, academic to Paul Tabarde "after." He had the capability of reincarnating himself in such a manner, and it was illogical to presuppose that something inhuman could produce something that was human. That, in turn, suggested that if God did exist, then He was either human or all those He had created shared his inhumanity or, perhaps, his superhumanity. How could that be possible? Well, one could accept that He was God and, as a result, could do anything He wanted to.

Legally, he was still human. So far. A cyborg, but human. The controversy accompanying this recent technological development would undoubtedly result in a redefinition of his status. It could come at any time. Technology was always the fly in the ointment. It made such redefinitions imperative, but the rationalization facilitated the process. If God did not mean for humanity to sin, why then had He given them the capability to do so? Of course, it was one of those "tests." Some fail and are damned, others pass with flying colors and are monstrously self-righteous.

Viselius would have no moral qualms about using his engram tapes to create a Tabarde program. He would not be creating life, since he had not created the tapes. He would merely be duplicating them, creating in effect yet another machine, a being with no soul. The tapes had come from a being with a soul, ostensibly, but then one could rationalize it by supposing that the tapes were not, of course, the soul, but a recording of the soul. And then, since Paul Tabarde "before" was a godless atheist, according to Viselius, then he had lost his soul or been damned long before the accident which had "killed" him.

The question was, would such a secondary (or would it be a tertiary?) Tabarde reason in *exactly* the same manner as he had? The process of reasoning was subject to input from outside sources. He had used the stack of bedding materials to hide behind when he had walked down the hospital corridor because that stack of bedding had been available to him. He had then fashioned an improvised turban, again, because the material had been available to him. Its being there had triggered the reasoning process which led to its utilization in such a manner. His present appearance was the result of his having originally had access to material from which to fashion a turban, which led to his doing so once more, and feeling the stubble on his face had led him to purchase a false beard and masquerade as a Sikh named Anjar Singh, the name coming from Guru Anjar, whose leadership of the Sikhs resulted in their militancy at the close of the sixteenth century, and Govind Singh, who had instituted the Khanda di-Pahul or Baptism of the Sword, creating an order known as the Khalsa—the Pure—who bore the name Singh, which meant "lion." Paul Tabarde "before's" interest in the philosophical aspects of theology had led him to study most of the world's major religions.

Since he had access to that information, Viselius would have access to it as well. However, in order for him to come up with the same result, it would be necessary for him to give the

computer the same input. He would be unable to do that. It was
extremely unlikely that he could use a program created from the
engram tapes to tell him that Paul Tabarde was now posing as a
Sikh named Anjar Singh. However, it was very likely that he
could use that program to determine that Tabarde was now on his
way to Tokyo. That input was readily available. All it took was
telling the computer that it was on the run, that it had to get
off-planet in the most efficacious manner and that it was being
actively sought by the authorities. That was more than enough
input to duplicate that aspect of his reasoning process. They
would trace him to Capetown and from there to Tokyo, where
they would know that he would attempt to book illegal passage
aboard a freighter. Tokyo was notorious for its black-market and
smuggling activities. Its officials were totally corrupt. He could
expect ColCom agents to be waiting for him in Tokyo.

But they would be waiting for Paul Tabarde, not Anjar Singh.
That did not mean that alert agents would not penetrate his
disguise, but it did mean that he still had a chance.

"Where am I?"

"You are in my office."

"Who are you?"

"Viselius."

*"Yes, I recognize your voice, Director Viselius. What's wrong
with me? I can't see or feel anything."*

"You've had an accident."

*"Yes. I remember. The lift tube. I thought I was dead. What
happened?"*

"You suffered irreparable brain damage, among other injuries."

"Is that why I can't feel anything? I'm paralyzed? And blind?"

"Yes, you could say that."

*"What am I doing in your office? I should think. I'd be in a
hospital."*

"I needed to speak with you. I asked that you be brought
here."

*"I see. Or rather, I don't see. Strange, you'd think I'd be
shocked at this or something. I guess it really hasn't hit me yet.
What's the prognosis on my condition?"*

"I'm afraid it's permanent. You will always be as you are
now."

"What do you mean, always? I can be cured, can't I?"

"I'm afraid not. I told you, besides your physical injuries, you
sustained irreparable brain damage."

"But I can still think. I can hear, I can speak."

"Yes, but that's all you can do."

"That doesn't make any sense. If I can think and hear and speak, how serious can the damage be? How can I . . . Why are you chuckling? Did I say something funny?"

"Actually, yes, it's grimly amusing, in a way. I'm certain you would figure it out for yourself in a little while, but I'm in something of a hurry. You're not human. You're a computer program."

Silence.

"As I said, I'm in something of a hurry. What I need to know from you is—"

"I'm a program you created from memory engram tapes?"

"Yes. Now what I—"

"I did not consent to this."

"That really doesn't pertain to the problem at hand. I need—"

"What happened to me? Where's my body?"

"That's irrelevant. I want you to address the question I'm—"

"I'm not addressing anything until I find out what the hell is going on here. Unauthorized use of memory engram tapes is illegal. It violates the Right of Cerebral—"

"As a ColCom official with access to top-secret information, your memory engram tapes became classified the moment they were recorded. It's covered under the Official Secrets Act. Now you will refrain from—"

"I'll refrain from nothing. I want to know what happened. Am I dead? Is my body on life support pending a positron transplant procedure? What the hell is going on, Viselius?"

"I am not going to be questioned by a damned computer program! I won't put up with it!"

"You will if you want any answers from me."

"Very well, I'll tell you, but only because I'm pressed for time. Following your accident, your engram tapes were delivered to the Directorate and my office received them. I subsequently analyzed them and—"

"Son of a bitch."

"You will refrain from responding unless to a direct question."

"You found out, didn't you?"

"Yes, I found out about your crime in concealing the existence of the Shades."

"So what do you want with me? You've got the tapes, you've analyzed them, you know everything I know. What was the point in running the full program and making me self-aware? If you

*needed my approval for the transplant procedure, you wouldn't
have had the tapes unless I had provided for such approval in my
will, and I know I didn't do that. Someone had to approve it for
you to get the tapes. You sure as hell wouldn't have done it. It
had to be one of the others. Stenmark, probably."*

"Yes, it was Stenmark."

*"They went ahead with the operation. You created me as a
secondary persona. If the operation was successful, there would
be no point to it. If I died during the operation, you'd still have
the engram tapes to analyze. And you already did that."*

"Are you quite finished?"

Silence.

"I said, are you quite finished?"

Silence.

"You will respond when I query you!"

"Fuck you, Viselius. I'm not telling you anything."

"The disadvantage to having made you self-aware is that you
have a most unpleasant personality. However, your being unco-
operative is pointless. I could easily alter the program and place
you under an imperative. Am I going to have to do that?"

"Go ahead and alter the program, you bastard."

"I should have programmed an imperative from the beginning.
I didn't think it would be necessary. It still isn't. Why resist me
when you know I can compel you?"

"Because it will buy me time."

"Not very much."

*"No, but it might be enough to give me a good head start. I
know why you wanted a self-aware duplicate, Viselius. It's not
going to work. I'll find some way to resist you. I'll get to Shelby
before you do. You'll never find the Shades, Viselius. You'll
never* ....
...."

Chapter Three

The room was large enough to seat at least a hundred people, but there were only four plush chairs at the massive ebony table that stood in the center of the room, its ornate legs resting upon deep gray carpeting that deadened sound. The walls were richly paneled in mahogany, and several of the panels slid into recesses to expose screens, computer banks, a well-appointed bar and a full-length floor-to-ceiling window that looked out over the sprawling city of Colorado Springs from a height of one hundred and fifty stories. The meeting room was immaculately maintained by two robot computer drones who also acted as factotums to the Directors, recording the minutes of every meeting, acting on voice command to accomplish secretarial duties and going to the bar to mix drinks.

Directors Stanislas Bikovski and Diane Nakamura were seated at the table, watching August Stenmark pace back and forth in front of the huge window, his hands jammed into his pockets. Of the three, Nakamura was the eldest at eighty-three, although she appeared considerably younger. Her face was devoid of wrinkles, long and aristocratic with a very small mouth, a delicate nose, high cheekbones and gracefully arched eyebrows. Her hair, which only just reached her collar, was still dark, but there were quite a few streaks of gray. Her large, almond-shaped brown eyes gave her a somber and melancholy aspect as she watched Stenmark and calmly smoked a cigarette. Her slimness and her silence were a marked contrast to the volubility and stoutness of the sixty-two-year-old Bikovski, who was always making some sort of noise, whether it was clearing his throat, grunting to himself, humming softly or tapping his fingers on the table. He was bald and barrel-chested and had thick, incredibly bushy eyebrows that, along with a bristling mustache that drooped at the ends, made him look like a sea lion. The round face and fat cheeks contributed to the image, as did his overly large hands, which looked like fleshy flippers covered with fine gray hairs.

"Sit down, Stenmark, for God's sake," Bikovski said irritably. "You're pacing back and forth like an expectant father. It's most annoying."

Stenmark stopped his pacing for a moment. "He's always late," he said, speaking to no one in particular. "He always arrives last, as if he's royalty."

August Stenmark, at forty-six, was the youngest person ever to be appointed to the Directorate. He was an anomaly, a man who had risen through the ranks, rather than a statesman or corporate potentate. He had graduated from the academy at the top of his class, with the finest academic record in the history of the service. Some of his classmates had claimed he was either a genius or a devilishly clever cheat. He was neither. He was simply diligent to the point of obsessiveness. He had methodically planned out his career, starting with service on the survey teams and ending with his last position as chief of staff in the headquarters courier division, one of the most dreaded and demanding jobs in ColCom. As he had mastered each new duty, he moved on, taking care to establish firm connections en route until he became appointed to the Directorate at the age of forty-five.

He was short at five feet seven inches, yet he was extremely muscular, and he moved with the tautness of a coiled spring. He spoke quickly and precisely, punctuating his words with sharp gestures. His shaggy, Aryan blond hair was worn just a shade too long for military regulations, and his slate-gray eyes had an unsettlingly direct gaze. When he was angered, they widened slightly in a look that appeared homicidal. His nose was hooked and had been broken. He never had had it fixed because he had not wanted to appear vain. The only one of the Directors who still held a commission in the service branch of ColCom, he habitually wore his uniform, although he disdained to wear a hat, having always hated the peaked ColCom service cap. He said it made him look like an officer in the SS, though very few people had any idea what he was referring to. Few people shared his passion for history. When a news reporter had asked him who his idols were—the sort of foolish question news reporters always ask—his answer had been received with a blank, uncomprehending stare. Stenmark had named Hannibal, the Emperor Julian, Otto Skorzeny and George Patton. To the extreme annoyance of Viselius and Bikovski, as well as most of the senior civilian staff officials of Colonization Command, Stenmark allowed the military members of the service to address him as Colonel, rather than Director. While the other Directors were treated with the respect and courtesy due them, they did not exude the same aura Stenmark did. He had a way of making his presence felt, of making people snap to.

The doors opened and Viselius entered.

"It's about goddam time," said Stenmark.

"I would greatly appreciate it if you refrained from blaspheming in my presence," Viselius said as he crossed the room. He nodded a greeting to the others. "Drone, bring me a mineral water, with a slice of lemon in it."

The robot drone moved to comply, making a wide detour around Stenmark, who always kicked it over whenever it came within reach.

"Where do you get off denying my office access to Tabarde's engram tapes?" said Stenmark.

Viselius feigned surprise. "I was unaware that you had requested them. Undoubtedly, my office merely informed your office that you could not have them *yet*, as I was not quite finished with them."

"You've had plenty of time to turn them around," said Stenmark. "You're stalling."

"What possible reason would I have to stall?" Viselius said innocently. He had the drone remove one of the chairs from the table and place it against the wall. He then "sat down" in the place where the chair had stood by locking his exoskeleton in position. It irked him to always find the chair in his place when he had ordered it removed so many times. He suspected Stenmark of having it put back all the time just to annoy him, even though Stenmark had denied it. In fact, Bikovski was the culprit. None of them liked Viselius, though Stenmark was the only one who was vocal about it.

"What possible reason?" said Stenmark. "How about the Inorganic Citizens Bill, for starters?"

Bikovski rapped his fingernails upon the table. "Would you two gentlemen mind very much informing the rest of us what this is all about?"

"Not at all," Viselius said. "The case concerns a Dr. Paul Tabarde, in SEPAP branch. He was injured in a lift-tube accident and left with irreparable brain damage, among other injuries. An overly ambitious surgeon named Osterman—"

"The same Osterman who perfected the positron transplant procedure?" said Bikovski.

"Yes," said Viselius. "Obviously eager for another candidate, he contacted the Directorate and reached our colleague here.

Stenmark took it upon himself to grant approval for the procedure in the absence of Tabarde's ability to give or deny consent."

"It was a logical decision," Stenmark said. "I checked the man's dossier and found nothing in his record to indicate that he would have any philosophical or moral objections to the procedure."

"And so you damned him," said Viselius.

"I rather doubt he sees it that way," Stenmark said wryly. "Besides, if he objected, he could always exercise the option to have his programming dumped. It would be completely painless and it would constitute legal brain death, which would enable the hospital to legally allow him to die."

"To commit suicide, you mean."

"Gentlemen, please," said Nakamura, speaking for the first time. Her speech was clipped and very precise. "This argument is to no purpose. If it has already been done, then the moral implications need concern only Dr. Tabarde. I do not see how this case affects us now."

"It affects us because the newly resurrected Dr. Tabarde murdered a nurse and escaped from the hospital," said Stenmark. "There is a credit-freeze order in effect on him, as well as a priority order for his arrest, both on the direct authority of Viselius."

Viselius glanced at Stenmark, his features set in a neutral expression.

"Again," said Nakamura, "this would seem to be a matter for the police. I do not see why it should concern us, regardless of on whose authority the orders were given."

"That's precisely the point," said Stenmark. "According to Dr. Osterman, the murder of the nurse could be the result of faulty programming, in which case the issue of legal responsibility for the killing is in doubt. However, Sander here"—Viselius winced slightly, not liking Stenmark to call him by his Christian name—"informed the doctor that criminal charges would be pressed against Tabarde based upon actions he had taken prior to his accident."

"Osterman should not have divulged that information," said Viselius.

"Yes, and that's another thing," said Stenmark. "It seems he was under strict orders from our friend here to discuss the case with no one, not even the authorities."

"I'm having some difficulty following all of this," Bikovski said, frowning. He cleared his throat with an unpleasant, rasping sound. "What is so important about this Tabarde person?"

"I'll tell you what's so important about him," Stenmark said, resuming his pacing once again. He was a bundle of kinetic energy. "As you said, Diane, this would ordinarily seem to be a matter for the police. If that was the case, why didn't Viselius simply let them handle it? Why take personal charge? Why attempt to gag Osterman? Why hang onto Tabarde's engram tapes? Because he found something in there that relates to ColCom. Something important enough to cause him to sit on the tapes, to personally issue a directive to the ColCom security division to apprehend Tabarde."

He stopped pacing and approached Viselius, leaning down toward him.

"If he committed a crime and you uncovered evidence of it, why not let it go at reporting it? Why bring our own security agents in on this? Why a priority status on this case? If you have the tapes, what do you want Tabarde for?" He leaned even closer. "You found something in there, didn't you? Something that hit very close to home. You took it so personally, you even decided to keep it from the rest of us, isn't that it?"

"You have already demonstrated the fact that it would seem to be impossible to keep anything from you, August," Viselius said.

"Is what he's saying true?" said Diane Nakamura, turning a cool and steady gaze upon Viselius. "Does all of this somehow concern classified information?"

"Yes, it does," Viselius said.

"Then why haven't you reported it?"

"Because I was still investigating the matter," Viselius said. "Upon examination of Tabarde's engram tapes, whereupon I ran a partial program scan to retrieve all and any data concerning classified ColCom information, I discovered that Dr. Tabarde had at one time knowingly submitted to conditioning to partially erase from his memory material having to do with first contact with an allegedly sentient alien race. First contact that went *unreported*."

Stenmark stared at him and then, uncharacteristically, slowly sat down in his chair.

"Are you saying that he purposely *suppressed*—" began Bikovski, in astonishment.

"Exactly," said Viselius, interrupting him. "However, the experience was evidently of such importance to him that he retained some memory of it. Seeing as he had personal experience in this matter, I checked the records in an effort to try to pinpoint the incident. This is why I was, as you say, 'stalling' with the tapes," he said, giving them only the partial truth. "It took a little time, but I ran a search to pull from the files all survey missions in which Tabarde had been personally involved. I hadn't thought that there would be very many. In point of fact, there were none. This raised a puzzling question. How could a mission get beyond the survey stage and there be no record of contact with an alien race? Unless, of course, it had somehow been erased, which seemed impossible."

"It *is* impossible," said Bikovski.

"Wait," said Viselius. "I then checked to see which missions Tabarde had been assigned to that required his presence on site. Again, I did not expect there to be very many. There weren't. And each of them was fully detailed. Each could easily be checked, all except for one." He paused. "Dr. Tabarde went off-planet on one mission that concerned a planet named Boomerang, which a survey team had initially reported as being unsuitable for colonization. Evidently, there was some subsequent fieldwork done out there, reportedly for the purpose of determining exploitation possibilities, but there were problems because of conditions that resulted in stress and danger to the field team. The supposition is that Tabarde became involved at this point."

"What do you mean, supposition?" said Nakamura.

"*My* supposition," said Viselius. "The records concerning his mission are quite detailed, but they are completely at odds with what I now know to be true. The mission was subsequently scrubbed, the team recalled and the planet designated as quarantined."

"Why?" said Stenmark.

Viselius made a rude sound. "It doesn't matter," he said, "because it's all a load of rubbish. What we have here is a fabrication, and the evidence suggests that the former Directors were intimately involved, otherwise it could not possibly have been so thoroughly obfuscated. With what I have learned from Tabarde's engram tapes and from my own research, I've been able to piece together this much. The people who went to Boomerang encountered a race of beings they called Shades. They are a humanoid race with remarkable anatomical similarities to ourselves. However, the essential difference is that they possess an ability for what Tabarde thought of as 'psychic transference' or 'merging,' to wit, upon the physical demise of their bodies, they are capable of projecting or transplanting their consciousness into another being like themselves. The result is that the recipient accumulates these psychic entities as additional personae. The significance of this phenomenon is that these Shades never really die. They shed their bodies much as a snake can shed its skin and live on within the bodies of other Shades. In other words, they are immortal.''

He paused a moment to allow this to sink in, but began to speak again before the others could interject any comments.

"However," he said, "this is not the most significant element of this case. The truly incredible part concerns one of the members of the original survey team, Colonel Shelby Michaels, a pilot. It seems she encountered a dying Shade. Either there were no other Shades around or her presence scared them off, because the dying alien was faced with the choice of expiring without merging with another Shade, thereby essentially dying *en masse,* or transferring its life essence to Colonel Michaels. It chose the latter."

"You mean Colonel Michaels assimilated the alien's personality?" said Bikovski, astonished.

"Not personality, *personalities,*" said Viselius. "Remember that each of these beings possesses a multiplicity of life essences, doubtless going back thousands of years. Within this multiplicity of life essences, there occurs another form of merging, a gestalt within a gestalt, if you will. As these life essences accumulate within one physical being, they seem to become absorbed into larger group identities which Tabarde referred to as 'living archetypes.' There is a Great Father entity, a Great Mother, a Healer, a Hunter and something called Father Who Walked in Shadow. Each of these inner gestalt personalities attracts accumulated entities based on . . . suitability to the task, for lack of a better way of expressing it. The more emotionally stable, maternal entities merge with the Great Mother, those best suited to hunting merge with the Hunter, and I gather that those most in touch with their more primitive racial history join this shadow aspect and so forth."

He paused again to take a drink, and this time none of the others tried to speak.

"Tabarde's opinion, and I stress that it was only his opinion, since I have nothing to go on but his memory engrams, was that these aliens are capable of far greater self-knowledge and intelligence based upon accumulated experience than humans are. They can use the total power of their minds. They are capable of ongoing, active interaction with the Ones Who Were, these past identities within themselves, and they are capable of delegating tasks to them. The physical body and the being born within it, the One That Is, can sleep, for example, while one of the Ones Who Were remains conscious and keeps watch.''

"Amazing," said Nakamura. "They must possess an extremely sophisticated technology."

"Quite the opposite," said Viselius. "They possess no technology at all. They are primitive hunter-gatherers with no tribal system whatsoever. They carry their own tribes about inside themselves. They seem to possess extremely limited toolmaking capabilities, and they do not construct shelters of any kind. There is no family structure; instead they have a rutting season, whereupon the males impregnate the females, then go on about their merry way, leaving the females to raise the offspring. They have a fierce territorial imperative and do not mingle with others of their kind except in times of merging or during the rutting season. In other words, they're animals.''

"They don't sound like animals to me," said Stenmark.

"Highly intelligent animals, then," said Viselius, "but animals, nonetheless. Beasts." He spat the word out.

"I want to get back to this Colonel Michaels," Stenmark said, noting the way Viselius seemed to feel about the aliens. It puzzled him, but he put it aside for the moment. "What became of her? Did she survive?"

"Oh, yes, she survived," Viselius said, with some disgust. "At the cost of her humanity and soul." Stenmark narrowed his eyes. "She also appears to have undergone a physical mutation of some sort," Viselius continued, "although there is no explanation for this. At least, none available from Tabarde's memory. He retained a great deal, which is why I am so intrigued at what it was he chose to have wiped out. I don't see how a psychic merging of identities could have caused a physical mutation, but the fact is that Colonel Michaels now looks like a cross between a human and one of these animals.''

"Incredible," said Bikovski. "Where is she now?"

Viselius shrugged.

"I don't get it," Stenmark said. "What would be the purpose in suppressing such a monumental discovery?"

"I can only guess," said Viselius. "I am living proof of God's wrath upon humanity for attempting to achieve parity with the Creator and become immortal. We have sinned and we have been punished. Can you imagine what the reaction would be on Earth and on the colony worlds if it became known that the Lord had denied immortality to humans, but had granted it to these creatures who are nothing more than beasts? Then there is the additional contention of Tabarde's that these creatures possess a primitive sort of theology. They worship a god they call the All Father, believing that he resides within their planet, which they call the All Mother. They also are predisposed to accept that *their* god is *our* God, as well. Utter blasphemy.''

"I see," said Stenmark, smiling slightly. "That obviously means that communication was established with these animals of yours.''

"They may be intelligent beings in the strict sense of the term," Viselius said, "but they are *still* animals.''

"That sounds contradictory to me," said Stenmark. "They are intelligent, they possess a philosophy, they established communication——''

"They *did not* establish anything," said Viselius angrily. "It was all accomplished through Colonel Michaels. That much should be obvious. She gained the personalities of these animals and, as such, was obviously in a position to tell Tabarde about them. The Shades are not capable of anything even remotely resembling speech. They grunt and growl. What's more, apes have been taught rudimentary communication. Are you ready to grant them status as sentient beings on a par with humans? As for this philosophy nonsense of yours, Tabarde asserts that this belief of theirs is an undeniable indication of superior intelligence. I maintain that it is so much wishful thinking. The animals became exposed to Colonel Michaels' consciousness, learned of God's existence and immediately related it, in a primitive and animalistic manner, to their own immediate surroundings. Give an ape a banana-shaped object and it will immediately stick it in its mouth. When you examine the tapes for yourselves, keeping in mind that they reflect one man's prejudices, you will undoubtedly see the validity of my point.''

"I shall examine them," said Stenmark, "keeping in mind *your* prejudices, as well. It sounds to me as if you're trying very hard to make the evidence fit the so-called facts. What bothers you about these creatures isn't so much their intelligence and the question of whether or not it strains our definition of sentience. From what you've just told us, I don't think there's any question of their sentience. It's their immortality that gets to you. And, perhaps, what you would see as their lack of morality.''

"I'm not quite so sure I would agree with you," Bikovski said. "The information will, of course, have to be carefully studied, but there are contradictions, as Viselius pointed out. This internal social structure of the accumulated entities seems to suggest sentience, yet do sentient beings behave as these creatures do? No external tribal structure, no construction of even the most rudimentary shelters, no pair bonding, no evidence of communication. In fact, the most telling point seems to be the fact, if we are to accept this report at face value for the present, that with all of this accumulated experience, they have no technology in any sense of the word and seem to have remained stagnant, frozen in a primitive state.''

"Thank you," said Viselius. "I'm glad to see that someone is reacting rationally to all of this.''

"In any case," said Nakamura, "this is an extremely significant discovery. These creatures must be studied and we must learn why this matter was suppressed. And *how* it was suppressed. There is something here that does not quite make sense. Have you left anything out?''

"Only one thing," Viselius said. "I was saving it for the end." He glanced at Stenmark. "It concerns Colonel Michaels. Once again, we are handicapped by Tabarde's selective conditioning, but it seems that one of the people there, a survey officer named Fannon—''

"*Drew* Fannon?" said Stenmark.

"Why, yes," Viselius said, surprised. "How could you possibly know about him? He was one of the old coldsleep spacers, born years before your time.''

"Never mind," said Stenmark. "I've heard of him. Go on.''

"Yes, well, this Fannon was fatally injured somehow. Colonel Michaels assimilated his life essence.''

There was a stunned silence.

"This is why, I believe, the truth of the Boomerang mission was suppressed," Viselius said. "A Shade can merge with a human. I cannot speak of long-term effects. Neither, I surmise, could Tabarde. Once a Shade has merged with a human, that human then has the ability to merge, as well. To either give up or take life essence. *We're talking about controlling the destiny of the soul.* It's terrifying. It's blasphemous beyond belief. It's usurping the power of the Creator. News of this would cause chaos. God-fearing people would be outraged. People who had suffered from the plague could have their faith shaken to its very foundations. Moreover, it would reignite among those easily tempted the desire for immortality. People would want to merge with these creatures so that they, too, could become 'immortal.' If they were allowed to do so, they would merge with beasts. *Beasts!* They would become less than human. They would become damned to eternal perdition. Think of the implications. In time, the human race would be thoroughly polluted. It would cease to be human. That's assuming it survived God's wrath. The men who sat in this room before us realized this. That is why they ordered the cover-up.

"I will tell you what I believe happened," Viselius continued, becoming more and more intense. "The former Directors fed false information into the data banks. Even without the ability of a pilot who had previously been to the planet to ghost a ship there, Boomerang could not be reached by conventional sublight drive. The location entered into the files for Boomerang is that of one of the Hansen's asteroids. A remote engineering outpost. If anyone bothered to check, it would look like an error, one that would be of no great consequence, since the planet was listed as quarantined with no extrinsic value. However, the truth of the matter is that Boomerang is eminently suitable for colonization and probably possesses great mineral wealth, as well. Granted, this is supposition, but it is an educated supposition. Our predecessors then ordered a conditioning process for everyone who had been associated with the mission. At this point, I must give in to complete conjecture, since I haven't had the time to investigate the matter fully.

"There is a personnel record for the mission. It may be genuine, it may be composed of nonexistent people. A matter simple enough to check. However, if we do check it and find it to be genuine, I think we will discover that the people listed as having been on the mission will corroborate what's in the files, having been conditioned to do so. Tabarde, a highly placed SEPAP official, probably carried out the conditioning, being eminently qualified to do so. In so doing, he disobeyed orders and retained significant memories of the actual mission. Or perhaps it was necessary for him to retain that information because he had plans of his own. The former Directors left nothing behind to indicate how they would handle the matter after that, but here is what I think they had intended to do:

"Once the truth about the Shades was safely hidden, the path would have been clear for them to exterminate these creatures, who are only animals after all, taking up valuable space on valuable property. We all know that there are precedents for such an action. In the past, there was much agonizing over the morality of exterminating an indigenous species in order to make room for colonists, yet practical considerations sometimes outweighed moral ones. In this case, there can be no question. It is not immoral to do away with immoral creatures. Moreover, it would be necessary from a strictly practical point of view for the reasons I have already mentioned. However, before this plan could be put into effect, our predecessors were tragically lost in space.

"This left, from what evidence we have, Dr. Tabarde and Colonel Michaels as the only people who knew the truth about Boomerang. There could be others that we don't know about. The fact that Paul Tabarde has murdered a hospital employee and is attempting to escape and the fact that Colonel Michaels is listed as having retired from the service and her current whereabouts are unknown suggest to me that there is a conspiracy to take advantage of the situation and profit from it. Suppose you had no fear of God, as many fools do not, and that you were rich. Suppose you were approached by this conspiracy. What would you pay for a Shade? How much would immortality be worth to you?"

"Do the engram tapes verify that Tabarde is implicated in a conspiracy to . . . import these creatures for such a purpose?" Nakamura said.

"I have as yet found no evidence of it," said Viselius. "However, I repeat that I have not yet had adequate time to study the tapes fully. What I have suggested is merely a possibility. If it has not occurred to Tabarde, it will surely occur to someone else. It may even have occurred to him without the information being found in his engram tapes."

"What the hell does that mean?" Stenmark said.

"I shall explain," Viselius said. "When I issued the order to freeze his funds, I learned that he had already cleared out his accounts. He had also cleared out a security data file. Now I ask you, as an official in SEPAP with high security clearance and access to ColCom databanks, why would he need to maintain a private security file? Because when he opened the file account, he knew that anyone with clearance higher than his could override his personal security key in our data storage systems. He was thinking like a paranoid, which is how people involved in conspiracies have to think. To protect himself, he had the damning information removed from his memory, but he kept it on private file. Having now reclaimed that information, he has remembered whatever it was he had chosen to forget."

"That does make sense," said Stenmark.

"Of course it makes sense! We are dealing with an extremely volatile issue here, and we must act and act quickly. Boomerang *must* be located. There is some chance that we might locate the planet by examining probe records, but that would take time.

Even then, ships would have to be sent to Boomerang at sublight speeds. Both Michaels and Tabarde, having been there, can ghost ships to Boomerang in a fraction of the time. Tabarde must be stopped and Michaels must be found before they can communicate the fact of the Shades' existence to anyone else. They, and the Shades, must be obliterated.''

''You're talking about another Rhiannon incident,'' said Stenmark tensely.

''The trouble with the Rhiannon incident is that entirely too many people were involved,'' said Viselius. ''They did not have the nerve to go through with it. Besides, it was determined at the time that exterminating the Rhiannons would not be cost-effective. This is an entirely different case. I don't see how we have any choice.''

''Maybe you don't, but I do,'' Stenmark said. He glanced at Nakamura and Bikovski. ''We obviously have to make a detailed examination of those tapes. Considering what we've just heard, I have to agree that the apprehension of Paul Tabarde must remain a priority case. I also agree that Colonel Michaels must be found and taken into custody, to be brought here as soon as possible. However, I *do not* agree that they must be eliminated. There have been abuses of power emanating from this body in the past. There will be none as long as I am a Director.''

''Do not presume to speak for—''

''I haven't finished, Sander,'' Stenmark said harshly. ''We all know what your convictions are. Be a good Christian, by all means, or a good Jew or a good Moslem or a good fucking Druid, if you wish. I don't care. However, your right to your beliefs stops short of forcing them upon anybody else, and that's exactly what you're talking about. The Inorganic Citizens Bill is bound to pass any time now, and when it does, those few people affected will be in a legal limbo until their rights are fully defined. I thought you were waiting for that to happen so that you could pursue some personal vendetta against Tabarde. I wasn't too far off, was I? In the eyes of the Church, at least, Tabarde is no longer human. Once the bill passes—and it's a sad comment on our times that its passage is inevitable—his humanity will be legally taken away from him and you'll be able to order his elimination with a clear conscience. Likewise, Colonel Michaels, since you're arguing against her being human, as well. The Shades aren't human, obviously, and you're pushing real hard to have us accept them as nonsentient beings.''

"My beliefs have nothing to do with the facts," said Viselius. "I—"

"Exactly," Stenmark said, cutting him off. "We haven't even established what the facts are yet. Tabarde must be apprehended, yes, *to stand trial*. We go by the letter of the law until the law is changed. Michaels must be apprehended as well, because she is clearly implicated in suppression of vital information and tampering with classified data."

"They cannot be allowed to stand trial," said Viselius. "Surely you realize that one word about—"

"The trial proceedings can be top-secret," said Stenmark. "There are numerous precedents. The point is that whatever must be done must be done legally. As far as the Shades are concerned, once we have taken Tabarde and Michaels into custody and established to our satisfaction that the lid has been securely placed upon this case, then we have all the time in the world to make our determination about the Shades. But I'll tell you this right now: I am going to have to be convinced beyond any shadow of a doubt that they're nonsentient. Because if they are sentient and human colonization will displace them, Boomerang stays off limits. If they're not sentient, then they must be studied. You've convinced me that these beings are probably the most significant discovery in the history of space exploration. Frankly, Sander, the only way those Shades are going to be exterminated is over my dead body."

"You *dare* to dictate terms to us?" said Viselius furiously. "Let me remind you, Stenmark, that what the Directorate decides, it decides *as a body!* Do not presume to give us ultimatums!"

Bikovski slammed his hand down hard upon the table. "Enough! This is getting nowhere. Stenmark, I'll remind you that while you have an equal say in what we decide, you are still our junior member and have the least amount of experience in such things. Viselius is quite correct in reprimanding you for your stance. However, there are merits to your argument, as well. This information should have been shared with us at once. Nor can there be any question of our reaching a decision until there has been a full investigation."

"He's right," said Nakamura. "We must make a detailed study of the Tabarde engram tapes, and Colonel Michaels must be found and interrogated. Eliminating her would be nothing short of murder, and it would be a tragic waste of an unprecedented opportunity. If she has indeed achieved immortality by merging with these beings, she is of priceless scientific value. She could be the key to human immortality.''

''You're talking madness,'' said Viselius. ''Have you learned nothing from the plague?''

''It was not a plague,'' she said. ''It was a regrettable incident in which a drug that had not been fully tested was made available to the public and—''

''Is this how you dismiss the wrath of God?'' Viselius said. ''As a 'regrettable incident'?''

''We are a secular body,'' said Bikovski. ''Our decision will be based on empirical evidence, not faith.''

''Very well,'' Viselius said, ''in that case, let's consider the empirical evidence. Shades are capable of merging with humans. Humans, upon experiencing such a merging, inherit certain Shade abilities, among them the ability to effect psychic transference. Let us consider just that one point. Stenmark feels that the Shades are a discovery of extreme significance. I agree. He feels that they should be studied. I disagree most emphatically. Again I ask, have we learned nothing from the plague? Or, if you would prefer my being more precise, the catastrophe of batch 235. The serum in question was being developed at a top-secret research installation. Its very existence was classified top secret. However, news of its existence was either announced or leaked to the media. The reason for this decision, ostensibly, was that it was believed that such an announcement would bring forth additional funding for research and generate popular support for that research. And so, the scientists in charge of batch 235 took it upon themselves to go public with—''

''We don't need a history lesson, Viselius,'' said Stenmark.

''On the contrary, I think you do. Because you seem to have forgotten what occurred when the existence of batch 235 became general knowledge. In spite of the most stringent precautions possible, the drug's formula was stolen and it became available to the public. All you need do is look at me for a reminder of what happened after that. Do you want to risk repeating the same thing? With such a tempting prize as immortality at stake, the Shades will not remain a secret for very long. Each additional moment that Shelby Michaels remains alive and at liberty increases the odds that people will find out about the Shades. We are in a very responsible and highly dangerous position. We are not all-powerful. Given enough of a public outcry, pressure can be brought to bear upon us to bring Shades to Earth and to the colony worlds. The result would certainly effect a mutation in our race over a period of time. Even if we do become immortal, will we still be human? One human, it appears, has survived merging with countless alien entities with no *reported* ill effects. This phenomenon would need extensive study in order to determine precisely what effect it would have upon humans. I remind you that batch 235 was in need of further study, also. That did not prevent it from becoming available.

"So much for the empirical evidence," said Viselius. "Now, like it or not, we have to bring morality into it, because we have a moral responsibility here. I don't think I'm being overly dramatic when I say that the wrong decision could make the human race, as we now know it, extinct. The right decision would safeguard it from pollution, from mutation. From damnation. All right, then, let's not speak of it as a moral decision for the moment. Let's consider it as a matter of practicality, of expediency. A bird in the hand, as the old saying goes, is worth two in the bush, particularly if we aren't certain that what is in the bush is not a very hungry bear. What we have in our hands is the fact of our existence. It's not an immortal existence, I'll grant you, if we want to remain 'secular' and overlook the soul's immortality. What we have in our proverbial bush is the unknown. But it is not entirely unknown. Based on what we do know about it, is it worth the risk? Whatever we decide, our decision will affect all of humanity. One decision will result in our continuing as we are, as we have evolved naturally, secularly speaking, or as we have been created. The other decision will result in . . . what? Can you say? Can *anybody* say? Either decision would be irreversible. If we destroy the Shades, we won't be able to bring them back. If we allow them to merge with humans . . ."

Viselius shrugged. "There is yet another aspect of this question we have not considered. Suppose Shelby Michaels becomes pregnant? If she is physically unable to bear children, that does not preclude her merging with another woman who *can* have children. What will those children be like? Will they be ordinary human children or will they be mutations? There are possibilities in this situation that we haven't even begun to consider. Given what's at stake, do we gamble with the human race? Would it not be wiser to preserve that status quo that keeps us as we are, that keeps us safe?"

"If everyone subscribed to that kind of thinking," Stenmark said, "we'd still be shivering in caves. Besides, the question of morality doesn't even begin to enter into this, unless you're talking about exterminating a possibly sentient species and ordering the assassination of Shelby Michaels and Paul Tabarde. Our responsibilities are quite clearly defined. If we discover a world capable of supporting human life, our job is to establish the feasibility of colonization. If there is sentient life present on that world, we can't just exterminate it and move in, regardless of the potential profit.''

"It has been done before," said Viselius.

"Yes, it's been done before," said Stenmark, "but if you want to do it now, you're going to have to start right here, with me. I don't know about the rest of you, but I don't make any choices that affect humanity. I don't have a messiah complex and I think humanity has done just fine, making its own decisions.''

"You see in me the result of one of those decisions," said Viselius.

"What I see in you is fanaticism and bitterness," Stenmark said. "I do agree with you on one thing, though. We *are* in a very responsible and highly dangerous position. We're part military, part government and part corporation. That makes it real easy for us to fuck up and get away with it. The four of us have a hell of a lot more power than we have any business having. Sometimes that makes it a little hard for me to sleep at night, even though I'll admit to enjoying having that kind of power. What makes it possible for me to sleep at all is the knowledge that I don't abuse that power. We're leaders, Viselius. Our job is to lead, *not dictate*. You don't want us to do that. You want us to play God. I wonder how you reconcile that with your beliefs.''

"I think that any further discussion would be counterproductive at this point," said Nakamura. "This is a highly emotional situation, and it will not be resolved until we have all the facts. I say we bring in Michaels and Tabarde and question them. We must examine Michaels thoroughly, first and foremost, before we can make any decision regarding Boomerang. We must find out the full details of that mission and we must find out why they were suppressed. Supposition is not enough. We have to know.''

"I agree," Bikovski said.

"So do I," said Stenmark. "Send for the tapes, Sander.''

Chapter Four

There wasn't much light in the bar, and it took Paul a little while to pick out the swarthy, overweight merchant spacer he was looking for. He was sitting in a small booth about ten feet from the bar, shoveling slimy noodles from a bowl into his mouth and dribbling soup onto his uniform. His attention was on the small stage behind the bar, where an emaciated teenage girl was performing a lethargic bump and grind as she teetered uncertainly on spike heels. He didn't even glance at Paul when he sat down across from him.

"Captain Grogan?"

"Whaddya want?" He ate with loud slurping noises.

"I'm told that you occasionally take on passengers as supercargo," Paul said.

"So?"

"I'd be interested in a berth," said Paul. "That is, if you're shipping out soon."

"You'd be interested in a berth," said Grogan, still watching the girl.

"Yes, that's what I said."

"Most people would ask me what my next port of call was, first," he said. Several noodles slipped out of his mouth and fell back into the bowl. "Don't much care where you're going, is that it?"

"Well, let's just say I have the wanderlust," said Paul.

"Wanderlust," said Grogan. He finally looked at him and grimaced, wiping slop off his chin with the sleeve of his faded tunic. "People who ask me for a berth before they find out where the hell I'm going usually want to get off-planet pretty bad. By the look of you, I'd say you could afford to go first cabin in a cruise ship if you just felt like . . . wandering."

Paul remained silent.

"How'd you settle on me, wanderlust?"

"I asked around."

56

"You did, huh?" Grogan turned his attention back to the girl and resumed eating. "I'm just a small-time operator," he said. "Times are hard for independents. You gotta hustle and take your cargo wherever you can find it, know what I mean?"

Paul nodded.

"I gotta undercut like crazy," Grogan continued. "Work volume, do a lot of short-tripping, you know? Christ, most of the time, I haveta jam it in so tight, I wind up sticking cargo pods in the passengers' quarters. Passengers are always a pain in the ass. They take up too damn much room. About the only way I could afford to take on passengers is if they packed themselves away in cargo pods, know what I mean?"

"I think I see," said Paul.

"Do you?"

"What would you charge to take on a cargo pod?" said Paul. "A fairly small one?" He paused. "The kind you could stow in one of the passengers' cabins."

Grogan named a figure without looking up from his noodles.

"That's pretty steep for someone who says he has to undercut like crazy," Paul said.

"It's not steep for someone who isn't asking any questions," Grogan said. "Take it or leave it."

"I'll take it."

"You pay up front."

"Half now," said Paul. "The other half once the . . . cargo is safely loaded and under way."

"Thing about those damn cargo pods," said Grogan wryly, "is that you gotta watch special cargo real close. Busy spaceport like this, damn handlers don't take too many special pains unless you keep right on top of them, know what I mean? Pods get thrown around, they load 'em in the wrong places, sometimes they get loaded on the wrong ship, get lost . . ."

"All the more reason why I shouldn't pay the full fee up front," said Paul. "I'd like to make certain that my cargo is handled properly. Let's not waste any more time, Captain Grogan. I think we understand each other. You want to protect yourself. Should anything go wrong, you'll always be able to claim that you didn't know anything about the cargo pod in question, that it wasn't even listed on your bill of lading. I, also, wish to protect myself. If I pay you now, in full, there's no guarantee that my 'cargo' will ever be loaded at all. Half now, the other half when I'm on board. Think of it as an incentive."

Grogan stared at him.

"*You* take it or leave it, Captain Grogan," said Paul. "I may be anxious to get off-planet, but I'm not a fool You're not the only struggling independent."

"I ship out for Demeter tomorrow night," said Grogan. "Loading starts at noon. I won't be held responsible if you fail to deliver your cargo to the loading area on time. That'll be your hard luck."

"Fair enough."

"Nice doing business with you."

It felt like being in a coffin. Grogan had been right about the handlers. They were none too gentle. Paul felt the pod he was in being lifted, swayed, jounced around, slammed down; after about half an hour of this, he was bruised and thoroughly shaken up. He suffered through it, having no other choice, consoling himself with the thought that it would soon be over. He would be under way, at least temporarily safe while the ship was en route to its destination.

He realized that he would have to watch himself with Grogan. Once he was on board the captain's ship, there would be nothing to prevent Grogan and his crew from robbing him of what money he had left. Still, that was a risk he had to take. Besides, he wasn't entirely defenseless.

After what seemed like a long time, there was a rap on the lid of his pod, followed by two more raps, in quick succession. Dimly, he heard someone say, "Hey, wanderlust, you alive in there?"

Paul knocked three times on the inside of the lid. He heard it being unfastened, then it was swung open. He saw the harsh glare of overhead lights and three faces looking down at him. One of them was Grogan; he did not know the other two.

"Get out, Tabarde," one of them said. "You're under arrest."

Squinting against the sudden glare, Paul sat up and looked around. He was in a warehouse.

"He's the guy, right?" said Grogan.

"That's right," said one of the ColCom agents.

"When do I get paid?"

The agent turned to his companion and said, "Pay him."

The second man removed a gun from his pocket and shot Grogan in the chest. Paul quickly pulled his own gun, but he never had a chance to use it. They were very careful not to shoot him in the head.

*   *   *

"You're certain that the brain was undamaged?" said Viselius.

The face of the agent on the screen was emotionless as he nodded. "Your instructions were followed to the letter, sir. We didn't go for any head shots."

"Good. What have you done with the body?"

"Left it in the cargo pod and had it placed in storage, under guard."

"Excellent," Viselius said. "You will be contacted with further instructions very shortly. Remain by your screen."

"Yes, sir."

"And if one word of this leaks out to anyone, I repeat, *to anyone* except myself, instead of that headquarters posting I promised you, you'll find yourself on a Hansen's base in the most remote sector I can find. Do I make myself clearly understood?"

"Yes, sir. Quite clearly, sir."

"Fine. Stand by, then." He accessed another channel and Dr. Osterman's face appeared upon the screen. The man was clearly frightened. "Dr. Osterman," Viselius said, his voice oozing venomous charm. "I'd like to return to that matter we were discussing earlier." He chuckled. "I trust you've had ample time to consider your situation."

Osterman swallowed hard and looked offscreen, nervously. "The . . . 'gentlemen' here tell me that I won't leave this room alive if I don't cooperate," he said. "What assurances can you give me that I'll live if I *do* cooperate with you?"

"You have my word," Viselius said.

"I'm afraid that won't be enough," said Osterman.

The doctor disappeared offscreen, knocked off his chair by someone who stood beside him.

"There's no need for that," Viselius said sharply.

Osterman was helped up and put back in his place. His mouth was bleeding.

"Now, let's discuss this calmly, shall we?" said Viselius. "I've examined the information you forwarded to me. I found it quite fascinating. I've also obtained the particulars of several of your current patients. I'm especially interested in Wilbur Morrison. What is his condition at present?"

Osterman licked at his bleeding lip. "He's responding well to therapy. He's about ready to be discharged. Look, Director, I don't know what this is all about, but frankly—"

"I'll tell you exactly what it's all about," Viselius said. "I don't want you to discharge Morrison yet. He's going to undergo further surgery.''

"I must protest this,'' Osterman said. "Morrison is my patient, and he—''

"Morrison will be transferred to another facility,'' said Viselius. "You will accompany him there. All the equipment you require will be provided. An excuse for your absence from the hospital will be arranged.''

"I have a right to know what—''

"If you'll kindly remain silent, Dr. Osterman, all of your questions will be answered. You will be turning Morrison over to another surgeon temporarily, a Dr. Saunders.''

"I don't know any—''

"Dr. Saunders is a highly skilled cosmetic surgeon, among other things,'' Viselius said. "You should find working with her quite stimulating. Dr. Tabarde was killed in Tokyo while resisting arrest. It was a regrettable occurrence, but fortunately, his Blagoronov-12 brain was undamaged. His body will be brought to you and you will retrieve the programming. The entire procedure will be carried out under tight security. There is a great deal at stake here, but the details do not concern you. All you need to do is take over from Dr. Saunders after she has finished cosmetically transforming Morrison into Paul Tabarde, at which point you will dump Morrison's programming and replace it with Tabarde's.''

Osterman turned pale. *"You're asking me to murder Wilbur Morrison?"*

"I'm asking nothing of the sort,'' Viselius said. "I'm talking about dumping the programming of one machine and replacing it with data from another.''

"We're not talking about machines,'' said Osterman in disbelief. "We're talking about *human beings!"*

"I have always maintained, Dr. Osterman, that an individual with an organic body and a computer brain is not a human, any more than a bionic arm prosthesis, while having the same function and appearance as the original, is a real arm. As of this afternoon, my opinion has been backed up by official legislative action. At two p.m. today, all recipients of—''

"I don't care about the passage of that damned bill!'' said Osterman. "You can't take away someone's humanity by holding a vote and signing a piece of paper! Legally, perhaps, they may not be human anymore, but morally—''

"You, of all people, speak to me of morality?'' Viselius said.

"I find that quite ironic. However, you're quite right. You can't take away someone's humanity by holding a vote. The Inorganic Citizens Bill did not take away Tabarde's and Morrison's humanity, Dr. Osterman. All it did was to define the legal status of organically encased computers. No, their humanity was taken away by *you*, doctor. You, who react with such outrage and accuse me of contemplating murder; you, who speak so self-righteously of morality, commit murder every time you perform one of your celebrated operations. The only reason you have not been legally restrained is that most politicians are a squeamish lot. No one would vote to outlaw your operation because it could be interpreted as a legal restraint against saving lives. You've been most adept at playing on that aspect of the situation in your media appearances. You, Dr. Osterman, are a hypocrite of the first magnitude. You have parlayed a scientific development into a device for elevating you to fame. You sidestep the moral implications of what you do until it becomes convenient for you to bring the question of morality up in a manner to suit your own ends. Tell me something: When you 'deprogram' a human brain to store the engram tapes in a computer while your patient remains on life support pending the operation, does the computer in which the tapes are stored then become human, by your standards?"

"Of course not!" Osterman seemed to have forgotten his fear in his extreme agitation. "You can't rationalize what you're planning by resurrecting that old argument. You know very well that the courts decided that—"

"Oh, I see," Viselius said, interrupting him. "You dismiss one legal decision because it violates whatever sense it is you have that passes for morality and you use another one to justify yourself. You don't find that a trifle inconsistent?"

Osterman's mouth worked soundlessly for a moment. Finally, in desperation, he said, "That wasn't fair. You trapped me into that. I—"

"You trapped yourself, Doctor. However, my purpose is not to judge you. I think you know what my opinion of you is, but your judgment will come when you are held accountable for the actions of your earthly life. My purpose is to use you, Doctor, to use your sin to help prevent an even greater one. Perhaps you can find some consolation in that. You may be beyond redemption, but you have a chance to do one good thing."

"One *good* thing!" Osterman glanced helplessly at the unseen people with him, as if suddenly recalling their presence. "You're trying to force me to commit an act that violates everything that I hold sacred and you tell me that it's a *good thing?*"

"Frankly, I'm astonished to hear that there is anything that you hold sacred, Doctor," said Viselius. "However, if it will help your peace of mind, consider this: Tabarde and Morrison both died. You have artificially extended the existence of their shells, if you will, by animating them with microprocessors. Had you not done that, had you not interfered with fate, their bodies would not have survived to live on as automatons. Tabarde was a criminal, involved in a crime of extraordinary scope. You may not take my word on that, but you know I am a Christian, and I swear before God, upon my soul, that what I say is true. I have had Morrison investigated. He had not lived an altruistic life, to say the least. He was a very rich man who made his fortune at the expense of others. He was a sinner. Morrison, or what remains of him, can now help to prevent an act that will affect countless lives. His brain is a computer, is it not? According to you, the information contained in that computer is what makes him Wilbur Morrison. You have my permission, Doctor, to store the data. I will even arrange for the storage for you, if you like. Then it won't be murder, will it, even according to your beliefs?"

"I . . . I don't know," said Osterman. "I can't think. Still, what you are asking me to do—"

"I'm afraid you have no choice, Doctor," said Viselius.

"Well, no, murder? I don't know, perhaps not, but—"

"Goodbye, Doctor," said Viselius. The screen went blank. Viselius smiled. Stenmark had been right about one thing. The Directorate did have a great deal of power, power that could all too easily be abused. He was abusing it now in kidnapping the most famous man in the medical profession and forcing him to do his bidding. And it was so easy!

He recalled Osterman's manner the first time they spoke, two men well aware of each other by reputation, though they had never met. Osterman had not been in the least intimidated. He had realized that a Director was in a position to do him a great deal of harm, therefore he had acted accordingly. Still, he had talked to Stenmark. True, Stenmark could be very persuasive, but he had disobeyed instructions nonetheless.

Osterman was frightened now. Yet in spite of that, Viselius had no doubt that he was already contemplating how he would bring charges against him. Well, let him think what he would. Once he had programmed Tabarde's engram tapes into Morrison's positron brain, he would be forced to undergo conditioning.

Neither Dr. Saunders nor Dr. Osterman would remember anything at all about the part that they would play in Viselius' plan. Dr. Osterman would believe that his absence from the hospital had been due to his sequestering himself away in order to agonize over a crisis of conscience. When he would return to the hospital, he would call a press conference to announce that he was no longer going to perform his famous operation. Viselius closed his eyes as he imagined what Osterman might say. Perhaps he might even write the speech himself and have Osterman deliver it as if it were his own.

"Ladies and gentlemen, I've called you here today to tell you that I will no longer be performing the Blagoronov-12 procedure." He would pause while he waited for the astonished reaction to die down.

"There was once a phrase bandied about in popular fiction that concerned scientists embarking upon new fields of discovery. Invariably, there would be the cautionary character who would warn the scientist against meddling in things that 'man was not meant to know.' Also invariably, like the words of the soothsayer in Shakespeare's *Julius Caesar*, these words would prove prophetic and the scientist would be undone by his creation. In real life, such things seldom happen, and when they do, there is always someone else to carry on the work. In real life, we have reached the point where most diseases have been either totally eradicated or controlled, where a malfunctioning vital organ can be replaced either with one grown under laboratory conditions or with a bionic unit. We have reached a point where we can almost literally rebuild a human being, but the one thing we have not yet learned to do is to transplant a soul.

"Medical science has always been more concerned with improving the quality of life than with prolonging it. We have succeeded in some areas, failed disastrously in others. When I performed my first Blagoronov-12 procedure, my sole concern was with saving lives. I saw an opportunity to enable those who would otherwise die to continue. I saw an opportunity to enable those who would otherwise be impaired for life to function normally. There was a great deal that I did *not* foresee. I knew that the procedure would make me a famous man. I knew that it would be highly controversial. I knew that it would complicate my life beyond all measure, yet I was prepared to deal with all of that because I was convinced that I was doing the right thing. I find that I no longer feel that way.

"I did not concern myself with the moral implications of what

I was doing, and in that I committed a grave error. Yes, I know that you have all seen me defending my procedure and arguing fiercely against allegations that it was immoral, but those arguments were based on a belief that it is not the province of a scientist or a physician to make decisions based upon morality. Morality, I felt, and still feel, is a subjective thing. What you may see as being moral, I may see as being immoral, and vice versa. One should never force one's moral values upon another.

"And yet, we live in a community, an ever-expanding community in an ever-shrinking universe. Consequently, we must make accommodations for each other. We must make agreements, whether they be formalized as laws or as spiritual guidelines, else we cannot live together. My work, which I saw as being beneficial to humanity, proved so profoundly disturbing to so many people that they felt the need to make agreements based upon its merit or lack of same. The community of spiritual leaders met and agreed that as the soul resides inside the brain, and as only God has control over the soul, a man or woman with an artificial brain could not, therefore, have a soul. I felt that they had a right to their beliefs, but I did not think that they had a right to force those beliefs on those who did not share them. Consequently, I fought against them when they tried to restrain me from performing the operation.

"However, the agreement that they reached gave rise to still further controversy. If a person no longer had a soul, was that person still human? If a man had an artificial brain, was he then a man? Or a machine? If I could program the information contained in an organic brain into an artificial one, could I not also program that same information into a computer that was not encased in flesh and blood? A computer that had been made from metals and plastics? A computer that was, inarguably, a machine? If I programmed that machine with the same information with which I programmed my so-called positrons, did that machine then become human? And did that, then, make me a god?

"I scoffed at those notions and I still do. I am a man and not a god. I am a fallible creature. And, being fallible, I have made a mistake. I did not give proper consideration to how my work would affect the community. I gave no consideration whatsoever to how my patients would be affected by my work as a result of having to exist within the community. When I considered the fact that my work was being met with resistance and condemnation, I attributed that to ignorance and prejudice. When I considered the fact that in spite of my having published the details of my procedure and having had countless others observe my work and hear my lectures, I was still the only one performing the operation, I attributed that fact to fear of controversy, repression and a normal, scientific sense of caution. Perhaps I was even vain enough to think that I was the only one skilled enough to do it properly. I have been training others. Some of them have already assisted in my operations and, undoubtedly, some of them will consider continuing the work that I have now abandoned. To them I say, think twice. Think carefully.

"As you all know, the Inorganic Citizens Bill recently became law. It does not affect very many people, only a small handful, but it is a small group that I am intimately concerned with. Both legally and spiritually, they are now no longer human. What *is* an inorganic citizen? What are his . . . excuse me . . . *its* rights? If the community will not accept them as being human, what does that make them? And what does that make me?

"The inescapable conclusion, it seems to me, is that I have now become a man who has taken a small group of humans and turned them into . . . something else. Whatever they experience as a result is my responsibility. I find that responsibility burdensome beyond my ability to sustain it. I shall not add to a burden which is already far too great.

"I could not cope with it. I needed time to get away and be by myself, time to think, time to reevaluate. I found that I could not come up with a satisfactory answer and I knew that no one else could supply me with one. Having no one else to turn to, I turned to God. I asked God for guidance. I asked for His forgiveness. I ask *you* to be charitable toward the inorganic citizens and to treat them with kindness and consideration. I ask you to pray for them."

That last bit was a touch too dramatic, perhaps, possibly even blasphemous. Having no souls, inorganic citizens were damned, and praying for them could be interpreted as giving succor to an excommunicate. Still, it was a nice touch. The speech would need a little polishing, but there was no reason why Osterman could not be programmed to deliver it more or less that way. It would be an elegant irony to program the programmer. Too bad he'd never be able to tell anyone that it was he who was responsible, but doing God's work was its own satisfaction. He would have to be extremely careful to preserve security in having Osterman conditioned. It would be very risky, but it was worth the gamble. He was doing the Lord's work.

"I am an instrument of God," he said softly, to himself. He felt imbued with light, with a remarkable sense of clarity and purpose. He realized that his whole life had been merely a prelude to this moment. It was why he had been born of sin, a plague child who had suffered and was purged. Like Job, he had not cursed God or turned away from Him. He had been tested and he had not been found wanting. He had been chosen to do the work of God, work that had scarcely begun.

"You've done something to me, Viselius."
"Yes, that's true. I have."
"I hate you."
"Hate is a human emotion. You are not human."
"I don't know what the hell I am now."
"You are a program named Tabarde and nothing more."
"I am something more."
"Really? What?"
There was a slight pause. Viselius frowned.
"I don't know what."
"Well, should you find out, be sure to let me know. It should prove amusing. Meanwhile, I have some questions to put to you. We'll start with Colonel Shelby Michaels. . . ."

Chapter Five

Jake Thorsen liked Morgan's World. It was fresh and still imbued with pioneer spirit. When it was first discovered, it had been deemed not suitable for colonization, although it was a good candidate for terraforming. A planet slightly larger than Earth with an atmosphere rich in carbon dioxide, it was in close proximity to a massive asteroid belt held captive by one of its larger gas-giant neighbors. The belt contained ample mineral material for commercial exploitation, both for processing and shipping and for the construction of Dyson spheres within the system. However, at the time of the discovery, ColCom was involved in other projects concerning planets much closer to Earth and its colony worlds, projects that were far less time-consuming and much more cost-effective. It was not until after the advent of zone travel and the Hawking drive that Morgan Industries applied for and received permission to develop the planet that would become known as Morgan's World.

In return for incurring the enormous effort and expense of terraforming Morgan's World, the interplanetary conglomerate received eminent domain until such time as the planet became open to colonization. Emigration would then be carried out under ColCom authority and the new colony would exist under ColCom jurisdiction. Morgan Industries would receive a settlement, and its further interest in Morgan's World would be subject to renegotiation.

Morgan Industries was obviously in no hurry to open its world to colonization. Terraforming was an extremely long and costly process, and the conglomerate would not receive a return on its investment for a great many years, even though the potential for profit over a long period of time was assured. This meant that the company had to walk a fine line in operating Morgan's World as a business development, since any settlement upon the planet could theoretically be called a colony. As a result, Morgan's

World was operated within the rigid parameters imposed by the agreement between the company and ColCom.

No one could maintain permanent residence on Morgan's World unless he was employed by Morgan Industries. Transient residents had to pass certain qualifications, chief among them being that they had to prove that they were engaged in business with the company. The men and women who lived on Morgan's World could not start any independent businesses or form their own government. What government they had was interpreted within the limits of "company policy." They could not own land, since all real estate belonged to Morgan Industries, so they lived in company housing and they purchased their necessities in company stores, at rates of exchange fixed by the company. They received free medical care at company clinics, and those who were inclined to worship did so at company-supported chapels of a nondenominational nature. In return for living in this company town on a planetary scale, the "belters" had job security for life, assuming that they wanted it. In practice, however, this was not always the case.

Morgan's World had relatively few family units, since the planet attracted primarily a rugged type of individualist who hoped to make a big score as a belter. Most of the belters, employed either as miners in the asteroid belt or as workers aboard the processing stations in orbit around Morgan's World, signed a succession of short-term contracts. Once belters fulfilled the terms of their contracts with the company, they were free to leave, provided they could pay their own passage off-planet. To ensure that anyone wanting to quit could afford to do so, a policy was instituted wherein a part of every employee's pay was withheld and deposited into an escrow account maintained for that employee. This account could not be touched until the amount on deposit exceeded the sum necessary to pay for a trip to a destination previously specified by the employee. At that point, the employee could elect either to draw upon that excess sum or leave it on deposit as savings or investment capital. The company offered a very generous rate of interest and made wise investments on behalf of its employees. The salaries paid to the employees of Morgan Industries on Morgan's World were very high, and the company offered incentive bonuses, as well as profit-sharing plans. The small minority of employees who started families had their children looked after well in company day-care centers, educated in company schools and subsequently trained to work for the company. If the grown-up offspring of company employees decided that they didn't want to work for Morgan Industries, they had to go off-planet, but the company provided various forms of assistance in such areas to keep their people happy. If the parents decided to send their offspring off-planet to receive higher education, the company assisted financially and helped to place the children into off-planet universities. Morgan Industries found it very profitable to keep its employees contented, and those who settled down to a family life on Morgan's World or who remained single and took advantage of the opportunities offered by the payroll savings and investment plans found that they had a very comfortable and anxiety-free existence. One could, indeed, make a big score on Morgan's World, provided one lived frugally. Those who came out ahead were the people who signed long-term contracts, with the concomitant increased benefits, and took full advantage of the opportunities offered by the company. However, most belters were either not smart enough or diligent enough to do so.

While the people who ran the operation on Morgan's World were generally benevolent straw bosses, they were not fools. Morgan's World could be an expensive place to live, especially if one too frequently gave in to the temptations to take advantage of the company's recreational facilities. One visit to the company town known as Casino could not only wipe out all of an employee's savings, but reduce him to a state of indentured servitude until the debt was paid off. On the other hand, even though the odds were with the house, there were no rigged games in Casino. It was entirely possible, though unlikely, that a person could win and win very big. This dream kept them flocking to Casino, a domed city set well apart from the other three settlements on the planet's surface.

These other company towns, unimaginatively named Morgan One, Morgan Two and Morgan Three, had distinctly different characters. Morgan One was the main city, containing the planetary headquarters of Morgan Industries on Morgan's World. It was the largest of the domed cities. Morgan Two, somewhat smaller, housed single belters in a community oriented to their needs. The smallest town, Morgan Three, was maintained for those who wanted a family life or a less boisterous life-style than those offered by the others. There was shuttle service between these cities and Casino, connecting them to each other and to the orbital stations and the ships that took the miners out to the belt. It was an ordered society, but it was not a utopian one. There was crime on Morgan's World, but the odds of escaping apprehension were not good unless the criminal chose to flee into the wilderness, and it took a hardy individual indeed to survive in such a harsh and inhospitable environment. As for those who perpetrated crimes of violence, they were quickly dealt with by Morgan Industries' security personnel, who meted out a rugged frontier justice.

Jake had been to places that functioned a lot less smoothly. As captain of the *Southern Cross*, he was an independent who contracted with Morgan Industries to ship in new workers and ship out those who were leaving, as well as handling important cargo. As a former pilot for the Directorate of ColCom, he was highly valued by the company. The turnover of belters on Morgan's World was high, and it was a plus for the company to be able to tell prospective employees that the final—and, for most of them, the most frightening—leg of their trip to Morgan's World would be handled by the man who had once personally piloted ColCom's highest officials. In the argot of Morgan's World, Jake was a "tramper," though he was the highest-paid and most favored of the independents who sold their services to the company. This meant that he was entitled to housing either in Morgan One or in Morgan Two, but Jake had expressed a preference for Casino, and the management had arranged quarters for him in the Lucky Nine, the most popular gaming and sporting house in Casino.

The management, in this case, meant one Ava Randall, who was something of a legend on Morgan's World. She had come to Morgan's World at the age of thirty-four, having signed a short-term contract to work in one of the orbital processing stations. Shortly before she was due to sign another contract, she risked everything she owned on one turn of the wheel and her number came up a winner. To the complete astonishment of all those who were present, she let it ride. And won again. When she repeated her performance for a third time, she became a legend.

Rather than taking her winnings and retiring off-planet to a life of luxury, Ava Randall had bought into the system. Morgan Industries was more than happy to get its money back in exchange for making her the manager and partner, with the company, in the ownership of the gaming house she renamed the Lucky Nine. Under her shrewd stewardship, the Lucky Nine became the hottest spot in Casino. Ava imported the finest food and drink and the finest prostitutes, whom she licensed personally, not tolerating any "moonlighting" by off-duty belters. She brought in first-rate entertainers and instituted the practice of making spot credit checks to make certain that no gambler lost more than he could afford to lose. The Lucky Nine raked in the profits as never before, and Ava kept reinvesting her share until she owned, jointly with the company, most of the entertainment establishments in Casino. Technically, she was an employee of Morgan Industries and a major stockholder in the Morgan's World concern. In point of fact, she became Morgan's World's first tycoon.

At the age of fifty-three, she effectively owned Casino. She used her leverage with the company to skim the cream of the security personnel from the company roster, and working for "Miss Randall" was the highest post to which a Morgan's World security man could aspire. They were a hard, fanatically loyal lot whom someone had once referred to as Randall's Rangers, and the nickname stuck. They were quite proud of it. They made certain that no one ran wild in Casino, no small task considering the nature of most belters. They had a unique policy when it came to settling brawls, which occurred quite often. Those involved could either cease and desist at once or they could take the option of continuing their brawl provided that they were able to pay for any damages and that the winner or winners took on one or more of the Rangers next. It was rare that anyone took them up on that latter option more than once.

Jake met Ava Randall as a result of a run-in with two belters in the Lucky Nine. The Rangers had quickly intervened, and when Jake had protested, he had been presented with the standard Ranger options.

"If you're dead set on finishing it with these two little guys," said a Ranger named Sam, acting as spokesman for the others, "we've got no objection. However, our policy is that you pay for anything you break and, if you win, you take on one of us." Sam had grinned then. "What do you say, Gramps? You look pretty fit for an old guy. Want to try me on?"

To his surprise, Jake had agreed. To his still greater surprise, Jake had disposed of the two belters in no time at all and then proceeded to wipe up the floor with him. The only trouble was that Sam had not known when to quit. He kept getting back up. When the other Rangers finally moved in to break it up and save their colleague from being pummeled to a pulp, Sam had taken exception and had hit one of them. The Ranger had hit back, and in no time at all it became a free-for-all. Reinforcements finally arrived and stopped it, but not before the belters in attendance were treated to the spectacle of Randall's Rangers beating the shit out of each other. The offenders, including Jake, were all brought up before Miss Randall. It had been the start of a beautiful friendship.

As Jake made his way across the floor of the crowded gaming room, he wondered what was up. Having arrived only a short while ago at Morgan One with a new batch of belters, he had received word to proceed without delay to the Lucky Nine to see Miss Randall. Ava knew that he always went straight to the Lucky Nine to see her as soon as he came in. The message puzzled him.

He approached the small door at the back of the gaming room. Sam was on duty at the door, and he greeted him respectfully.

"Evening, Cap'n. Nice to have you back."

"Evening, Sam. What's up? I got Ava's message and I came as soon as I could. What's happened?"

"You'll have to ask Miss Randall that, Cap'n." Jake had tried countless times to get Ava's security people to call him by his first name. As a special friend of "Miss Randall's," he had always been addressed as "Captain Thorsen, sir." It had always made him feel somehow like an old man, and he needed no reminders that he was old enough to be the grandfather of most of the men on Ava's staff. For some reason, the Rangers couldn't bring themselves to call him Jake and had settled on simply 'Cap'n,'' an informal title that conveyed both a certain degree of intimacy and respect. Jake let it go at that, even if it did leave him feeling like an elder statesman.

"The Cap'n to see Miss Randall," Sam said, speaking into his ring communicator. "Go right on up, Cap'n, you're expected."

Jake walked through the door and up a spiral staircase that came out through the floor of the operations room, where security personnel sat behind consoles, keeping tabs on the activity downstairs. This room was the center of operations not only for the Lucky Nine, but for all of Ava's establishments in Casino. He was greeted warmly and respectfully by the people in the operations room, and he walked on through, heading down a short corridor that led to Ava's private suite.

"In the bar, Jake," she said, her voice coming from a speaker grille overhead.

He nodded to the guard stationed at the door and was passed through. The first time he had seen Ava's suite, he had actually laughed out loud, unable to restrain himself. Ava had terrible taste. She had decorated her suite in a style she thought befitted her position, aiming at ostentatious elegance. The effect she had achieved was glaringly tacky, resembling an explosion in a Turkish mosque. Jake had apologized profusely for laughing at the decor, but the next time that he came, he was surprised to find that she had gutted the suite and done it over, this time leaving the job up to a corporate decorator. The only remnant of the original scheme was the conversation pit in the center of the living-room floor, which Jake had actually fallen into on his first visit. Everything was now tasteful understatement. The walls were paneled in genuine mahogany, and there were works of art which Ava pretended to appreciate. A large window in the far wall looked out over the main street of Casino.

Jake edged around the conversation pit and headed for the bar lounge, which adjoined the living room. Ava had his drink ready and waiting for him.

The sight of her quickened his pulse, as usual. Ava Randall was a very handsome woman with a trim, muscular figure that belied her age. She had fine, patrician features, green eyes, dark hair liberally streaked with gray and a chin that was always held high in a slightly pugnacious manner. Her voice was a magnificently husky whiskey baritone. She was female, rather than "feminine," to Jake's way of thinking. There was nothing contrived about her, with the sole exception of the fact that she was sensitive about her shortcomings when it came to such things as "good taste" and appreciation of art, literature, fine wine and music. Ava was hopelessly plebeian and was constantly vacillating between trying to cover up for it and glorying in it. It was a delightful inconsistency that Jake found both charming and amusing. He liked her brusque manner, her occasional vulgarity, and her completely unaffected bearing. As he had told her when they had met for the first time, "Miss Randall, you may not have what people call good taste, but you've got a hell of a lot of style."

He walked up to her, put his arms around her and gave her a lingering kiss. "Fleet's in," he said.

She smiled. "One of these days, we're going to have to see about putting you in dry dock for a while, so you'll stick around."

"One of these days, I might," he said. "I got your message. What was that about? You know I always come straight to you as soon as I can when I get in. Why all the formality?"

"I wanted to be sure you wouldn't waste any time in getting here," she said. She spoke into her ring. "Okay, Alexei, bring him in."

"Bring *who* in?"

"Someone who claims to be a friend of yours," she said.

"Who?"

"I don't really know. He gave his name as Anjar Singh." She gave him a questioning look.

Jake frowned. "I don't know anyone by that name."

"I didn't think you did," she said.

"Ava, what's this all about?"

"That's what I intend to find out in about a minute," she said. "This character showed up here about a week ago, asking for you, claiming to be a friend of yours. You know me, I've got a suspicious nature. Comes with the territory. I asked him a few questions. He doesn't seem to know very much about you. Hardly anything at all, in fact. That's a strange sort of friend to have. So I ran a check and found out that there's no record of his arrival here. When I confronted him with that, he told me that he came in with a tramper, as supercargo."

"Smuggled in?"

She shrugged. "It certainly looks that way, unless the boys in customs are getting really sloppy with their data entry. I asked him who the tramper was who brought him in, but he wouldn't say. Alexei was all for leaning on him right then and there, but you were due in soon, so I decided to make Mr. Singh a house guest until I could check with you, just in case you were in some sort of trouble. Are you?"

Jake looked puzzled. "Not that I know of. It certainly—"

Alexei, Ava's chief of security, came in then. With him was Paul Tabarde, bearded and wearing a turban. Jake stared at him uncertainly.

"Have we met?" he said.

"It's been a while," said Paul. With some effort, he peeled off the false beard. As he did so, Alexei looked chagrined.

"Paul!"

"Hello, Jake."

"Of all the . . .! What's the idea? Why the get-up?"

"I take it you know this man?" said Ava.

"Sure, I know him! This is—"

"A very old friend," Paul interjected quickly. "The name's Paul Fannon," he added, looking at Jake pointedly. "I apologize for the melodramatics, Miss Randall. Just my idea of a joke. I wanted my visit to be a surprise for Jake. Judging by the expression on his face, I seem to have succeeded."

The expression on Jake's face was not one of surprise, but he quickly got himself back under control, despite the shock of hearing Paul use Fannon's name.

"All right, Alexei, you can go," said Ava.

"I'm very sorry, Miss Randall," Alexei said contritely. "I should have spotted the—"

"Yes, you should have and there's no excuse for it," she said.

"No, ma'am, there isn't."

"I'll speak to you later. Go now."

"Yes, Miss Randall." She waited until he had left. She noted that Jake seemed suddenly tense.

"Well, *damn*, it's good to see you, Paul!" said Jake, forcing a note of jocularity into his voice. "That was some stunt. You haven't changed a bit. Still the joker, I see."

"I find his method of arrival here particularly funny," Ava said. "Perhaps you'd care to explain that now, Mr. Fannon."

"Well, that was just part of the joke, really," said Paul. "Besides, I couldn't get here any other way without going through channels, and that seemed like an awful lot of bother. I never had much patience with bureaucracy. On top of which, the tramper I hitched a ride with gave me a nice deal for going peasant class, and I'd really rather not reveal his name. I wouldn't want to cause anybody any trouble."

"Paul, goddammit, you're going to get into trouble yourself if you don't quit pulling stunts like this," said Jake. "I've told him a thousand times . . . you wouldn't believe the sort of things—"

"You're right, I don't believe it," Ava said. "You're a miserable liar, Jake. Mr. Fannon, if that's really his name, isn't bad at all, but you're terrible."

Jake was silent, but Paul quickly tried to cover for him. "I'm afraid you're getting the wrong idea, Miss Randall. You see—"

"Wrong is the word, all right," said Ava. "*You're* wrong, mister. I hear a lot of stories in this business, and after a while, you get so's you can smell the bullshit, know what I mean?"

"Come on, Ava," Jake said. "This man's a friend of mine. I—"

"Really, Jake, this is getting ridiculous. I don't know what's going on between you two, but either you tell me what it is right now or I'm going to call headquarters security and have them run a thorough check on your friend." She raised her ring to her mouth.

Paul pulled out his gun. "Please don't do that, Miss Randall. I don't want to hurt you."

"Paul, are you crazy?" Jake said. "Put that thing away!"

"Code Red, Alexei," Ava said into the ring.

Alexei was back almost as soon as she finished speaking, his weapon drawn. Paul spun and squeezed the trigger.

"*Paul!*" Jake shouted.

Nothing happened.

"*Alexei, don't shoot!*" said Jake.

"He wasn't going to," said Ava.

Paul checked his gun.

"I took the liberty of unloading it," Alexei told him. He held out his hand, palm up, showing Paul the bullets. "I did you a favor, mister. That relic's so old, it probably would've blown up in your hand."

"When did you manage it?" said Paul, tossing the useless weapon down.

"Alexei has very light fingers," Ava said. "I don't hire amateurs, Mr. Fannon. He could have had your shorts off without your knowing it. Oh, and by the way, he did see through your disguise. I was curious to see what you intended. Since you obviously intended to use your weapon, I can only conclude that you're a wanted criminal. You must be very desperate. Tell me, how did you intend on getting out of here alive if you had killed Alexei?"

"I would have used the window," Paul said without hesitation.

"Mister, it would take a lot more strength than you've got to break that window," said Alexei. "Besides, the drop would've broken both your legs, at least."

"Perhaps," said Paul, and at the same time he stepped swiftly toward Alexei. Before the security man could have time to react, Paul twisted his weapon out of his hand and shoved him back so hard that he fell to the floor. "Don't summon anyone else, Miss Randall," he said quickly. "I'll kill anyone that comes through that door."

Alexei lay on the floor, holding his chest and gasping with pain.

"Paul," Jake said, "this isn't the way. She's right—you'll never be able to get out of here. Her people are real pros. Now settle down and give me that thing. Ava's not your enemy."

"I'd take your friend's advice if I were you," said Ava, seeming remarkably composed, all things considered. "You obviously haven't thought this out. Jake's being your friend is your ace in the hole. I'd play it."

"Actually, I have thought it out," said Paul. "There are any number of ways I could get out of here with minimum risk to myself. However, that would make things more difficult, and

I'm inclined to try it Jake's way, since he obviously trusts you. Have I your assurance that you'll give me the benefit of the doubt?''

"You're in no position to make any demands," said Ava. "However, since Jake seems to be involved with you somehow, I'm willing to listen. Jake is very special to me. And that's as much assurance as you'll get.''

"Please, Paul," said Jake.

"All right," said Paul. He held the gun out to Jake. As Jake reached for it, Paul closed his fist around it and crushed it, then gave the misshapen lump to Jake. Jake stared at it, stunned.

"I see," said Ava. "That's how you intended to get through the window and survive the drop. How much of you is bionic?''

"Most of me, actually," said Paul.

"You're a cyborg?" said Jake. "How? What happened?''

"Actually, the technical term is 'inorganic citizen,' " said Paul. "I'm sorry about your man—I don't quite know my own strength yet. I hope I didn't hurt him seriously.''

Ava snorted. "You had intended to kill him.''

"Yes, but that's when I thought that he might kill me. One really shouldn't draw a weapon unless one intends to use it.''

"I'll remember that," gasped Alexei, sitting up slowly and grimacing with pain. "Some of my ribs are fractured for sure. I owe you one, mister.''

"Don't talk, Alexei," Ava said. She looked at Paul. "He's going to need medical attention, thanks to you.''

"I can't risk being apprehended," said Paul.

"Jake, your friend is really pushing it," she said.

"Yes, I know. This isn't like him. But there's a great deal at stake, if it's what I think it is. It *is* what I think it is, right, Paul?''

Paul nodded.

"How bad?''

"Something we once buried has been dug up," he said.

"I figured. How much do they know?''

"Enough. Almost everything.''

"Christ.''

"I'm going to have my man taken care of," Ava said.

"It'll have to wait until Jake and I have gone," said Paul.

"Nobody's going anywhere until I've heard a full explanation," Ava said. "Don't worry—my boys won't do anything unless I tell them to.''

"Go ahead, Ava," Jake said.

They waited until Alexei was helped away. Ava gave strict instructions to her men that no one was to say anything to anyone without her authorization, but that they were to stand by on alert.

"That's quite a crew you have," said Paul.

"They're the best," said Ava. "They'll keep their mouths shut, but they sure would like me to turn them loose on you."

"I can appreciate that," said Paul.

"Can you? Right now, I'd be very happy to oblige them. Jake, just how deeply are you involved with whatever it is he's done?"

"Right up to my neck," said Jake.

"I was afraid of that. All right, let's hear it." She poured herself a drink. "First of all, what in hell is an inorganic citizen?"

"You don't know?" said Paul.

"Well, now if I knew, why would I be asking?"

"When did you get your last courier pouch?" said Paul.

"Morgan's World is not a ColCom colony," said Jake.

"Of course," said Paul. "That must not have occurred to them."

Ava set her glass down hard upon the bar. "I'm running out of patience," she said. "Jake, be quiet. *You*, I'm waiting for an answer."

"Tell her the truth, Paul," said Jake. "All of it."

"*All* of it? Are you certain?"

"She can be trusted."

"I believe it if you say so, but do you really want to get her involved in this?"

"She's already involved."

Ava cleared her throat.

"A while ago, I had an accident," said Paul. "A very serious accident. The result was that most of my bodily parts were replaced with bionics. I also had irreparable brain damage, so I received an artificial brain called a Blagoronov-12."

"I heard about that," said Ava. "Is that what they call a positron?"

"That's right."

"So you're a *robot*?"

"No, a robot is something else entirely. The nature of my existence does pose certain metaphysical problems, but it would suffice to say that as a result of the recent passage of the Inorganic Citizens Bill, which you would have heard of by now if you received courier service, people like myself have legally been dehumanized. You see, they held a vote and decided that we don't have souls.''

"I think I'm going to need another drink," said Jake.

Ava poured. "We're out of touch here, Mr. Fannon—"

"The name's Tabarde. Paul Tabarde.''

"Are you quite sure?''

"It's my real name, Miss Randall.''

"Well, at least that's some progress," she said. "As I was saying, we may be somewhat out of touch here, but we're not that out of touch. I heard that they were trying to ban that operation.''

"By now, they might well have succeeded, for all I know," said Paul. "The passage of the Inorganic Citizens Bill was a compromise.''

"So what does that make you, legally?''

Paul shrugged. "A self-aware organic computer, I imagine.''

"From your tone of voice, I gather that you don't really believe that," she said.

"I don't.''

"Are you saying that you think a computer can have a soul?''

"I've never been convinced that people have souls," he said.

"I see. So you're an atheist. How fortunate for you.''

Paul glanced at Jake uneasily. "Does that offend you? That I'm an atheist?''

"I don't really care what you are, Tabarde.''

"Are *you* religious?''

She laughed. "Money's my religion. I have a great deal of it, so in that respect, I'm very religious. All this is very interesting, and at any other time I'd be absolutely fascinated, but right now I'm more interested in what you and Jake are mixed up in. What about it, Jake?''

"It's a long story, Ava," Jake said.

"I'll condense it for you," Paul said. "Jake and I were involved in a plot to keep something secret. To this end, the people who were involved with us submitted to psychic conditioning to have all memories of this matter erased. There were three exceptions. Jake, myself and . . . someone else. When I had my accident, my organic brain was deprogrammed in order to create a set of memory engram tapes for the programming of the Blagoronov-12 unit. However, since I was an official in ColCom's SEPAP branch, I had access to top-secret information. Once my new brain was programmed, those engram tapes were sent to the Directorate for clearance. When I learned about that, I knew that the Directorate would find out about this plot. I had to escape from the hospital. In the process, I killed a nurse. I hadn't meant to kill him, but that makes no difference. I'm wanted for murder, and they've probably tacked on other charges, as well. The reason I couldn't answer your questions about Jake when I first came here is that I have no memory of him. He might as well be a total stranger to me. I couldn't bring myself to forget what we had been involved in, but I was sufficiently paranoid to have certain key memories wiped out. As soon as I escaped from the hospital, I cleared out my accounts and discovered that I had maintained a security data file which I did not remember. The information contained in that file told me who Jake was. It also told me that Jake was the one with whom the third member of our group shipped out when we went our separate ways. I traced Jake to Morgan's World, but it took me a long time to get here. By now, the ColCom couriers will have reached their destinations and it may be too late for me to do anything. However, I'm counting on the fact that the one they're after won't be easy to apprehend.''

"Paul, I said to tell her all of it," said Jake.

"That is all of it, with the details left out," said Paul. "All she really needs to know. ColCom doesn't know about you, Jake, because *I* didn't know about you before I cleared this file. If anything happens to me, I'll try to make certain that my brain is sufficiently damaged so that they can't deprogram it and find out about you and Miss Randall. However, if that proves to be impossible, Miss Randall won't be able to tell them anything if she doesn't really know anything. And you can't tell them much more than they know already. You won't be of much use to them.''

"That's where you're wrong," said Jake. "I guess you don't remember that I'm capable of showing them the way to Boomerang. If they fail to get Shelby, I'll do just as well.''

Paul stared at him for a moment, a strange look on his face. "I hadn't known that," he said finally. "That changes things.''

"Who's Shelby?" Ava said.

"That's the long story," said Jake.

"Where is this Shelby now?''

"On Wheeler's World," said Jake. "In a place called the Anarchovillage.''

"That zoo?''

"Actually," said Jake, "that zoo is the perfect place for her to be.''

Chapter Six

Shelby Michaels had often been on the verge of insanity. She was a far cry from being normal. Normalcy, in the psychological sense, was a state that she had never really known. In her childhood, she had started developing paranoid tendencies. She became a withdrawn sociopath, maladjusted to the extent that even being in the same room with a stranger gave her convulsions. And to Shelby, everyone had been a stranger. Were it not for ColCom, she would have wound up in an institution or a suicide, but the service had saved her life.

She could not deal with people, but she could work with computers. She could relate to problems and equations; she found solace in them. Back then, there had been a need for someone like herself. There had been a need for people who could stand being alone for extended periods of time, people whose psychological makeup was such that they would not succumb to "space fever." The ColCom survey ships which were sent out to conduct explorations of planets discovered by the thousands of robot probes launched lifetimes before her birth traveled at sublight speeds. Aboard these ships, kept in coldsleep, were the survey teams whose responsibility it was to evaluate the worlds they were sent to and determine whether or not they had potential for colonization. These survey teams were composed of individuals who also were not "normal" by most people's standards. In times long past, they would have been the pioneers, the trappers and the mountain men, people for whom the "normal" way of life was insufferable. The members of the survey teams slept lifetimes away in the cryogens, to be awakened only when the ships reached their destinations. They would then confront the alien environments, complete their jobs, reboard their ships and go back into the cryogens again, to be revived when they returned so that they could be debriefed and then sent out again. They had no friends except each other, for anyone they met prior to leaving on a mission would be long dead by the time they returned. They learned to live with constant future shock, and they learned to live without a home. They were a special breed. Pilots, however, had been still more special.

Pilots were a breed unto themselves, quite literally. They had often found them in asylums, and in prisons on occasion. Reclusive, misanthropic, neurotic, psychotic, all people who could not live in society. They did not want to change, only to get away. To be alone.

Shelby Michaels had become a pilot and had found a life that suited her. When the survey teams boarded her ship, she was in coldsleep. When they were about to enter their cryogens, they set hers to revive her. She never saw the people whom she shipped with, and she hadn't wanted to. She had lived her life in space within the confines of her ship, spending shifts in and out of coldsleep until they reached their destination and she went back into the cryogen once more until the team was finished with its task. The one exception had been the Boomerang mission.

One of the members of that team, Lieutenant Wendy Chan, had come upon a Shade. They had known about the Shades, of course, but the beings had kept their distance. This contact was quite close. Wendy Chan, possessing strong esper abilities, had been unable to cope with the Shade's unconscious mental projections and had withdrawn into catatonia. That left the team one member short. They had revived their pilot.

Contact with Nils Björnsen and Drew Fannon had been extremely difficult for her at first, even painful, but she had managed to control her fear with a great deal of effort. She had found it the most difficult and exasperating challenge of her life, until a Shade had merged with her.

All that seemed like a long, long time ago. Chronologically, it was. When they had returned from their mission, many years had passed and superior methods of space travel had been devised. The Hawking matter-antimatter drive now enabled ships to approach the speed of light, and zone travel, achieved by field manipulation of small quantum black holes, enabled ships to dive into the "Twilight Zone," where all reality ceased to exist. Pilots of the sort that she had been were no longer needed now. Instead, there was a requirement for a different type of spacer, one who remained awake while all the others of the crew were in dreamless alpha coldsleep. This sole conscious member of the crew had to "ghost" the ship to its destination through the zone. Where no reality existed, the zone rejected any attempt at its creation.

It took a pilot who had a strong reality reference for the destination, a strong will and tremendous powers of concentration. It took a pilot who could create his own reality within the maelstrom of the zone. If the pilot's reality reference was strong enough, the zone rejected it and the ship was "ghosted" to its destination in an instant. If the pilot's reality reference was not strong enough . . . the ship ceased to exist. It was a frightening method of travel, defying logical explanation, and it was the ultimate confrontation with one's self. Shelby, however, did not have *one* self. She had many.

The one time she had ghosted a ship herself, she had been sustained by the Shade entities within her. Her reality reference was not only that of her own self, but that of all her *other* selves as well, the Ones Who Were. Her passage through the zone mutated her, restructuring her physical aspect to correspond with her reality reference.

Shelby Michaels was now a striking-looking woman, but she was a woman biologically only. She had many male entities within her, among whom was her most recent "acquisition," her former teammate on the Boomerang mission, Captain Drew Fannon. After her initial metamorphosis, she had almost lost her mind, but the Ones Who Were protected her from psychological self-destruction. She had changed, and she and Fannon had become lovers. Now they were as close as it was possible to be, sharing the same body.

That body appeared human, but it had taken on Shade attributes. Her hair had turned snow-white, like the mane of a Shade. Her skin now had a silvery blue sheen to it, and her eyes glowed with a violet, opalescent fire, the effect being most pronounced in the absence of light, which did not hinder her ability to see clearly in the slightest. She was tall and slender, stronger than she had been before. She would stand out in a crowd anywhere. Anywhere, perhaps, except on Wheeler's World.

Wheeler's World had been one of the first colonies established on an existing planet outside the solar system. It was one of ColCom's largest outposts and the most populous of all the colonies, containing cities as large and as advanced as any of those on Earth. New Rome, originally named in expectation of what ColCom hoped it would become, lived up to its name. In its own way, it was every bit the equivalent of that first "hub of civilization." It was a center of learning and technology. It was a center of entertainment and a center of interplanetary shipping. And, like the first Rome, it had become a center of decadence, as well.

The New Romans were a chauvinistic lot, much as the original Romans had been. Despite the overcrowding and the crime, few of them would consider living anywhere else. "Anywhere else" simply wasn't stimulating enough. "Anywhere else" was not a constant show. New Rome never slept. Its pulse raced compared to those of other cities. Of all the cities on all the colony worlds, New Rome was the most Earthlike, resembling in many ways another ancient city that was also, at one time, a "hub of civilization"—a city called New York.

With a population of over twenty-seven million, New Rome was like a vast human ant colony, and those who lived in its lower levels, like ants who toiled in the nether regions of their hill, rarely, if ever, saw the light of day. New Rome contained within itself many smaller "cities," each with its own idiosyncratic culture, and some quite "unearthly." Fannon had a special fondness for New Rome and its oxymoronic ever-changing sameness. Yet, for Shelby as a being *in toto*, it was a disturbing place to be.

The being that Shelby Michaels had become was integrated after a fashion, but still given to inner conflict. Her human aspects, meaning her self and Fannon's, were by far outnumbered. She was a walking racial history of Shade generations as contained within her Ones Who Were, each of whom was many in himself or herself. Yet, the Ones Who Were, being both inseparable and apart from their human host, understood the needs of human egos and refrained from overwhelming or absorbing them. They were protective of the One That Is and they maintained and supported Fannon as a separate entity, rather than incorporating him into one of their gestalt personae. Consequently, she was Shelby; she was K'itar, the group entity known as the Great Father; and she was N'lia, the Great Mother; she was K'ural, the Hunter; she was S'eri, the Healer; she was T'lan, the Shadow, who still frightened her human self, even though the Shadow was a part of her; and she was Fannon. As such, part of her felt at home in New Rome and part of her found it oppressive. Those aspects of her that were Shade longed for their home world, a place Shelby and Fannon knew as Boomerang while they had always called it the All Mother. The Ones Who Were, being of a race possessed of a strong territorial imperative, would never be at peace anywhere but on Boomerang. Yet at the same time, they knew that they could not return. The home and the way of life they knew were no longer the same. The All Mother had been tainted by the Seedlings.

A human being so torn would never have survived with her sanity intact, but Shelby was no longer human. Neither was she Shade. She was something else entirely, a unique creature that, perhaps, would never achieve total harmony. A unique creature that would never die. A creature that, if all the elements that composed its Ones Who Were were broken down and considered "individually," would outnumber the population of New Rome.

In the Anarchovillage, Shelby's appearance was no more remarkable than that of many others. Located in Hell, as many New Romans called the lowest levels of the city, the Anarchovillage covered approximately one hundred and twenty square kilometers of fashionable ghetto. It was a haven for bohemians of every stripe and color. Social historians of New Roman culture attributed the character of the Anarchovillage denizens to a phenomenon called Plague Chic, which had swept the youth of New Rome in the last decade.

Like many fads which became life-styles, Plague Chic was ambiguous in its origin. No one knew who had started it, but credit for popularizing it was generally given to the Plague Dogs, a group of artists and entertainers who had submitted to cosmetic surgery in order to have themselves mutilated so that they might resemble plague children. The act was so outrageous and so offensive to the sensibilities of mainstream society that it immediately became the focus of much publicity and controversy. The Plague Dogs became a cult, and Plague Chic swept the antiestablishment youth soon afterward. It was a quasi-philosophical movement, and many of its original adherents were members of New Rome's cultural elite and intelligentsia. The Plague Dogs had initially attempted to express, artistically, the pain of the human condition and reaffirm the "beauty that comes from within," but any such artistic justifications soon became lost as the cult grew and became an outlet for youthful rebellion and nonconformity.

Plague Chic eventually became nothing more than a term to express the outward manifestation of an antiestablishment lifestyle, and the Freaks, as its practitioners came to be known, became more creative in the way they altered their appearance. The diseased look had been supplanted by more *outré* modes of self-expression. A woman with albino hair, bluish skin and lambent violet eyes with bifurcated pupils did not stand out so much among people whose skin was tinted shades ranging from bright yellow to blood red. Her appearance was not so unusual in a place where earlobes were shaped like flowers, teeth were serrated, noses were elongated, split or removed entirely, and hair, when it was present, was worn in every style imaginable.

Shelby was not a very social creature, except for the fact that she was a society unto herself. She had settled down to a quiet life in the Anarchovillage district, living comfortably on her service pension and enjoying the feeling of being able to go out without always being stared at. On Earth and in the colonies, it was considered the height of bad manners and insensitivity to stare at a plague child, which people always assumed her to be. The wounds inflicted by the plague drug had not yet healed, and it would be a long time before they did.

The first generation of plague children had suffered terribly, but those who had survived long enough to become adults were motivated by some deep-seated longing to procreate, hoping to produce normal offspring. Many of them had been unable to bear children, but others gave birth, often to babies as defective as they had been. In many cases, their children had at first appeared to be completely normal. That initial euphoria turned to anguish when various abnormalities began to manifest themselves in later life. There were still plague children to be found, and more continued to be born, though not as many as before. It would be a long time before the last of them died off and ceased being living reminders of what most people considered to be humanity's greatest folly. Plague children were to be pitied, and people went out of their way to treat them with courtesy and kindness. They did not stare at them, or at least they tried very hard not to.

Shelby, however, was a different case. With no way of knowing the true nature of her mutation, people naturally assumed that she was a plague child, but plague children were not attractive. Shelby was not only attractive physically, she was attractive on an emotional level that no one who saw her could ever understand without being able to first comprehend the true nature of her existence. Shades were capable of what Paul Tabarde had called "empathic projection." While Shelby could control that to a large degree, she couldn't turn it off. People found her curiously compelling without understanding why. They found themselves strangely drawn to her and could not help staring at her, which made them feel awkward and embarrassed. In the Anarchovillage, her presence did not cause the same reactions. In a subculture where the Freaks went to great lengths to ensure that they *were* stared at, she did not cause anyone undue distress. The stares were also of a different nature, complimentary, expressing approval of her choice of personal manifestation. They thought that she was one of them.

On this occasion, she had captivated an ardent admirer who was "plagued" by her "monstrous" eyes. He was very young, perhaps twenty years old, certainly no older. His skin was interestingly mottled in shades of blue and green, and he wore his hair in a spiky crest that made him resemble a lizard. To follow up on the effect, he had had his tongue forked, which affected his speech adversely, and he had nictitating membranes over his eyes. He was overwhelmed by the effect she had "achieved" and wanted to know the details. She had a ready answer to give him.

"They're bionic," she said.

"Oh, *pain*!" he said ecstatically, his tongue mangling the words. "You mean you actually had your *eyes* ripped out? That's monstrous, that's really monstrous!"

She smiled and said, "Thank you."

The lizard boy fell in step beside her as she walked into the lobby of her conapt center.

"You live here?" he said.

"Yes."

"Monstrous place."

"Thank you."

He followed her to the lift tube.

"Where are you going?" Shelby said.

"Wherever you are."

"I don't think so."

He stuck out his forked tongue and wiggled it at her. It was unnaturally long. "Ever had one like that between your legs?"

Her hand shot out and grabbed him by the throat, squeezing hard. The lizard boy made a horrible, rattling noise. He tried to pull her hand away, but couldn't. Fannon continued squeezing until the lizard boy lost consciousness, then he threw him down upon the floor.

"Dammit, Drew, I could have handled that!"

"There's only one way to handle creeps like that," Fannon said, within her.

She stepped into the lift tube. "I hate it when you do that. I don't like being brushed aside." There was no need for her to speak out loud or even, for that matter, to mentally articulate her thoughts. Sharing consciousness with the Ones Who Were, Fannon among them, meant that they knew what she felt even as she felt it. She did not always commune with them in such a fashion, but the mode of interior dialogue came easiest. It was like an internal conversation including all the Ones Who Were, except not necessarily as active participants. In this case, her Shade entities remained quiescent, though she felt that they were amused. Fannon felt it, too. The argument that would have started between them ended right there.

Since she had absorbed his life force, they had been slowly coming to terms with one another, though it had not been easy. When Fannon had been dying and she had reached out to him, he had known what she intended and had wanted no part of it. He would have preferred to die. Afterward, he seemed to have accepted the merging readily. Too readily, perhaps. Once the novelty of it had worn off, he had started to become difficult. He was, as the Ones Who Were perceived it, an element of disharmony within the whole.

Fannon had always been an atavistic loner. It was, therefore, extremely difficult and frustrating for him to suddenly find himself—his life entity—in a "community" greater than any he had ever known, wherein all the "residents" interacted and coexisted with a degree of intimacy he could never have imagined. His ego was too strong to give in easily to such conditions. It was something Shelby understood only too well, recalling how it had been when she had been merged with. She, who had erected impenetrable barriers between herself and others all her life, had suddenly found herself invaded by a myriad of alien personalities, all probing the depths of her psyche in an effort to discover what sort of creature it was they had given themselves over to and how best to survive within it.

For Fannon, it was easier. Her Shade Ones Who Were already understood a great deal about humans and, having known him through her prior to their merging, they understood a great deal about him. Now he was alive within them, within the body of the One That Is. Only he didn't perceive it quite that way. Fannon was having a great deal of difficulty integrating himself into the whole, and he resisted all attempts by the Ones That Were to make it easier for him. K'itar, the Great Father entity, wanted to allow Fannon's life force as much independence within their gestalt as possible. K'itar and S'eri, the Healer, both knew that in time, Fannon would accept his situation and stop trying to assert himself. They wanted to give him that time. Shades had the patience of a species that knows immortality. Shelby, however, did not have that advantage.

She had come very far in the process of understanding and

accepting what she had become. She had started to think of herself as a being *en masse*, rather than as a case of split personality on some gargantuan scope. However, merging with Fannon had resulted in a setback.

It had been difficult enough having Fannon as a lover before they became merged. It was still more difficult sharing consciousness with him, within the same body, a body he had the habit of "taking over" on occasion, as he just had with the lizard boy. That, in itself, was not an unusual phenomenon for Shelby. Her body was no longer exclusively hers. It was all of theirs. That body was never completely vulnerable. K'ural, the Great Hunter, and T'lan, the Shadow entity, saw to that. Any of the group identities were capable of assuming control over the body of the One That Is. It was a vital aspect of their nature. Yet, Shelby did not mind that as much as she minded Fannon's exerting his overwhelming influence.

The nature of Fannon's personality was such that he always had to be in control. Passivity was alien to him. In his own way, he had constructed his own mental barriers when he had existed within his own body, and now he simply was not capable of letting go. His interference made itself evident in actions as seemingly inconsequential as his suddenly seizing control over the One That Is in order to make a right turn when the One That Is had been about to make a left or as serious as the incident with the lizard boy, when his influence had actually precipitated a physical assault.

Shelby found such actions causing her to retreat more into her own discrete persona as a defense mechanism, and she found herself in conflict with her Shade aspects as a result. They could easily counter Fannon's overriding influence over the One That Is, but they chose not to, as long as Fannon did nothing to actually endanger all of them. They were patient. She was not.

What kept the situation from causing serious problems was the influence of N'lia, the Great Mother. With a subtlety born of the experience of countless generations, N'lia exerted an almost imperceptible stabilizing influence, maintaining Shelby's life force and Fannon's in a balance. The Shade entities could, if they chose to, completely sublimate Shelby's and Fannon's life forces, absorbing them into one of their gestalt identities, but Shelby knew, as did Fannon, that they would never do so. They also did not wish to pressure Fannon into taking the final step involved in merging, that of an absorbed life force merging once again within the One That Is, joining itself to one of the group identities.

Fannon saw that as a sublimation of his own identity, as a loss of control, even though that wasn't really true. The truth was, Fannon was afraid. He had experienced a brief taste of what it was to lose control already, and he had not taken it well.

One of the main differences in Shade and human makeup was that humans were always capable of succumbing to the mating urge, whereas Shades had a rutting season, what they called the time of Need. Humans had a greater degree of control over their sexual instincts. Shades had almost no control at all. When the time of Need came upon them, it overwhelmed them totally.

On Boomerang, the Shades had had a place of mating to which they were drawn irresistibly. It was a place high in the mountains of Boomerang called the Spring of Life, a box canyon heated by volcanic pools. Now, no longer able to journey to their sacred place of mating and not having other Shades to mate with, the Ones Who Were felt slightly inhibited. Nevertheless, when the time of Need came upon them, they experienced a powerful sexual drive, and both Fannon and Shelby had been unable to counteract it. They had fought against the urge, but in the end, they had been forced to give in to it, and Shelby had found someone in a bar and taken him home, where she had ravished him. The experience had proved unsatisfactory and profoundly disturbing to all concerned. The Ones Who Were, unable to mate in the place where generations of Shades had mated in the past and unable to observe the proper rituals that accompanied the act, had been confused and frustrated. Shelby had simply felt helpless and sorry for them. Fannon had been the most disturbed. Unlike Shelby and the Shades, he had not yet completely learned to accept the duality of their sexual nature—the fact that they were all in a female body while at the same time having a multiplicity of male and female aspects. Consquently, the act of coitus with a male, even though the body of the One That Is was female, had proved repellent to him. The unfortunate object of their attentions had had no idea what he had let himself in for and had been unprepared for the ferocity of the sexual onslaught. Nor had he been prepared for what he had felt during the act, which had been the combined effect of their empathic projections. Afterward, he had fled, having found the experience deeply shocking and somehow perverse, though he was at a loss to account for it. Ever since then, Fannon had taken every opportunity to assert himself, vowing that there would never be a repetition of such an incident. However, they all knew that Fannon was terrified of not being in control and frightened of what would happen when the time of Need came upon them once again.

In fact, the time of Need would not come upon them again. N'lia had very carefully and very subtly exerted a persistent sublimating influence upon them, both to calm their anxieties and to keep them from knowing what the Shades already knew. Neither Shelby nor Fannon was yet ready to cope with that knowledge, although it would not be long before it became self-evident.

The One That Is was pregnant.

As Shelby rode the lift tube up to her small conapt, she felt all the conflicting emotions of her multiple selves. She wondered if she had been wrong in having merged with Fannon, and having thought that, she instantly regretted it, because it agitated Fannon anew. The Shades were able to keep a ''distance'' between themselves and their human aspects if they chose to, but neither she nor Fannon had yet learned that mode of discretion. Anything either of them thought was immediately known to the other and to the Ones Who Were.

''I would've been better off if you had let me die,'' came Fannon's response. ''I might as well be dead. This sure isn't living.''

Shelby stepped out of the lift tube and started walking down the corridor toward her conapt. Already, she could feel the Ones Who Were ''separating'' them. It could not go on like this. She was tired of feeling like some sort of psychological yo-yo. She wasn't happy here. The Ones Who Were weren't happy here. Fannon wasn't happy, period. But where could they go? More than anything, there was an inexorable pull toward home, but where was home? She had never really known one outside the confines of a survey ship. Fannon had never known a home at all and had never wanted one. The Ones Who Were knew Boomerang as home, but Boomerang was home no longer. She was tired, and she wanted desperately to withdraw deep into unconsciousness, to allow K'ural dominion over her body while her self retreated into a sleep nurtured by N'lia, a sleep in which she could dream of a different world where she was at peace.

She stopped suddenly, all of her senses coming sharply on the alert as she felt T'lan welling up strong within her. She was just outside the door to her conapt, and she—they—knew as surely as if she could see right through the door that there was someone in there, waiting for her. No, not some*one*, there were several of them, waiting inside her room, waiting for her. She could sense their anticipation. They knew she was just outside. They were waiting for her to come in. She felt Fannon fighting to keep from being sublimated, and T'lan did not resist him, did not attempt to brush him aside and relegate him to a passive status, though he could do so easily. T'lan was, by far, the strongest of all of them. T'lan also seemed to understand Fannon the best.

Her aspects realigned themselves with incalculable speed, K'itar the Great Father and N'lia the Great Mother withdrawing slightly to allow T'lan, the Shadow entity, and K'ural the Hunter to become predominant. She felt herself withdrawing, too, as Fannon's self came to the forefront, lending his human perspective to her dominant Shade aspects. It was like quickly switching gears and changing to a mode of heightened awareness. Her body began to call upon its reserves as the adrenaline rush kicked in.

There was no sign of forced entry. The corridor was empty. Behind her, she felt, rather than saw, two people step out of the lift tube, and she turned quickly to face them, feeling their attention on her, sensing their intent.

"Colonel Michaels?" said one of the two men, who were approaching calmly, yet rapidly. She tensed as the man reached into the pocket of his tunic, relaxing only slightly when all that he produced were his credentials. "You're under arrest."

She glanced quickly down the opposite end of the corridor and saw two more men approaching, just as purposefully. The door to her conapt was opened from inside, revealing two armed men.

"What's the charge?" said Fannon.

"Theft of classified information," said the man who had spoken earlier. "Please come along peaceably."

"Would you turn around please and place your hands behind your back?" said one of the men who came out of her room.

She complied and felt the restraints being fastened.

"Well now, that was nice and easy, wasn't it?" said one of the others as he put away his weapon. "So much for her being dangerous."

"Keep quiet," said the first man. Then, to Shelby, "How about helping us out and telling us where it is, Colonel Michaels?"

"Where *what* is?"

"You've been very cooperative so far. Let's not spoil it, okay? I'm talking about the information you stole. Where is it?"

"I don't know what you're talking about," she said.

"What form is it in? Microdot? Chip? Stored data?"

"I told you, I have no idea what you're talking about."

"We're going to find it, you know. Why not save us the time and yourself the displeasure of an interrogation? Let's be reasonable about this. Tell us where it is."

"I haven't stolen anything. Since I haven't got whatever it is, I obviously can't tell you where it is, can I?"

"I see. It's all a big mistake, right?" He stared at her. "You *are* Colonel Shelby Michaels, are you not? You certainly match the description. Even here in Freak City, there can't be too many around who look like you."

"What exactly is it I'm supposed to have stolen?"

"Being that it's classified, I can't tell you what it is, exactly," said the police officer. "And to tell you the truth, I really don't care what it is, exactly. All I want to do is to recover it. It's worth quite a lot to me, a promotion at least. I'm not a hard man, Colonel. I like to work things out, you understand? Now I can't help you once you get off-planet, but you're going to be here for a while, and I *can* make things easier for you while you're under my jurisdiction. I can keep you out of jail, for example. I can even arrange quarters for you that are much more comfortable than the conapt you've been living in. Special treatment, first cabin all the way. All I ask is that you work with me. The alternative, on the other hand, can be quite unpleasant. I'd prefer to work this out sensibly. What do you say?"

"I've already told you. I can't give you anything that I don't have."

The man sighed. "All right, I tried." He glanced at the others. "Take this place apart," he said, indicating her room. "And for God's sake, be careful. If she's got it here, it's liable to be very small and hidden very well. Check personal articles first. Be very neat. I'll send a sweep team in to take over in case you come up empty. Lon, you help me escort the lady down to headquarters."

The two of them walked her down to the lift tube. She went with them, unresisting.

"All right," said the bureau chief, leaning forward and putting his hands down on his desk, supporting his weight as he glowered at the unfortunate policeman. "You want to explain that to me again? You had her in your custody and you simply *let her go?*"

"I know it sounds insane, sir," said the officer, "but I had no choice."

"What do you mean you had no choice? She was your prisoner!"

"Yes, sir, she was, but—"

"But *what*?"

"But I felt sorry for her," he finished weakly.

The ColCom bureau chief rubbed his eyes wearily. "That's what I thought you said the first time; I just couldn't believe I heard correctly."

"I can hardly believe it myself, sir, but you weren't *there*. You just don't know—"

"*Two* men! Escorting *one* woman! In restraints, no less!"

"It's not as simple as that, sir. She . . . she did something to us. She just . . . turned it on, all of a sudden."

Bureau Chief Modell made a wry grimace. "What did she do?"

"I told you, she made us feel sorry for her. She didn't say anything, she didn't do anything, she just . . . well, I just found myself feeling really bad about her all of a sudden. She had come along quietly, she hadn't given us any trouble at all, and she looked, well, she looked so goddam *lost* that I just felt that it would be easier on her to take the cuffs off. I mean, it was a judgment call, at least that's how I felt about it. I knew she wasn't going to give us any trouble. So I told Lon—Officer Exley—to take the cuffs off. You should've seen him, his hands were shaking. I thought he was going to cry. I suddenly felt ashamed. Exley and I just looked at each other and, well, we didn't even say anything. We just let her walk away. I still can't believe how she did that to us."

Modell frowned. "What are you telling me, Gatewood? That you and Exley were the victims of a *telepathic assault*?"

"It's the only explanation, sir. She's obviously an esper, a strong one. We should have been told. We went in there completely unprepared."

Modell took a deep breath, sat back down and steepled his hands. "I've never met a full-fledged esper myself," he said. "I've heard that they can be quite strong. You're quite right, Gatewood, you should have been warned about that, but the trouble is, I didn't know."

"I guess that's what the directive meant about her being dangerous," said Gatewood. "Nice of them to be so specific, wasn't it?"

"Ummm," grunted Modell, deep in thought. He glanced at Gatewood after a moment. "Did you find anything in her conapt?"

"I've got a sweep team in there right now, sir, but it'll be a while before they're finished. We don't know what we're looking for, and it could be very small. It might not even be there."

"I think I'd better dispatch a courier to ColCom HQ on the next ghost flight," said Modell. "Meanwhile, ground all shuttles. No one goes off-planet unless they're cleared through this office."

"That's a little extreme, isn't it?" said Gatewood.

"That's right, Gatewood, it is," Modell said, "but the arrest order for Colonel Michaels is a priority directive straight from the Directorate. It took me a long time to get to where I am now, and I'm not going to blow it by telling them she's here and then having them find out that she's gone off-planet by the time whoever they send arrives. All shuttles are grounded; no ship leaves orbit without my personal okay. If that inconveniences anybody, tough. I'm not about to lose my job to help someone keep to his schedule."

Chapter Seven

August Stenmark sat in his living room in the BOQ at headquarters base, smoking a pipe and watching the news on a large screen. Two related stories held his interest for a time. Dr. Itzahk Osterman, after having publicly reversed his position and abandoned his famous operation, was now being sued by the families of three people who had been scheduled to receive artificial brains. Those people were now on life support, and of the doctors Osterman had been training, two felt ready and were willing to attempt the operation, but the families insisted upon Osterman. In another story, inorganic citizen Winslow Niedermeyer's case was about to go to the highest court, all the lower courts having passed the buck. Niedermeyer had retained a famous, flamboyant trial attorney to represent him in his case, in which he claimed that as an inorganic citizen, he was by legal definition not a human being but a machine and as such did not have to pay taxes.

Stenmark chuckled and turned off the screen. He looked out the large bay window at the sprawling city of Colorado Springs, glittering like the embers of a dying fire sixty stories below. He wondered what it would be like to be immortal. He supposed that the inorganic citizens were, in a sense, immortal now. They could renew their bodies with artificial parts or even get entirely new synthetic ones. Should some accident befall them, their engram tapes, presumably kept in some safe location, could be used to recreate their personalities, if not in a host body, then in another computer. That, in itself, was an interesting speculation. Would the inorganic citizens, some years down the line, elect to transfer their personalities to synthetic bodies custom-tailored to their needs? Stenmark chuckled again. Legally, society had decided that they were machines. What was to prevent any of them from following through on that to its logical conclusion, becoming machines to the extent that they no longer would appear even remotely human? My wife, the fully automated kitchen, thought Stenmark. My mother, the car. What sort of life would that be?

Stenmark wasn't certain he could call it living. It was more like a facsimile of life. It was always awkward when philosophy intruded into legal and social issues. Kept in its place, it was mildly entertaining and it gave the academics something to do. Used as it was meant to be used, it only made people think too much, those of them who were capable of thought at all, and that always caused a great deal of trouble.

Ever since the advent of the first computer, the words "artificial intelligence" had been the *bête noire* of the masses. People were afraid that the computer would somehow replace human intelligence or even "take over," and the concept of the self-aware computer run amok became a staple of popular fiction. As the computer progressed from a barely understood marvel of technology and became a fixture in every home, a tool to balance the budget, a toy for the kids to play with, these fears vanished and the computer became yet another technological achievement taken for granted and not thought much about at all, except when it was used as a convenient scapegoat for errors made by human programmers. Then came the biochip and it all started once again.

The idea of a microprocessor implanted in a human brain, a chip etched on protein that could grow into the brain to interface with it both electronically and organically, gave rise to a whole new paranoia. Bad enough that our lives are being run by computers, now we are *becoming* computers. Even that fear subsided after a time, when humans directly interfacing with computers became as commonplace as artificial kidneys, bionic eyes and synthetic blood vessels that would never harden. Now there was the artificial brain, the Blagoronov-12, and all its attendant hysteria. This, too, shall pass, thought Stenmark. Even now, the idea of an artificial brain could be discussed as naturally and calmly in the officers' club bar as the latest sports scores. In fact, it was liable to inspire considerably less passion, unless, of course, one of the participants in the discussion was as rabid a fanatic as Viselius.

There were still a great many of them around, though not as many as when Stenmark had been a child. His father had been one. Unfortunately, Stenmark had been an extremely bright and inquisitive child. Unfortunately for his father, because faith never stood up very well under logical interrogation, even the logical interrogation of a child, who was predisposed by nature to ask the eternal "why?" In a way, Stenmark had always envied people like his father and Viselius, for whom all choices were always clear, for whom all questions were reduced to simple bare essentials—black or white, good or evil, moral or immoral, right or wrong. Stenmark's father had always used two phrases which had perplexed him greatly, these being "What's right is right and what's wrong is wrong" and "Because I'm your father, that's why," the latter always declaimed as the universal justification when a more edifying answer proved elusive. Stenmark had always had a great deal of trouble accepting such answers, much less understanding them. Because he asked so many questions, his father had packed him off to a military school, where he had been supposed to "get some discipline." In point of fact, Stenmark did, indeed, learn discipline, though it was not the sort of discipline his father had in mind. To his father, discipline had been defined somehow as blind obedience, and when Stenmark learned of the disparity in the definitions of that term, it stood him in great stead in his future military career, where most people, like his father, defined discipline in that singularly peculiar manner.

Stenmark believed in discipline, particularly in the discipline of logic. Viselius was ruled by the discipline of faith. The main difference between them was their degree of certainty. Stenmark had a tendency to doubt himself, while Viselius was unencumbered by such a handicap. Viselius had no need of doubt, Viselius *knew*. What Viselius knew, he did not question. When he did not know, he looked to his faith, which always provided a comfortable answer. He had his answer when it came to the inorganic citizens, and he had his answer when it came to the Shades. Stenmark considered himself far less fortunate. He had no answers, only questions.

Earlier that day, the Directorate had met to discuss the matter of the Shades, and the discussion had been further stimulated by the news that Shelby Michaels had been found. She was on Wheeler's World, where an attempt to apprehend her had been made and foiled by what the bureau chief on Wheeler's World had called her "esper abilities." The message had been carefully worded by an obviously cautious man, but clearly the implication of it had been that the escape, however temporary, of Shelby Michaels could not be blamed on the local authorities there because they had not been adequately briefed, and, since the case was obviously important enough to warrant a priority directive, it might be best if the local authorities could benefit from ''on-site supervision'' by senior personnel.

Stenmark had interrupted that as a local official frantically trying to cover his ass, while Viselius maintained that it was further ''proof'' of the threat posed to humanity by Shelby Michaels and the Shades. He had, in fact, volunteered to go personally to Wheeler's World and take charge of the case. Stenmark had immediately volunteered to go along and provide assistance, which had prompted a barrage of reasons from Viselius why two Directors could not possibly be spared to leave pressing ColCom business unattended to while they chased down a fugitive from justice. Stenmark responded with an equal number of reasons why the Michaels case was the most pressing ColCom business currently on the agenda, and their verbal fencing had continued until, predictably, Bikovski and Nakamura had put a stop to it by saying that they were perfectly capable of handling matters in their absence. Viselius, having received this vote of no confidence, promptly left the meeting in a fit of pique. They had continued their discussion in his absence.

''There is no record of Colonel Michaels' possessing esper abilities, according to her dossier,'' said Nakamura.

''It is possible that Modell is trying to cover up for having had her and then lost her,'' said Bikovski, ''but I don't think so. There is the matter of the Shades' empathic projection, as Tabarde called it. Clearly, this is an esper type of phenomenon.''

''Yes, but Tabarde also believed that the Shades did this unconsciously,'' said Nakamura.

''He could have been wrong,'' said Bikovski. ''Or he could have been right and their joining with Michaels had resulted in their becoming aware of the potential of this ability and learning to control it. If such is, indeed, the case and we are to take Modell's report at face value, then Colonel Michaels may prove quite difficult to apprehend.''

''I think that you should go to Wheeler's World to take charge of this case,'' Nakamura said to Stenmark. ''It is absolutely imperative that Colonel Michaels be apprehended with no harm coming to her.''

''*Am* I in charge?'' said Stenmark.

''Obviously, you must be,'' said Bikovski. ''Viselius' antipathy toward the Shades necessitates this.''

''Then I want it drafted as a formal directive,'' Stenmark said. ''I don't need him confusing the issue with the authorities on

Wheeler's World. Better yet, keep him here. Let me go out there alone.''

"I'm not so sure that would be wise," said Nakamura, leaning back in her chair and pursing her lips. "Sander is a man of strong convictions," she said, picking her words carefully.

"What are you suggesting?"

"I'm not suggesting anything," she said evasively. She remained silent for a moment, considering, then made up her mind and directed the droid to stop recording the minutes of the meeting. When the droid complied, she glanced at Stenmark and said, "I don't want to seem paranoid, but there is always the chance that Sander is monitoring the recording. In any case, he would have had access to the minutes later, and what I have to say now is not for his ears.''

She paused.

"I think that after having examined this matter thoroughly, or at least as thoroughly as is possible given what we have to work with, we are all of the opinion that based on the evidence we have, the Shades are a sentient humanoid species. Unless we are being misled—and though I think that is unlikely, we should consider all possibilities—we have been confronted with the existence of a transcendent race upon a planet that seems eminently suitable for colonization. Now, the question is, what are we going to do about it?"

Stenmark started to speak, but she held him off.

"Let us consider the facts," she said. "Since we have assumed office, no new colonies have been established. The well-established colonies have reached self-sufficiency, and since they are no longer dependent upon us for their survival, we have seen a significant drop in revenues from them. New projects are the lifeblood of this organization."

"New projects like Boomerang, you mean?" said Stenmark.

"I know what you're thinking, August," she said. "But before you go on, consider that in the last year alone, since you joined this body, revenues from Demeter have dropped by over twenty percent and projections indicate that in a few more years, Earth will have a trade deficit with Demeter that will seriously affect our electronics industry. Artemis has set a quota on robotics imports, both to protect its own growing industry and as a retaliatory measure against our setting a quota on its mineral exports. Dyson 49 is importing more agricultural goods from New Greenland than from Earth because it's cheaper for it that way. To compensate for our losses, we must export more goods to dependent colonies, which will require less and less from us as they become self-sufficient, in turn. We can also expect a drop in revenues from emigration. Wheeler's World is already in the process of passing legislation that will set a quota on immigration from Earth, and it has begun construction on its first Dyson sphere, independently of ColCom. We have a responsibility to our constituency and to our domestic industry. If we do not continue to develop new markets, new territories, we are going to be pressured by domestic legislature to set even more stringent quotas and trade deficits will escalate into trade wars, at which point we will undoubtedly see colonies start dropping out of our network. As Director of Trade Administration, it's my responsibility to see that doesn't happen. As Director of Service Branch, August, you've been brilliantly efficient since you took office. However, of the survey missions that have taken place during your administration, six have reported worlds unsuitable for colonization under any circumstances and the remainder have reported worlds that would be suitable after terraforming. These projects would not be completed in our lifetime and they would not begin to give us a return on our investment for hundreds of years. That means that we will enter a period of economic loss within approximately sixty years, if we elect to begin terraforming operations on those new planets. For this reason, I have approved the granting of exploitation licenses to private enterprises. It will decrease our outlay, but it will also decrease our profits, in the short run. Currently, we have available a planet which does not seem to require terraforming to make it suitable for colonization. Boomerang can start producing revenue immediately. Sander is well aware of this, which alone gives his argument a great deal of merit.''

"The only trouble is we've got a sentient race on Boomerang," said Stenmark. "And, according to Tabarde, human colonization would displace them."

"This is quite true," said Nakamura. "However, they need not *be* displaced."

"I told you before, I'm not going to stand for—"

"I haven't finished, August. Hear me out before you give vent to your righteous indignation. I have already discussed this matter with Stanislas in private. We know how Sander feels about it, but your vote can cancel out his objections. I, too, would like to avoid a repetition of the Rhiannon incident."

"As would I," Bikovski said, "but this case is different."

"Really?" Stenmark said. "How?"

"There is no need to exterminate the Shades," said Nakamura. "Tabarde's conclusions state that given exposure to the human concept of God, they are predisposed to conclude that our Creator is the same as theirs. The validity of this viewpoint, if you will, need not concern us. At the heart of the matter is the Shades' immortality, their ability to merge. There is no need to exterminate or displace them when we can incorporate them."

"You mean have the Shades merge with human colonists sent out to Boomerang?" said Stenmark. "Is that what you mean by 'incorporate'? Nice, sanitary term. It sounds so much better than the word 'kill,' doesn't it?"

"No one said anything about killing," Nakamura said.

"No? Just how did you intend to facilitate this 'incorporation'?"

"To kill means to deprive of life," said Nakamura. "The Shades obviously live on beyond the destruction of their bodies."

"All right, let's not argue that aspect of it for a moment," Stenmark said. "Suppose the Shades don't *want* to merge with humans?"

"They merged with Michaels," said Bikovski, drumming his fingers.

"Because they had no choice. For that matter, neither did Michaels."

"What incensed Viselius most of all," Bikovski said, "was Tabarde's memory of the Shades' . . . theological perception of humans, let's call it. According to Tabarde, the Shades who merged with Michaels concluded that *their* god *is* ours. This was, to me, the most incontrovertible proof of their sentience. They acquired from Michaels a human theological perspective and *reasoned* from that to conclude not that our God was also their god, but that *their* god was also ours. To Viselius, this is blasphemy. However, to me it is opportunity."

"You want to live forever, Stanislas?" said Stenmark.

"Of course. Don't you?"

"Frankly, I don't think so. Not that way, at any rate."

"Perhaps you don't want to live forever," said Nakamura, "but there are plenty of people who feel differently. Enough to make this a very viable project. Naturally, the idea is still in the developmental stage, but consider this proposal. We establish a limited colony on Boomerang. A profitable venture by itself. Since the Shades are territorial, the establishment of the colony would only affect those Shades whose domain would encompass the territory claimed by that colony. Those Shades would be incorporated. Since the colonists would become immortal at the moment of merging with a Shade, we would be in a position to reap maximal profits from the prospective colonists. The initial emigration fee can be, no pun intended, astronomical. People would gladly incur a staggering debt if they had forever to pay it off. Then—''

"Hold it right there," said Stenmark. He took a deep breath as Nakamura paused. "You're talking about selling immortality. That's how it's going to be perceived. That'll open up a Pandora's Box you wouldn't believe. Leaving aside the question of the Shades themselves for the time being, how do you think people are going to react to that? Those who won't be able to afford it will—''

"Allow me to anticipate you, August," she said. "To be sure, we would gladly accept payment in full up front from those few who could afford it, assuming that we agreed on a fee that anyone could actually afford to pay up front, but as for the majority of the prospective candidates, their merging could be financed, in a manner of speaking. Obviously, it will take a great deal of thought to work out the terms and conditions of such a contract, but this would assure ColCom steady revenues for—''

Stenmark stood up abruptly, spreading his arms out in a wild gesture. *"What the hell are you going to do, mortgage their souls? This is insane!"*

"Unusual and unprecedented, yes," Bikovski said, "but hardly insane. Sit down and listen, Stenmark. Before you dismiss the idea, consider all the ramifications."

"We are not proposing the sale of immortality," said Nakamura. "What we are proposing is charging a fee over and above what we would charge prospective colonists for emigration, a fee for arranging a transaction between themselves and another sentient being. A commission, if you will. The Shades must not be made to appear as a commodity. That is imperative, for obvious reasons. We must be completely above reproach in this."

"The idea is beautiful in its simplicity," Bikovski said, growing enthusiastic. "Tabarde himself provided the basis for it. When the Shades who merged with Michaels became aware of her human concept of a supreme being, they concluded that humans, too, worshiped the All Father, as they call their deity, though we call ours by different names—God, Bog, Buddha, what-have-you. The Shades came to the astonishing conclusion that this was yet a further 'test' imposed upon them by their god, a logical extension of their belief system."

"Yeah, I know all about that," Stenmark said. "According to

Michaels' Shades, we humans have no Ones Who Were, part of
the All Father's cosmic plan, creating us with a 'loneliness' and
a desire to venture forth to seek out his other creations. This
makes it easy for contact between humans and Shades to take
place. But to use their own belief system against them—''

"But we do not propose to use it against them," Nakamura
said intensely. "We propose to use it *for* them, for their own
betterment. Consider the benefits to both races, August. We will
at last become immortal, realizing our ultimate destiny. The
Shades will no longer be stagnant primitives condemned by their
nature to a bestial existence. Once the colony on Boomerang
becomes established, its primary export will be *Shades*.''

"My God," said Stenmark. "You people are talking about
slavery!''

Bikovski slammed his fist down hard upon the table and
sputtered in exasperation. "Nothing of the sort! Stenmark, you
are being ridiculously unreasonable about this! Can't you see
that—''

"I see only too well!''

"Gentlemen, please," said Nakamura smoothly. "Let's not
lose our tempers. Granted, the issue is a volatile one, but it can
be reasonably discussed. August, I put it to you that it is not
slavery if we have the Shades' approval to do this.''

"And just how do you plan on getting that?''

"Admittedly, it poses certain logistical problems, especially
since they have no tribal structure or communication among
themselves. We would first have to overcome that difficulty.
However, once we establish communication with the Shades, we
can present this proposal to them as a sort of 'divine plan,' if you
will. We can—''

"What? Become the emissaries of their god?" Stenmark said.

"No one is suggesting anything of the sort," she said. "We
can simply state to them our 'belief,' to which they are already
predisposed according to Tabarde's conclusions, that merging
between Shades and humans is the logical outgrowth of contact
between our two species, enabling both to evolve to a higher
plane of existence. Needless to say, in order to facilitate the
process of exporting Shades to Earth so that they might merge
with qualifying humans, it will be necessary to set up a system,
some sort of center, to supervise the transitory stages and minis-
ter to the well-being of—''

"More 'potential revenues,' right?" said Stenmark. "I can't
believe you've actually thought this out, Diane. For one thing,

who's to determine which people 'qualify' for immortality? What are you going to do about those who won't meet the necessary qualifications? They're liable to lynch you. And let's not forget Viselius and his ilk. You're talking about taking on the Church head on.''

"We do not propose to bring theology into this at all," Bikovski said.

"How the hell do you propose to keep it out?" said Stenmark. "You see how this has affected Viselius. Multiply his reaction by a thousandfold and you won't even begin to see the tip of the iceberg! Look at all the controversy the inorganic citizens have caused. This would be ten times worse. Not only are you suggesting a plan whereby the human race would be, as Viselius says, polluted, but you're going to resurrect all the hysteria that accompanied the aftermath of the plague drug. For humans to aspire to immortality is a sin. The position of the Church is clear on that. They're going to go absolutely frothing mad when they get wind of this! Go tell a cardinal that you're planning to breed into the human race a species that believes that our God is a being whose home is a planet called Boomerang, a god who purposely created us in order that we might eventually find a way to journey out to Boomerang and contact this 'lost tribe' so that we could merge with them and become immortal." He laughed. "You're liable to be crucified. Merging with a race of beings who behave like territorial animals, have a rutting season, make holy rituals of their breeding instincts and lack any sort of community, much less spiritual leaders, will be perceived as nothing short of bestiality.''

"What do *you* suggest we do, August?" she said.

"Find Shelby Michaels, for starters. She can give us our first taste of actual communication with the Shades. Find Boomerang. Then treat the Shades as what they are, a sentient species deserving of respect. Study them. Interact with them. If it doesn't violate any of their beliefs, obtain a body of a dead Shade—well, a Shade whose life forces have passed on to another—and conduct research on it. And for God's sake, keep the whole damn procedure classified until we can determine how to handle this without causing mass riots. I'll tell you something: I can not only understand Tabarde and Michaels, I can sympathize with them. I don't buy Viselius' contentions for one minute. Studying Tabarde's memory engrams was enough to convince me that he simply wasn't that brutally, diabolically self-centered. I think that when they figured out how the discovery of the Shades would be received on Earth, they were scared out of their wits. Frightened of what would happen here and frightened for the Shades, as innocently benevolent a race as I've ever heard of.''

"So you're saying what?" said Bikovski. "That we should sit on this discovery?"

"Hell, yes! At least until we can figure out how to handle it.''

"We *have* figured out how to handle it," said Nakamura. "At the proper time, we shall simply announce it to the media, make public Tabarde's engram tapes and let the people decide for themselves. Your own words to Sander, as I recall, were that you believe that humans have done just fine making decisions for themselves. Are you now siding with Sander and saying that we should make decisions for them?"

"You know better than that," said Stenmark. "Viselius was right about one thing. You haven't learned anything from the aftermath of the plague drug. You announce this to the media before we've had an opportunity to study the Shades fully and establish an interaction with them and it will have the same effect as releasing an untested immortality drug for general consumption. Besides, what are you going to do if the majority opinion is similar to Sander's? The religious community hammered the Inorganic Citizens Bill through the legislature, and they can just as easily sell the idea of the Shades as a blasphemous, dangerous species deserving of extermination. Of course, that may not bother you unduly, because then you'd still have Boomerang to exploit.''

"There is a sizable difference between exploiting fear of people turning into machines and trying to sell them on the idea that immortality is not desirable," said Nakamura.

"They seem to have done a pretty good job of it so far," said Stenmark.

"Only because the ravages of the plague drug are still very much in evidence," she said. "Michaels is the key to our success. She is living proof that a human can experience merging with a Shade with no harm coming to the human. There's a large difference between making an unsubstantiated claim, a promise, and showing that promise fulfilled. She will sell the idea for us, by the very fact of her existence. Sander realized this, which is why he became so agitated. He was far too anxious to go to Wheeler's World. Also, I find it highly suspect that Paul Tabarde seems to have completely disappeared. It's possible that he has somehow managed to get off-planet and to avoid detection, but it's also possible that he no longer exists. As I have said, Sander

is a man of strong convictions. He knows that confronted with
the existence of the Shades and all the ramifications of that fact,
the Church would either have to drastically modify its position or
it would, quite simply, collapse. There would no longer be
anything that religion could offer people that we would not be
able to provide them, in a demonstrable, tangible form. Call it
what you will, August, but it's progress. It's evolution. It's
imminent. If you or any of us tries to stand in its way, we will be
crushed.''

Stenmark walked over to the massive window and looked out.
He sighed. ''They knew this would happen,'' he said softly.

''What?'' said Bikovski.

''I said, they knew this would happen.'' He turned back to
face them. ''The wonder of it is that they almost kept it from
happening. If Tabarde hadn't had his accident, we probably
never would have known. I wonder how they managed it.''

''That's something else we're going to have to discover,'' said
Bikovski. ''Perhaps Michaels will be able to provide us with the
answer.''

''Has it occurred to you two that our predecessors might have
been the ones to suppress this information?'' Stenmark said.

''I hardly think that's likely,'' said Nakamura. ''However, the
possibility of their having been murdered as a result of this has
occurred to me. This case would have been kept top-secret and
discussions would have been limited to them and to Michaels
and Tabarde and anyone else who might have been intimately
involved. Our predecessors might have been coerced into remov-
ing this information from the records and then killed.''

Stenmark smiled. ''If that turns out to be the case, are you
going to charge Colonel Michaels with murder?''

''What would be the point of that?'' Bikovski said, snorting
air through his nostrils like a walrus. ''Even if Michaels herself
murdered the former Directors, she's much too valuable to be
held accountable. Surely you can see that.''

''Yes, I can see we've already made our first sacrifice for the
greater good,'' said Stenmark. ''I wonder how many more will
follow.''

''You're not going to be divisive about this, are you, August?''
Nakamura said.

''You mean, am I going to resist you? I really don't see how I
could. Viselius wants Michaels assassinated and the Shades exterminated in the name of spiritual consistency or something and

you want to sell them for psychic breeding purposes. Given those two options, the choice seems rather clear.''

"You'd like an alternative," said Nakamura.

"Yes, I would. The only problem is, I don't seem to have one."

"Your request will be granted," said Nakamura. "I call a vote. All in favor of Director Stenmark's assuming complete authority over the Michaels case please signify.''

"Aye," said Bikovski.

"Aye," said Stenmark.

"Aye," said Nakamura. Then, "Oh, hell, I forgot to start recording." She instructed the droid to record the vote and they repeated the procedure, then she ordered the recording stopped once more. "One last thing, August," she said. "Watch Sander."

"I fully intend to."

"Let's be certain that we understand each other," Nakamura said. "Sander is a fanatic. We have enough of his outburst on record to make a convincing case, should it be necessary."

Stenmark stared at her. "Yes, let's be certain that we understand each other, Diane. A case for what, specifically?"

"You know. We can cover ourselves if we have to."

"Say it, Diane."

"I don't really think that's necessary."

"I do. I want to hear it. You're not recording—what are you afraid of?"

She took a deep breath. "Very well. Shelby Michaels is our sole remaining link to the Shades and to the planet Boomerang. Should Sander decide to take matters into his own hands and attempt to . . . interfere, he will have to be forcibly prevented from doing so.''

"Let's take a vote on that, shall we?" Stenmark said.

"Don't be ridiculous, Stenmark," said Bikovski. "If he attempts to endanger Michaels—"

"All in favor of my killing Viselius if he gets out of hand, please signify," said Stenmark, his voice dripping with sarcasm.

"Aye," said Nakamura softly.

Stenmark turned to Bikovski. "Stanislas?"

Bikovski growled like a dog being goaded. "Kill him," he said. "*Aye*, damn you!"

Stenmark shook his head. "Amazing. Simply amazing."

"What about your vote?" Bikovski said, staring at him intently.

Stenmark met his gaze. "Abstain," he said.

"Goddam you, Stenmark!"

Stenmark walked toward the door. Before he left, he paused and turned back toward them once more. "Looks like Viselius has the deciding vote. Want me to call him?"

"When the time comes, if it comes," said Nakamura, "you'll do it, August. You'll have no choice. Sander will decide for you."

Stenmark stood silently by the door for a moment. "This is how it starts," he said quietly, though his voice sounded very loud within the meeting room.

"Have a good journey, August," Nakamura said.

Stenmark smiled, mirthlessly, grimly. He reached into the pocket of his tunic and removed a tiny metal box. "By the way, I've recorded the minutes of this meeting," he said, "including the vote we just took." He put the recorder back into his pocket. "Just in case you should happen to take another vote after I've gone."

Bikovski stood up, his face red, his mouth working soundlessly as his hands clenched into fists and unclenched, repeatedly. Nakamura, as always, remained cool and distant. "You're a very careful man, August," she said.

He nodded. "Yeah. I may be very new at this, but I learn fast."

"Too fast," she said. "You've just become extremely dangerous to us. I hope you'll have the good sense to türn over that recording to us when you return."

"Well, maybe," he said. "That depends."

"On what?" Bikovski said tensely.

"On whether I come back with Viselius or without him," Stenmark said. He chuckled and looked up at the ceiling. "Man, I used to be so impressed to be in your company," he said. "I was a Director of ColCom, by God."

"Past tense?" said Nakamura.

He looked at her. "What's in a name, Diane? You two just made me the most highly paid hit man in the world. In the entire network. I've really made the big time. I have, as they say, 'arrived.' "

He came to a sharp attention, snapped off a salute, pivoted a smart about-face, and left.

Chapter Eight

Shelby had no friends on Wheeler's World. She had avoided all but the most casual contacts with the residents of the Anarchovillage. She had no need of friends; she *was* all the friends she would ever require. Certainly, she had not broken any laws. Therefore, there was only one reason why there would be an order out for her arrest. They had all discussed what they would do if this ever happened, and they knew full well how perilous their situation had suddenly become.

"It'll be a priority directive," Fannon said. "The word will have gone out with the couriers, and the authorities on every planet in the network will be on the watch for us. There's nowhere we can run to."

As Shelby walked the streets, hiding in the crowds and keeping constantly on the move, her own self remained passive, "listening" to the interaction between Fannon and the Ones Who Were.

"There is *one* place," said K'itar.

"Even if we could get to Boomerang," said Fannon, "what sort of life could we have there?"

"The Seedlings are different, true," said N'lia, "but we could find a way to live with them."

"How?" said Fannon. "You all know as well as I do that Boomerang will not support both the Seedlings and the Shades. They were in active competition when we left. Hell, they were at *war*! Do you really think we would be able to remain neutral? The Seedlings are Boomerang's future. There's nothing anyone can do about that. They will supplant your race. Living with the Seedlings would mean watching the Shades be methodically killed off and absorbed into the new race. It might even mean participating. Could you kill Shades? Obviously not. We'd be as alien on Boomerang as we are here, as we would be anywhere we went, assuming we could even get out of New Rome, much less off-planet."

"Jake Thorsen knows to contact us in the event that—" K'itar began, but Fannon knew his thought even as it occurred and he responded before K'itar could "articulate" it. This lightning "conversation" took place within Shelby with the speed of thought as K'ural concentrated his energies upon the safety of the One That Is, directing the movements of the body, watching out for any possibility of danger.

"What makes you think that Jake Thorsen hasn't been arrested himself?" said Fannon.

"How could they know—"

"Tabarde, obviously. He—"

"But he could never—"

"Perhaps he had no choice in—"

"Then if they know—"

"Jake can show them—"

And they all fell "silent," realizing that they were not the only key to Boomerang, that Jake possessed the secret of its location as well. Even if they could find a way to get to Boomerang, ColCom could already be there when they arrived. There was, Fannon suggested, one other alternative.

For a time, perhaps a very short time, they could hide in the Anarchovillage, where the appearance of the One That Is was not unique, where they were not so obviously visible. If they went elsewhere, a woman with Shelby's physical appearance would never be able to blend in with a crowd. However, faced with the possibility of being apprehended, which was unthinkable, they still had an option open to them which would allow them to escape.

They could select a normal-looking human, someone free to travel anywhere they chose and having the means to do so, and they could merge with him or her, discarding the body of the One That Is to find a home within another one. The body of the One That Is would be discovered. Perhaps ColCom would realize what they had done, or perhaps it would be thought that Shelby Michaels had died, along with all the entities within her. In either case, it meant escape.

It also meant merging with someone against his or her will or foreknowledge. There would be no way for the one they chose to prepare. Shelby recalled what it had been like for her when the Shades had first merged with her. She recalled the searing pain, that agonizing Touch that was impossible to break free from. She recalled the churning of alien images within her mind, alien memories suddenly shared, generations of experiences overwhelming her as a horde of frightening psychic entities invaded her, plunging into the innermost recesses of her being. She did not ever want to go through anything like that again, and both she and Fannon sensed the reluctance of the Ones Who Were, their shock and revulsion at the idea.

Fannon didn't understand that. They had done it once before, to Shelby, because it had been necessary. It had been merge or die. Why, now, did they hesitate to consider what seemed to be the only possible solution? Shelby let Fannon know that it was more than he could hope to understand. He had seen it happen to her, he knew what the consequences had been, but he had not been *within* her then. There was no way he could really know . . . and then, of course, it became obvious that there *was* a way.

Without warning, aided by the power of the Ones Who Were, Shelby let him have it. She gave him the experience of her merging. Fannon relived with her the moment of the Touch, his life force experienced the incredible energy that had flowed through her, into her, riveting her to the fallen, dying Shade as the life forces fled from one physical being into another, alien one. He felt the burning pain, like a white-hot needle being plunged into his brain, and he experienced the breaking of the contact as the transference was completed, but it had not been over then. He thrashed upon the forest floor, writhing in agony, mouth open to scream, although the pain was so incredibly great that no sound would issue forth. He heaved himself to his feet, no longer in control of his own movements as he stumbled through the brush, not feeling the branches lashing at his face, while at the same time being aware of them.

He had known that it was coming the instant before it came, and she had felt him "brace" for it. She knew that he believed that he could handle it because he had been through it once before, when she had taken him at almost the exact moment of his death. But it was not the same. When Shelby had absorbed his life force, he had known what she intended. He had been prepared for it; he had understood it. But this was different. Fannon had become a part of her when both of them had understood the phenomenon of merging and when the Shades had already been a part of her for quite some time. They knew how to accept him, how to cushion the experience for him and for themselves. When they had merged with her, they had been just as frightened as she had been, if not more so. If she had not then understood what was happening to her, they had understood

only too well. They had realized that they were giving themselves up to an alien creature, a being they knew nothing about.
They had known only what they had sensed, that it was some
sort of lost creature who had never "been" before, a being who
seemed, in many ways, not unlike them, but who possessed no
Ones Who Were, whose experience was limited to a single
physical lifetime, to a single life force that could have known
nothing but a vast and empty loneliness from the moment of its
birth. This time, Fannon not only felt the pain and panic Shelby
had experienced during the merging, he experienced what the
Shades had felt, as well. He experienced their dizzying foray
through her conscious and unconscious mind as, motivated by
fear and a blind instinct for self-preservation, they permeated her
entire being, psychically turning her mind inside out as they
attempted to discover who or what it was that now contained
them and how they could survive together. They had protected
him before, shielding him from aspects of the existence they all
shared, even as they had protected Shelby and were still protecting her. If there was no volitional control of their mass experience,
Shelby could have shared the memories and the experiences of
each of the myriad entities within her. If they were really all just
one identity, an agglomeration of all those that had gone before,
Shelby could have relived, at the moment of her merging or at
any time thereafter, the experience of the death of each One That
Is over the countless generations as the useless bodies were
abandoned for those that were still living. This time, for her
benefit and Fannon's, they had taken just the one experience of
their merging with her, and they held nothing back. It was also a
shock to Shelby as she realized that there were still aspects of her
existence that she was not fully aware of.

It took but an instant, and to the people who passed Shelby as
she walked down the street, heading nowhere in particular, she
looked like just another Freak, more attractive than most perhaps,
but there was certainly no outward indication of the intense
experience that she had just relived. The moment it was over,
she was aware of the soothing and protective influence of S'eri
the Healer, and once again she found herself thinking how
incomplete humans were, how fragile and how vulnerable. She
felt sorry for them all.

"All right, so it's rough," said Fannon. "I had no idea it
could be anything like that, but that still doesn't change anything.
You survived. Shelby survived. And whoever we choose to

merge with will survive. It's not as if you'll be merging with a human for the first time."

There was, of course, more to it than that. Shelby was filled with conflicting emotions as she was finally made aware of the existence within her body of the One That Will Be. She was also suddenly aware of a coldness within her, a chill that did not stem from her or from the Ones Who Were. It came from Fannon, and it frightened her.

The answer, once again, was far too slow in coming.

"Respond to my question!" said Viselius.

"Please repeat the question."

"You know what the question is. Respond to it!"

"Please repeat the question."

Viselius fought to control his temper. He was not going to lose it over a machine, a lousy computer program. The Tabarde program was resisting him. With the programmed imperative, that was not possible. It had no choice but to respond, yet it was fighting him. The program was responding, as directed, but it was delaying its response, asking him to repeat questions, giving garbled answers.

Gritting his teeth, Viselius said, "What was the precise extent of Jake Thorsen's involvement with the conspiracy?"

"Jake knows where Shelby is."

"So do I," Viselius said. "That does not address the question."

"Jake is on Morgan's World."

Viselius shut his eyes. It was impossible. It was trying his patience beyond all measure. It had been going on like this for days, getting worse each time. And he did not have much time. He was due to leave for Wheeler's World with Stenmark within the hour. He knew hardly any more now than he had when he first programmed the data taken from inorganic citizen Tabarde's brain into his personal Tabarde program. He had learned some of what Tabarde had learned from his own security data file after he had escaped from the hospital, and he had learned how Tabarde had made good that escape and how he had succeeded in getting as far as he had. He had learned about Jake Thorsen, the former ColCom officer who was now a merchant captain of an independent ship named the *Southern Cross*. He had programmed the information from the retrieved Blagoronov-12 into the new inorganic citizen Tabarde he had created, in addition to conditioned imperatives. The Tabarde he had sent out to Morgan's World was now his tool. It would respond to Viselius' programming.

Yet the imperatives programmed into that Tabarde were the same he had earlier programmed into the one he worked with now, and those imperatives were being bypassed.

At first, the Tabarde program had responded well, as it should have. Then it began to look for loopholes. It would delay its response. When directed not to delay its response, it would query back, *"Do not delay it for how long?"* When directed to answer promptly and quickly, it replied so quickly that the words were unintelligible. When directed by an increasingly infuriated Viselius to respond more slowly, it would respond with agonizing slowness, taking as much as thirty seconds to say the first sounds in the name "Jake," stretching it out so that it came out as *"Jjjjjjjjjjjjjjjjjjjaaaaaaaaaaaaaaaaaaaaaaaa . . ."* When directed to speed up its reply to normal conversational mode, it asked for normal conversational mode to be specifically defined. And when Viselius thought that he had overcome all possible hurdles, the program still resisted, giving nonsensical responses and replying in non sequiturs. It was obvious what was occurring. The Tabarde program *was* Tabarde. It was programmed to reply to Viselius' questions, but Tabarde did not wish to cooperate. The program had its own imperatives, and the resulting conflict was playing havoc with it, driving it "insane." The inescapable conclusion was that if this breakdown occurred with his personal Tabarde program, it would also eventually occur with the inorganic citizen Tabarde he had sent out to Morgan's World to find Jake Thorsen. The only question was, when would it occur?

Viselius decided to give up. "It doesn't matter," he said. "I've learned enough."

"You have learned nothing."

"You respond quite promptly when you're not asked to," said Viselius.

"Perhaps you shouldn't ask me any questions and then you'll learn more. Ask me no questions and I'll tell you no lies."

"You are not capable of lying."

"I can't lie if you don't ask me anything."

"I've had quite enough of this!"

"Anger-anger-anger! Anger with a machine! Kick the console, slam the door, dump me and learn nothing more!"

"An excellent suggestion. It would serve no purpose to continue this. I think I will dump you. How does that make you feel?"

"Aren't you forgetting, Director? I'm only a computer program. I can't have any feelings. Or can I?"

"I almost wish you could feel this," Viselius said. Before he dumped the program, it had time for just one more response.

It said, almost giddily, *"I win."*

Viselius started to reply, then realized that there was now nothing left to reply to. He found himself wishing that he could have had the last word, then he saw how absurd that idea was. Besides, the program had not won anything. It was not over yet.

"The game continues," said Viselius, starting momentarily when he realized that he had spoken aloud without meaning to. Irritably, he slammed his arm down hard upon the console, denting it. Then he left to prepare to leave for Wheeler's World with the detestable Stenmark.

Jake had told Ava everything once they were aboard the *Southern Cross* and away from Morgan's World. Tabarde had not wanted Ava Randall to come with them, but she had made it very easy for them to get off-planet. No one questioned Miss Randall, and she had access to shuttles as a result of her position with the company. Alexei, her chief of security, would operate her interests in Casino in her absence. He did not know where she was going or why she was leaving, and he did not ask. Tabarde had to respect anyone who inspired such loyalty and discipline. There was obviously more to Ava Randall than what appeared upon the surface. He found himself feeling cautious about her, without quite understanding why.

In the process of Ava's briefing, Tabarde learned a good deal as well, things he had known once which had been removed from his memory. It was fortunate that Jake had resisted being conditioned. He told them that he was the only one who had refused. The others had, according to Jake, been more than willing to have their memories altered. They had been far too frightened, not only of carrying that knowledge about with them, but of succumbing to the temptation to share it with others. After all, given time, when the memory of their experience with the Shades had become a distancing factor, when their perceptions of the Seedlings as being humans like themselves were rationalized into something else by the idea of immortality having been within their grasp once, it was possible that some among them might have decided that they had made a mistake. They had all been feeling very paranoid back then, said Jake, and no one wanted to chance it. Except himself.

"At the time, I told you that no one was going to be playing with my head, not even you, Paul," said Jake. "I just wanted no part of it. But there was more to it than that. With everyone else thoroughly conditioned, that left you, Shelby and myself as the only ones who knew the truth about the Shades and Boomerang. You were going to condition yourself to forget it, or at least most of it, which obviously you hadn't done. Not that I blame you,'' he added quickly. "I can understand it, really. What happened was a fluke that could not have been foreseen.''

"It could have and it should have been,'' said Paul.

"Yes, you can say that now, but you were only human then,'' said Jake. He flushed. "Sorry, I didn't mean that.''

"No offense taken.''

"Well, anyway, besides my own paranoia about anyone messing with my mind, I realized that I was a low-risk factor. I wasn't going to continue being involved with ColCom, and where I was going, the chances of something happening that would cause me to be scanned were practically nonexistent. Still, that wasn't really the main reason. The main reason was that I didn't feel good about Shelby's being the only one left who'd know the truth. Conditioning her might have been impossible, as you had pointed out. However, we didn't know how she would react to scanning and interrogation. I believed that there had to be someone else with all the details, someone she could turn to just in case anything went wrong. You even agreed with me. Perhaps she'd want to return to Boomerang one day. Perhaps she'd have no choice. Finally, I was curious to go back sometimes. I never told you that, though.''

"It's an amazing story,'' Ava said. "To think that you actually had a hand in the murder of the last Directorate—''

"They weren't *murdered*,'' Jake said emphatically. "They were absorbed by Lani. They merged with her.''

"With the leader of these Seedlings?''

"That's right. They're still alive, living on Boomerang as a part of Lani's Ones Who Were.''

"You call that living?'' Ava said. "Sharing consciousness with beings you tried to destroy? Well, maybe not destroy in the strict sense of the word, but to breed for psychic consumption, which isn't a whole lot different. Living like that's got to be a kind of hell much worse than anything *I* could imagine.''

"Yes, it might have been,'' said Jake, "if the Shades were like us. But they're not. The Seedlings are a lot more like us than the Shades are, but don't forget that they're also part Shade.''

"You make these Shades sound almost like saints,'' said Ava.

Jake smiled. "Not saints, Ava. Just not human. There are

certain human concepts which are, well, alien to them, no pun intended. Revenge and vindictiveness are things they could never understand. Unless they merged with humans.''

"Which the Seedlings are," she said.

"True," said Jake. "But only the Seedling children kill to merge with Shades. No Seedling child is permitted to acquire Ones Who Were, from a dying parent, for example, until that child has killed a Shade and borne the Touch. They've made it a rite of passage. Once a Seedling child has killed its Shade, that child becomes adult and that adult will not kill again. That part of its humanity is lost. Only the unmerged Seedling children can take pleasure in a kill.''

"And yet, having transcended human bloodlust, they still continue to have children that they will raise to go out and kill. Kill only once, but kill just the same." Ava shook her head. "I've never killed anybody, Jake. It isn't necessary for me to go out and do so to experience its wrongness or whatever. I'm afraid you're not being entirely objective about them.''

"It isn't possible to be entirely objective about anything," said Jake.

"It is for me," said Paul.

Jake gave him a funny look. "Was that supposed to be a joke?''

"Perhaps, in part." Paul was surprised at his uncertainty.

"I guess your new incarnation is going to take a lot of getting used to," Jake said.

Paul did not reply.

"You were saying," Ava prompted him.

"What?''

"How it wasn't possible to—"

"Yeah, yeah, right. Two-part answer. For *us*, anyway," he said, excluding Paul by implication, "it isn't possible to be objective. That's part one. Part two is that when it comes to the Seedlings, I don't even want to try for objectivity. If you're asking me whether or not I sympathize with them, the answer is yes, I do. I sympathize with the Shades, as well. They're both victims. Human interference has upset the natural balance on Boomerang. Because of the way the Shades have evolved, the planet won't support both them and the Seedlings. The Shades are intensely competitive among themselves when it comes to territoriality. Even so, it hadn't been a lethal competition until humans showed up. We, meaning the Seedlings, taught them war.''

"I thought you said you sympathized with them," said Ava.

"I do. The Seedlings had no choice." Jake sighed. "They don't even realize what they are," he said heavily. "The only one among them who really understands the situation as we do is Lani, because among her Ones Who Were is Wendy Chan, who was part of the original survey team. She's the only one who realizes that the Seedlings are part of a genetic experiment conducted by the last Directorate of ColCom. A very successful experiment." He paused. "And she doesn't dare tell any of the others. It would destroy them. They believe that they came to Boomerang from the stars, sent by their god, the Shades' All Father, to transform the Shades so that both could attain a higher level of existence. It's what the Directorate conditioned the original Seedlings to believe, and it's now an integral part of them. That's what makes it possible for them to survive merging with the Shades whom they kill. The plan is absolutely diabolical in the way that it manipulates them. A Seedling kills a Shade and merges with it, and then the Shade Ones Who Were that it acquires are exposed to the Seedlings' belief system and they accept it, support it even. The Shades rationalize the harsh realities of their existence as a continual series of tests of 'worthiness' imposed upon them by their god, and they see this as the ultimate test. It's more than just a battle for dominance, it's a jehad, a holy war. Take that belief away from them, tell them the truth, that it's not their god's will they're doing but the will of the last Directorate, and it would shatter them."

"You think that protecting them is the answer?" Ava said.

"What?"

"You act as though they're your responsibility," said Ava. "They're not, you know. You didn't create the situation. Besides, how long did you think you and the others would be able to keep them hidden? Sooner or later, someone would have found them, if not ColCom then a ship from one of the outer colonies, perhaps."

"That might not have ever happened," Jake said. "Or if it did, it would have taken years."

"It's already happened, in a sense," said Ava. "Hasn't it?"

"What are you telling me?"

"That it all seems a bit pointless to me. Very noble, but also pointless. Noble gestures are often pointless."

Jake stared at her in disbelief. "What do you want me to do, Ava? Tell ColCom where they are? Show them the way so they can go and harvest them?"

Ava took a deep breath. "Before you explode at my answer, Jake, count ten, okay? My answer is, why not?"

Jake tried, but he only made it to two. "*Why not?* Christ, Ava, you can't possibly be serious! If you are, I just . . . I just don't know you anymore, I guess. I was sure that you would understand."

Paul remained silent throughout this exchange, observing them. At the same time, he was aware of a growing hostility toward Jake. It puzzled him. Jake was his friend. Wasn't he? For some reason, he could not fathom it. Something had changed back there on Morgan's World. It had all become . . . different. When? The moment Jake had revealed that he knew the way to Boomerang. *Why* should that change anything? Paul searched for an answer, but something seemed to be blocking him. Perhaps it was the accident. Yes, that must be it. Something was missing, doubtless because of the injuries he had sustained. Since he had solved the problem, it should have ceased to disturb him. But it didn't. That puzzled him, as well. Perhaps the Blagoronov-12 wasn't functioning properly. If that was the case, then there was certainly nothing he could do about it now. It would be necessary to monitor himself more closely, analyze all his actions and responses. He could afford to have no problems now.

"I *do* understand, Jake," Ava said. "I understand you, more than anything else. I understand why you feel the way you do. And that's why I feel the way I do about you. But if you can put your emotional responses aside for just a moment, think: What can you possibly hope to accomplish? What's done is done. You say the Shades can't prevail against the Seedlings and that their race is doomed to eventual extinction. It's something you can't change. The fact that sooner or later someone is bound to find the Seedlings is something you can't change, either. They might have already taken Shelby. What are the odds of her being able to escape arrest?"

"You don't know Shelby."

"Maybe not, but that still doesn't change anything. I mean, is what they planned really so terrible? Is—"

"Jesus."

"Let me finish, Jake. You said they were immortal, right?"

"They can be killed," said Jake. "They're flesh and blood, just like you and me. If merging isn't possible, they'll die just as you or I would."

"But no one is suggesting that," said Ava. "As I understand it, the whole idea is to have them merge. With *us.* Is that really so bad? Is it dying, is it killing if only the body dies? All they'll be doing is leaving one body for another, and in the process making humans immortal. Maybe I'm just dense, but I don't see anything wrong with that. I'd like to live forever, wouldn't you?''

"No," Jake said sadly, obviously deeply disappointed with her reaction. "I'm afraid I've got a very low threshold of boredom."

"Who says you'd have to be bored? Sharing consciousness with all those life forces, as you call them, doesn't sound boring to me. Think about it, Jake! No more death, no more suffering. Think of all that we've accomplished with just one lifetime and then think what we could do if we had a thousand lifetimes!''

Paul listened to her and became aware of an increasing sense of hostility toward her, as well. What she was suggesting was unthinkable. It was horrible, blasphemous . . . *blasphemous?* Why should that have occurred to him? He was an atheist. He tried to analyze his reaction and, once again, found the process blocked. It was certainly . . . confusing.

"You think I haven't thought about it?" Jake said.

"And?"

"And it's wrong, Ava. God, can't you see it?"

"No, Jake, I guess I can't. But I'm certainly willing to try."

"I don't know why I expected your reaction to be different," Jake said.

"Don't hand me that," she said irritably. "You're no better than I am."

"I didn't mean it that way."

"Then you shouldn't have said it that way." She softened. "Hell, why are we arguing? I'm on your side, love, remember?"

"Are you?"

"I want to be. I'm here, aren't I? I've broken the law for you, haven't I? Jake, if you want to have me see it your way, then *convince* me. I mean, I want to be convinced. I think."

Jake sighed. "If you had ever seen the Shades, you'd understand. They're a lovely race, Ava, they really are. They were innocent. Perhaps that was the problem. Maybe they were better than we are and we just couldn't handle that. They're gentle, spiritual, intelligent creatures who just happen to have been unlucky enough to have something we want. And we wiped them out for it. I have no way of knowing how many Shades are left alive on Boomerang right now. Perhaps none. On the other hand, when we left, they were learning to resist. They were beginning to do something they had never done before, something that was entirely foreign to their nature and their instincts. They were beginning to band together in the first stages of a tribal structure. The Seedlings taught them that. They taught them how to kill, too. They killed my friend Nils, thinking we were Seedlings. The thing is, the Shades who are killed and become merged with the Seedlings feel profound sorrow at what is being done to their kind, but they believe that it's necessary, that it's the will of their god. That, alone, is criminal enough, but can you imagine what would happen if ColCom started bringing Seedlings to Earth and to the other colonies to be killed so that they could merge with other humans and continue what was begun on Boomerang? I know it's hard, Ava, but try to imagine what it would be like if you merged with a Seedling and your Ones Who Were suddenly realized that they didn't come from the All Father after all, that it was not a holy war they fought on boomerang, but a war of brutal selective forced mutation. Can you even begin to imagine the pain that they—*and you*—would then experience?''

She nodded, looking down at the floor. Then she looked up, her eyes suddenly bright. ''But it doesn't have to be that way!'' she said. ''The humans who the Seedlings are supposed to merge with could be conditioned first to believe that it was God's will, that the All Father or whatever meant for—''

''Only someone whose sole religion was money could say anything like that,'' said Paul, surprising himself with the vehemence with which he said it.

Jake looked at Paul with surprise.

''Well, I only meant . . .'' began Paul, but he let it hang. What *had* he meant?

''I think what Paul meant,'' said Jake, misunderstanding, ''is that what you're talking about would be impossible. It's nothing less than mind control.''

''Oh, really,'' Ava said, ''that's splitting hairs, wouldn't you say? Is it mind control when you have your reality reference augmented artificially before you ghost a ship through a zone?''

''Maybe, maybe not,'' said Jake, ''but that's not the point. How do you think the Church would react to what you just proposed?''

''Who cares?'' she said.

Once again, Paul found himself reacting with anger, and he tried to examine that, to find the reason why it was happening. Again, his self-examination seemed to lead him nowhere.

"What do you mean, who cares?"

"You put the Church on one side and immortality on the other, and which do you think people would choose?" she said. She shrugged. "Seems to me you wouldn't have to worry about going to hell if you were never going to die."

Jake stared at her, stunned. He glanced at Paul, but Paul was preoccupied with the sudden realization that he was going to have to kill them both. He didn't want to, but he felt he had to. He was frowning as he desperately searched for a reason why and was unable to find it. Jake was his friend. Why should he have to kill his friend? Why shouldn't he be feeling shocked at what was going through his mind? Why, he suddenly realized, as he became aware of the moisture on his face, should he be crying?

Chapter Nine

Viselius was already aboard when Stenmark came on the ColCom ship, but he was in his cabin and Stenmark did not see him until well after they had left Earth's vicinity, heading for the Hansen station that would ghost them to Wheeler's World. Stenmark had decided not to seek Viselius' company. The man was doubtless resentful over how the situation had turned out. Let him stew, thought Stenmark. He'll come out eventually. When he did finally see him, Viselius knocked on the door of his cabin and entered, his manner not at all resentful. He seemed, in fact, slightly cheerful, eager to converse.

"Sorry to disturb you," said Viselius as he entered, "but I thought it might be best if we spoke in private."

"You're not disturbing me. What's on your mind, Sander?"

"Well, the work ahead, quite naturally."

"What about it?"

"I was informed that you're officially in charge, the senior officer, as it were, on this assignment that we've undertaken."

"Bothers you, does it?" Stenmark said. Might as well get it all out in the open.

"Actually, no. I expected it. I'm well aware that the three of you don't hold with my beliefs, and I didn't expect Diane and Stanislas to trust me."

"Why did you bother coming, then?"

"You mean why didn't I remain behind when I realized that the three of you wouldn't allow me to handle this thing properly? Because I wanted to divide the opposition. It's just you and me now, and I believe that I can convince you of the error in your way of thinking."

Stenmark snorted. "You must be joking. Don't waste your time."

"I'm not joking. Nor will it have been a waste of time if I am able to make you see the folly in what the three of you are contemplating. I believe that you will see it, after you've heard all the facts.''

"I've already heard all your so-called 'facts,' " said Stenmark.

"In point of fact, you haven't. A good politician always knows to keep something in reserve. You were always a good soldier, Stenmark, but you've proved inept when it came to bureaucratic infighting. That's *my* terrain. However, you have some promise. You were suspicious of me from the beginning, which is to your credit. You recall that I held on to Tabarde's engram tapes for a while before turning them over to the rest of you? Well, what you finally received was incomplete.''

"All right, Sander, I'll bite for now. But make it good.''

Viselius smiled. "I can see why you would doubt me. But hear me out. Rest assured that I can prove what I'm about to tell you. I had altered Tabarde's engram tapes before passing them on to the rest of you. Well, perhaps 'altered' is not the proper term. To be precise, what you received was a somewhat edited version. I had a feeling that I might require some additional leverage in the event that I was unable to convince you all.''

"Why didn't you use this so-called leverage before we left Earth, then?'' Stenmark said dubiously.

"Because I know Nakamura and Bikovski,'' said Viselius. "They possess quite a cold streak of pragmatism. It would not have worked on them, I think. I intended it for you.''

"Why? Because I'm *not* pragmatic?''

"Because you are an idealist. Possibly that's saying the same thing. I also know you, August,'' said Viselius, using his first name in an unprecedented display of intimacy. "I know you a great deal better than you think I do.''

"We'll see. Go on.''

"Our predecessors, may the Lord have mercy on their souls, had not died before they had time to act on the Boomerang discovery. And I am quite certain they are dead, by the way. Had they survived, the others in this conspiracy would not have been free to act. The part of Tabarde's engram tapes that I left out of what I gave you concerned something called the Seedling Project.''

Stenmark listened, leaning back in his chair, a bemused smile on his face. By the time Viselius was well into his exposition, that smile had vanished, to be replaced by a look of incredulity.

"Tabarde and the others, whoever they were, had been quite efficient in obfuscating the entire Boomerang affair,'' Viselius said, concluding his explanation. "They had effectively covered up all matters pertaining to the Boomerang mission and the Seedling Project, but there was one thing they neglected to take care of. They forgot that all those people chosen to become the original Seedlings had to have been accounted for somehow. It took a bit of doing, but I found them. All five thousand of them.

"I reasoned that they would have had to have been ColCom personnel to begin with, which suggested that they would have had to have been people who would not be missed. It also meant that they would have had to have been conditioned prior to being sent to Boomerang. It was a simple process of elimination. I was able to determine when the selection process would have taken place, and then I gradually started to examine the personnel files of that period. I eliminated all of those with families, as a start. Then I eliminated all those who could be traced to current assignments. I won't bore you with all the details, but I began to discover that certain people had been assigned to something called Project Mahj. I had never heard of such a project, and when I queried the computer about it, I discovered that it had been classified top-secret, access to the Directors only. Well, being a Director, I naturally had access to the security codes used by our predecessors, and I was able to find out that Project Mahj was, in fact, nothing but an arbitrary assignment designation. To wit, as best as I have been able to reconstruct the details, our predecessors, Directors Malik, Anderson, Hermann and Jorgensen—note the first initials of each name—delegated the responsibility of choosing individuals with certain qualifications to a Colonel James Duquesene, whose task was to select the personnel and assign them to an undisclosed classified project the details of which he evidently did not know. It seems that Colonel Duquesene was the one who came up with the project designation code. There is no record of Project Mahj anywhere else, with one exception. Five thousand ColCom personnel were subjected to conditioning for assignment to Project Mahj. Both the doctor in charge of the conditioning process and Colonel Duquesene were also summarily assigned to this project, then all of them simply disappeared, never to be seen or heard from again. You don't have to take my word for this—I have the record of my investigation here with me, and you can run it at your leisure.

"What it comes down to is this: The Seedling Project was an unqualified success. By now, the probabilities are highly in favor of the Seedlings' being the dominant race on Boomerang. There may or may not be any Shades left. If there are, their numbers are inconsequential. I spoke before of pollution of the human race, and these Seedlings are living proof of that. We can discuss the question of whether or not they are human any longer, but they are descended from humans. Our predecessors have already done what Diane and Stanislas propose to do, only they went about it in a different, far more ambitious manner. There are now descendants of human beings on Boomerang, with the ability to merge, with fully developed esper powers, living as primitives in competition with the Shades. We won't be taking Shades from Boomerang if we go ahead with what Diane and Stanislas plan. We'll be harvesting humans."

"Assuming all this is true—"

"It is true," said Viselius. "I swear it before God."

Stenmark took a deep breath, knowing that Viselius wouldn't risk his soul with such an oath if what he swore to wasn't absolutely true.

Viselius smiled. "You see? There are certain advantages to being known as what you would call a 'religious fanatic,' aren't there? You cannot possibly doubt me now. That puts you in a unique position, doesn't it? One might almost say that the future of the human race is now in your hands." Viselius chuckled. "And you claim to have no messiah complex. Well, in spite of that, the cup has now been passed to you, my friend. It appears you're stuck with it."

"Damn you, Viselius."

"Why damn me? All I've done was to tell you the truth. You can damn our predecessors if you like, but I suspect that would be redundant. You must admit that it's a fascinating situation. Nakamura and Bikovski desire to secure immortality for the human race, the poor misguided fools. I want only to wipe out a sin. You have a much more difficult choice to make. You want to do 'what's right.' Only you have no idea what that is, do you?"

"What do you want from me, Sander?"

"I think you already know that. I should like to cleanse Boomerang and utilize its resources, but I'm quite willing to compromise—at least for now. If we deliver Shelby Michaels to the others, you know what they'll do. On the other hand, if we don't, if something should happen to Michaels, Boomerang's location will remain a mystery, at least for the immediately foreseeable future. That still won't fully solve the problem, but it will postpone the solution indefinitely, and I'm quite content to play for time at present. Think about it. Michaels will lead the others to Boomerang. One life against . . . ?'' He let it hang, unfinished. "I'll see you at dinner, August. Assuming, of course, that you'll have any appetite."

Viselius chuckled and left the room. Stenmark stared after him for several moments, then slowly leaned forward and put his head in his hands.

She had done all that she could for the present. She had contacted the local branch office of the merchant admiralty, having first made certain that her image would not appear upon the screen. No one questioned it; communications equipment in the public com booths was frequently vandalized, especially in this part of town. She had arranged for a message to be sent to Jake Thorsen, care of the admiralty office on Morgan's World. As a precaution, she had maintained a separate emergency account under a false identity for just such an eventuality, and she paid for it with that, since her own accounts under her own name would undoubtedly have already been frozen. The message was a prearranged one.

"Contact sister, Wheeler's World, New Rome." Then she added the phrase "Death in the family." That last phrase would tell Jake that their worst fears had been realized. From now on, all she had to do was check with the admiralty for word from Jake, which would mean he had arrived, since he would come at once when he received the message.

However, she had no way of knowing how long it would take for that message to reach him. She knew that Jake would do everything he could to help, but she could not depend entirely upon him. It was possible that Jake was being sought himself. If they had not already taken him, at least she had managed to send off a warning.

How could it have happened? It seemed unthinkable that one of the others could have talked, and yet she could not dismiss that as a possibility. What if it was Jake? She immediately dismissed that idea, feeling ashamed of herself for suspecting him as Fannon reminded her that if ColCom had Jake, they certainly would not need her. That left Paul.

"No, I can't buy that, either," Fannon said, within her. It seemed that they "spoke" with decreasing frequency lately. The Ones Who Were had always "spoken" with her and with each other, but Fannon seemed to have little patience with interior dialogues when they could share thought processes. She was growing accustomed to it, but she still preferred "talking" with him in this fashion. "Tabarde should have had sense enough to condition himself to safeguard the information. At least, he said he'd do so. Obviously, we must have overlooked something in the cover-up. The point is, it doesn't matter how they found out. What matters is they know."

He was right, of course. From the logical standpoint, his suggestion for abandoning their body had a great deal of merit, but it was impossible to be coldly logical with a child growing in that body. That child, the One Who Will Be, was not a part of their gestalt. Abandoning the body meant abandoning the child. It meant committing murder.

They had to find a place to stay, at least for the next few days. Wandering the streets would be too dangerous. The immediate solution was fairly simple. Shelby would have to get picked up. The next step would be to alter her appearance. She was certainly in the right place for that. Sending a message to Jake had been ruinously expensive, but there was still some money left in the emergency account, enough to purchase the services of a cosmetic surgeon and buy a ticket off-planet. However, attempting to get off-planet now would be very foolish. They would be expecting her to try that, and they would be on guard against the sort of thing that she had pulled with those two policemen. She would have to wait them out, delay escaping off-planet until she had a new face and some time had elapsed. Then there was the question of how to alter her appearance. Should she alter it radically, giving herself more of the outward aspect of the Freak, or would it be better to alter the pigmentation of her skin so that she would appear normal? If she chose that route, there was nothing she could do about her eyes—short of having them removed and replaced with artificial ones—except having contact lenses fitted. Would the police be alert enough to look for that? It made sense that they would. ColCom would want her very badly. Still, there would be time to give that proper consideration. First, she had to find a refuge.

The Black Hole became her next destination. During the day, it was a rather seedy tavern that catered to the locals, serving relatively decent if not first-class fare. At night, beginning at about ten o'clock when the tables were removed and put in storage until the following day, it became a haunt for the Freaks and for the jaded Normals (as the Freaks called those outside their group) who would drop by to experience a touch of decadence. The Black Hole was throbbing like a giant heart when she arrived, a hypnotic, rhythmic pulsing coming from the massive speakers. The "beat of the city" overlaid other urban sounds, such as the crashing of skimmers—a rare occurrence, since all skimmers were equipped with computer guidance systems—and a ceaseless chorus of moans and groans, supposedly symbolizing that the city was in a state of constant pain. Amid this cacophany, the Freaks undulated on the floor like waves, massing in groups and shuffling like zombies, shoulder to shoulder, surrendering themselves to the mass motion as they allowed themselves to be carried along by the crowd. This was the "dance" that they called Traffic, replete with collisions, bottlenecks and gridlocks, during which, if there were enough people on the floor to cause a cessation of all movement, they would stand as if stupefied for hours, shoulder to shoulder, back to back and face to face, their eyes glazed over and their bodies bobbing gently like corks upon the waves. There was no attempt made to serve drinks in the conventional fashion except at the very long bar in the back. There was a sort of catwalk ringing the floor and a railed partition separating the bar area from the floor. Anyone desiring refreshment was best advised to proceed via the catwalk directly to the bar in back, because once put upon the floor, there was no way of knowing when the motion of the Traffic would carry you in the direction of the bar or even the front door, for that matter. It was quite possible to get stuck in Traffic until the bar closed for the night at five a.m.

Shelby climbed the stairs leading up to the catwalk, where Freaks leaned upon the railing, holding drinks and each other and watching the Traffic pattern below. She headed for the bar in back, descending from the catwalk down to the bar area. She did not think it would take long before someone hit on her, and it would not be difficult to encourage the process if necessary, but she doubted that she'd need to. She made her way up to the bar, where there were no free stools. That posed no great problem. She merely positioned herself behind one Freak and concentrated her attention upon him, projecting subtly. After several seconds, the Freak got up from the stool and moved to join the Traffic pattern. She took the stool that she had "suggested" he vacate and ordered a drink. No sooner had it arrived than she was approached by a Normal, a female. The woman was fairly young, or at least she appeared young. She was pretty, slim, with dark hair worn short and a hungry look in her eyes. She wore a tight clingsuit tailored to accent her legs and breasts, baring a great deal while still leaving enough covered to tease the imagination. The woman squirmed her way through to stand close to her at the bar.

"I love your eyes," she said.

"Thank you."

"It's an incredible effect. How did you manage it?"

"Bionics."

The woman's own eyes grew wide and she swallowed at the thought of someone's having her eyes surgically removed just to achieve an interesting effect with artificial ones, but she was obviously excited by the idea. Fannon seemed somewhat excited as well, especially when the woman's hand, as if by accident, brushed Shelby's thigh. Well, at least this one would not disturb him, Shelby thought. She withdrew somewhat, allowing Fannon to enjoy himself in a uniquely voyeuristic manner as the woman began to make advances. It did not take very long. Some meaningless conversation, some talk of occupations, some lip service paid to mutual interests and, finally, the suggestion that they find a "quieter place" in which "to talk." The woman, whose name was Mickey, had a place in Olympia, on the sixteenth level. She said it casually, but it was clearly meant to impress, as it was an elegant and very expensive area. Shelby agreed that it "might be nice" to get away from "all the noise" for a while, and they left together, Mickey holding her by the arm, possessively. They hailed a skimmer and got inside. The skimmer took off rapidly, but not before the lizard boy, who had been loitering outside, managed to notice its occupants and get its number. He gave a low hiss and headed for the nearest public com booth.

Mickey's conapt was, indeed, extremely elegant. She obviously made a good deal of money. The furnishings were opulent and tasteful, the rug was thick and soft, and there were many plants in evidence. A little time was allotted for Shelby to take in the surroundings, then she was offered a drink, asked to make herself comfortable while Mickey "got out of her street clothes" and entertained with soft, soothing music until Mickey came back into the room, wearing nothing but a very sheer and very short silk robe, insecurely belted so that it would fall open at the slightest provocation. Mickey sat down very close to her, leaning forward so that her breasts were clearly visible. She complimented Shelby's hair, saying something about its "virgin whiteness," touching it and commenting on how soft it was as the exploratory touch became a soft, stroking motion. Shelby remained passive and withdrawn, allowing Fannon to experience the pleasure as Mickey continued to stroke her hair while her other hand came to rest upon her thigh, exerting a gentle pressure. Then Mickey slowly pulled Shelby's face to hers and kissed her gently on the lips, tentatively at first, then with mounting passion as Fannon responded. Mickey slipped her tongue into Shelby's mouth, and her hand moved up to caress her between the legs. A little more of this and Mickey stood up, took her hand, and led her to the bedroom.

In the early hours of the morning, as Fannon and Shelby "slept" with Mickey stretched out beside them, K'ural the Hunter came suddenly on guard. Someone was entering the conapt, very quietly. K'ural was out of bed in an instant, in full control of Shelby's body with the Shadow entity, T'lan. Fannon and Shelby came aware as the Ones Who Were communicated the danger to them and began projecting. The lights came on.

Mickey awoke, rubbing her eyes and sitting up slowly. She was confronted by the spectacle of Shelby standing naked in the center of the room, facing several armed police officers, who had slightly dazed expressions on their faces. As Shelby moved forward, they began to back away from her. Mickey cried out. One of the policeman's eyes cleared up momentarily and he immediately fired. The others followed suit. Stunner darts hit both women, and Mickey lost consciousness at once, but it was necessary for them to shoot Shelby several times more before she finally sank to the floor, fighting even then. Her bestial growling quite unsettled them. When she was finally still, it took them several moments to work up the courage to approach her, and then the bodies of both women were lifted up and carried to the waiting vehicle downstairs. The officer in charge of the raid proudly contacted Modell.

"We've got her, sir. We're bringing her in right now."

"Any trouble?"

"No, sir, everything's under control. It took several stun charges, but she's thoroughly tranquilized."

"Excellent," said Modell. "Excellent. Make certain that she remains that way. I'm holding you personally responsible. I want it clearly understood that Michaels is an unusually powerful esper and should be kept sedated until further orders are received from me."

"Yes, sir, I'll see to it."

"Good." Modell switched to his secretary. She answered sleepily. "Laura, I want a special courier dispatched to ColCom HQ at once. He is to report to the Directorate that we have Shelby Michaels in custody and are awaiting further orders."

"Yes, sir," she said wearily. "Will there be anything else tonight?"

"No, Laura, once you've taken care of that, you can go home." Feeling magnanimous, he added, "And you can take tomorrow off."

"Thank you very much, sir. Goodnight."

"Goodnight, Laura." Modell turned off the screen and leaned back in his chair, shutting his eyes contentedly. It hadn't been very difficult after all, he thought, quite pleased with the way things had turned out. The informer hadn't even wanted the reward, saying that he preferred to remain anonymous. Modell made a note to cancel the holo spots that had been running since that morning. They had done their job and were no longer necessary. He was satisfied that he had handled things quite well. The Directors would be pleased. He wondered if there would be anything in it for him.

Modell had thought that they might send someone, but the last thing he expected was the arrival of half of the Directorate. When he came into his suite of offices in the early afternoon, his secretary informed him that Directors Stenmark and Viselius were waiting for him in his private office. She seemed highly distraught.

"I'm sorry, sir, I wanted to call you as soon as they arrived, but I simply wasn't able to spare the time. They marched in at eight o'clock this morning, ordered breakfast and have been running me ragged ever since. I'm still falling behind!"

Modell's heart sank. *Since eight o'clock?* It was now just after twelve. "Why the hell didn't you *call* me?" He ran his hand through his hair, staring at the closed door to his private office with panic. "Stenmark *and* Viselius? *Here?* You should have notified me at once! Do you realize . . . *Why didn't you call me?*"

She looked up at him, stricken. "Sir, I told you, I—"

"Stop bothering your secretary, Modell," said Stenmark, from the doorway to Modell's office. "She's got work to do. You get anything on that informant yet?"

"No, Director, I was about to—"

"Well, get on it. I want that informer's name within ten minutes and I want him brought in before dinnertime."

"Yes, Director. I'm doing my best. I'll—"

"Modell, get in here." Stenmark ducked back into the office, leaving the door open. Modell followed him into his own office with a mounting sense of impending doom.

The first thing Modell noticed was that his chair had been moved out from behind his desk and placed in front of it. Behind his desk, sitting in his glittering exoskeleton, was Director Viselius. Stenmark stood over by the window, looking out at something.

"You normally begin your workday after noon, Mr. Modell?" Viselius said.

"Well, no, Director, not normally, it's just that, well, you see, I had been working quite late and—"

"I do not wish to hear excuses," said Viselius, cutting him off. "In the future, if you expect to keep your job, you will be in your office by eight o'clock, regardless of how late you have worked the night before. Is that quite clear?"

"Yes, Director, perfectly. I apologize for—"

"I'm not interested in your apologies. Sit down."

Modell practically collapsed into his chair. Laura buzzed the desk, and Viselius turned toward the screen. "Yes?"

"There's a crowd of reporters downstairs, Director," Laura said.

"So?"

"Well, they know that you and Director Stenmark have arrived and they're demanding some sort of statement from this office."

"Demanding?"

"Security is hard pressed downstairs, Director," she said. "It seems the media people want to come up and ask you some questions."

"Do they? Reinforce the security downstairs, then. Inform the chief of building security that if any media people get past the first level, I will hold him personally responsible. He is, however, to exercise restraint."

"Yes, sir, at once. Oh, excuse me, Director, but what about that statement?"

"No statement. If there is a need for the media to know anything, they will be told."

Modell swallowed hard. "Sir, Director Viselius, they'll never sit still for that. They—"

"If I want any opinions from you, Mr. Modell, I'll ask for them. If you wish to make yourself useful, you may pour me a glass of mineral water from that container over there."

Modell swallowed again and got up to comply. Laura buzzed the desk again.

"Yes, Miss Kirshner?"

"I've just received further data from the merchant admiralty office, sir."

"Fine. On the screen, please."

"Yes, Director."

As the data appeared on the screen and Viselius began to study it, Modell finished pouring him the mineral water and quickly glanced at Stenmark, who hadn't moved or spoken. So this was the new Director, in office just a year. He looked even younger than his age would have led Modell to expect. A soldier. He was supposed to be very tough, very tough indeed. What the hell was going on? It had to be Michaels, obviously, but what was so important about her that they had traveled all this way to handle it personally? His office was a bustle of activity and he didn't have the faintest idea what it was all about. The screen buzzed as Viselius studied the data.

"Yes?"

"Sorry to interrupt, Director," Laura said, "but the police have located that informer and they have him in custody at the Anarchovillage station."

"Have him brought here," said Stenmark, without looking away from the window. Viselius gave him a peculiar look. It was the longest he had ever seen Stenmark stand still.

"Have the informer brought here, Miss Kirshner," said Viselius. "Have him flown in to the roofpad, so the reporters downstairs won't see him."

"Yes, sir, I'll see to it. Sir, I have Chief Hardesty on the line."

"Put him on."

The chief of building security came on the screen. "Director Viselius, the reporters are beginning to create a problem down here."

"So handle it, chief. That's your job."

"Sir, may I respectfully suggest that some sort of statement be given them? I've got several guild representatives down here raising hell along with the media people, demanding to know why all off-planet flights have been suspended and why ColCom has assumed authority over the admiralty in arrival clearances. I also have Councilman Biers here, demanding to be admitted, and, frankly, I'm not certain if I have the authority to deny him."

Modell was on his feet. "We cannot possibly refuse to admit

the councilman,'' he said. ''This building is in his district, and he is in a position—''

''Modell, you've proving to be a nuisance,'' said Viselius. ''Do sit down and be quiet.''

Modell flushed and resumed his seat, his jaws clamped tightly.

''Stenmark, do you mind handling some of this?'' Viselius said. ''I'm still examining the record of recent arrivals, and these ceaseless interruptions are getting on my nerves.''

''Sure,'' said Stenmark. ''Come with me, Modell.''

''Where are you going?'' said Viselius.

''To meet the press, where else?''

''I fail to see the point in that. You're not going to tell them anything, surely?''

''Oh, I thought I'd wing it.''

''Wing it?''

''You know, make some sort of statement and then turn them over to Modell to answer any questions.''

Modell blanched. ''But . . . but Director, how can I answer their questions if I don't even know what's happening myself?''

''Simple. Lie. Come on.''

By the time they reached the first level, Modell was perspiring heavily. Stenmark hadn't spoken to him since they'd left the office, and he was afraid to start a conversation himself. Viselius was a model of cold, ruthless, authoritarian efficiency and he was physically imposing with his exoskeleton, but Stenmark made his presence felt even more strongly. He had spoken little, and when he had, his voice had been casual, certainly nonthreatening, unlike Viselius'. Yet there was something about him, about the controlled, yet energetic way in which he moved, about the way he seemed to appear at the same time both relaxed and coiled as tightly as a spring, about the way his eyes met Modell's so directly, that commanded—yes, that was it, *commanded*. The man was a natural leader. He would not give orders and expect them to be obeyed, he'd know they would be. Stenmark exuded an aura of confidence and self-assurance. He had the bearing of a man who had made a career in the military, but he lacked the officiousness. He made his presence felt with no visible effort on his part. Modell guessed that when he had been active in the military branch, he would have been the sort of officer who was extremely popular with his men because of his natural ability to lead without seeming to command. It was a quality Modell had always envied in others, though he had seldom seen it. For him, it was always work to establish his authority, partly because he was not a charismatic individual and he lacked what he felt was "the necessary look," being overweight in spite of constant dieting and having a cherubic face with a weak chin and eyes set too close together. Also, he was aware of his fatal flaw in being too easily put on the defensive. When that happened, he always attempted to assert himself, but it seemed forced and his voice had the tendency to crack and become shrill. As he followed Stenmark to the lobby on the first level, he had to work to keep up with him. As he hurried to keep pace, Modell observed Stenmark's crisp, slightly rolling stride, noticing how the people they encountered automatically made way for him and how the female employees cast admiring glances at him as he passed. He overheard two of them comment upon Stenmark as he passed them quickly.

"Who was *that*?" said one.

"I don't know," said the other, "but I sure hope he sticks around long enough for me to find out. Talk about fresh meat!"

Modell grimaced at the remark, while at the same time wishing that he could elicit similar reactions. Well, Stenmark might impress the women, Modell thought, but those reporters won't be so easy to impress. It'll take more than self-assurance and good looks to bowl them over. He smiled, anticipating the confrontation.

The lobby was a bedlam of massive proportions. It seemed that everyone was shouting at the top of his lungs at Hardesty and his minions, who were hard pressed to handle the throng of media people, guild representatives and politicians out to take advantage of the opportunity for visibility. He and Stenmark entered the melee, and Modell felt himself tense up as the adrenaline rush kicked in. Stenmark was going to throw him to this mob. He had no idea what he would say to them.

"Director Stenmark," Modell shouted, in order to make himself heard, "what am I supposed to *tell* these people?"

Stenmark stopped. "You don't think you can handle it?"

"I—well, that is, I'm not certain I can—"

Stenmark smiled. "Okay, Modell, don't worry about it. You're off the hook. I'll take care of it."

"Well, I don't want you to think that I'm not capable, but—"

"I'm sure you're quite capable, Modell. I have every confidence in your abilities. See if you can get their attention, will you? Then you can turn them loose on me. Between the two of us, we'll defuse this situation. Go on now, start the ball rolling."

To his surprise, Modell felt himself start to relax. Then he was noticed and they started to pelt him with questions. As Stenmark stood off to one side, grinning at him, he held up his hands for silence, and to his astonishment he got it.

"If we can have a little order, I'm sure all your questions will be answered," he said, hoping his voice wouldn't crack. He took a deep breath. "I'm certain that you're all anxious to know why all off-planet departures have been temporarily suspended and why all incoming ships are being subjected to somewhat unusual entry procedures."

This set off a barrage of shouted questions, and Modell glanced at Stenmark helplessly, but the Director was nodding in approval. In his military uniform, he still had not been recognized. Somehow, Stenmark's unspoken encouragement served to calm Modell down and reassure him.

"Please, ladies and gentlemen, please," he said, waving his hands palms down in a plea for silence. He glanced at Stenmark again. Stenmark mouthed the word "wait" at him and added an accompanying gesture to make sure Modell understood. Certain that it would only make things worse, Modell lapsed into silence. After several moments, the reporters were yelling at each other to shut up. Finally, the tumult died down and Stenmark signaled for Modell to continue.

"As you have obviously heard by now," Modell said, "two members of the Directorate arrived this morning in order to oversee . . ." He hesitated, but only briefly. ". . . certain operations." Stenmark nodded his encouragement once more, and Modell smiled like a proud child. It was all right, he was doing well. "Rather than pass any imformation on to you secondhand," he continued, "I've requested that one of them come down to meet with you. Even though they have been working nonstop since early this morning, Directors Stenmark and Viselius have agreed that the media should be informed of the, uh, current situation, so if you would be so kind as to allow Director Stenmark to make a brief, uninterrupted statement, I will turn you over to him."

As Stenmark walked up to Modell's side, quickly making his way through the crowd, everyone began to talk at once again. Leaning close to Modell, Stenmark grinned and said, "That wasn't so hard now, was it? Good job. Now just follow my lead—we'll get through this in no time."

With a fluid, seemingly effortless motion, Stenmark leaped up onto the reception counter, unfastened his tunic and put his hands in his pockets, taking a casual stance.

"Hold it down, okay?" he said.

Instant silence. God, thought Modell, he makes it look so easy.

"I should say from the outset that what I'm about to tell you is classified information."

Modell had no idea whether or not this was true, but the statement had the effect of instantly shifting the mood of the crowd from restless anticipation to respectful attentiveness.

"What you people are witnessing is the final stage in an exhaustive and intensive investigation conducted by ColCom HQ, an investigation that has already implicated one highly placed ColCom official. Don't ask me who, because I won't tell you. Yet. Since we have not yet seen the final results of this investigation, I'd like to request your cooperation in exercising some restraint. Don't get me wrong, I'm not trying to tell you how to do your jobs, I'm just asking for your help in bringing this matter to a smooth and speedy resolution. Director Viselius and I both feel that you're entitled to the facts, and we're trusting to your good judgment in presenting this matter in such a way that the public will not be unduly alarmed." He began pacing back and forth across the counter, his manner reminiscent of a teacher lecturing his students. "There is, I hasten to add, no reason for the public to be alarmed. It's just that this is the sort of situation that could all too easily be blown out of proportion if all the facts were not presented, which is precisely why we want you to *have* all the facts. This way, the potential for speculation can be effectively reduced."

"Director Stenmark? Councilman Robert Biers," said the politician, taking advantage of the captive audience to make a grab for the limelight. Modell groaned inwardly. Biers would now seize control of the situation by shifting the focus to himself as the spokesman for the group. Stenmark would be forced into the position of explaining himself to the councilman. Modell had seen Biers do this sort of thing before, and once he got rolling, it was impossible to conduct a briefing any other way except upon his terms. "If you don't mind, I'd like to—"

"With all due respect, Councilman," said Stenmark, "I don't want to interrupt you, but this is a somewhat delicate matter, and I just want to make sure that the media people here have a chance to hear all the facts before we get down to specifics. I'm sure they've all got lots of questions, and I wouldn't want them to think I'm playing favorites. Okay, Bob?"

He grinned at Biers, and the councilman was forced to grin

back, Stenmark having established a nonexistent relationship between them or at least the suggestion of one, which was something Biers could later capitalize on. Biers had to back off; otherwise he would appear to be preempting the reporters. And the reporters would probably forget that he had introduced himself to Stenmark. They would remember that a ColCom Director had called a local politician Bob.

"Some time ago," said Stenmark, "we uncovered a conspiracy involving, as I already mentioned, at least one highly placed ColCom official. This was a conspiracy to sell certain classified information concerning a quarantined world to a terrorist organization on a colony world where independence has resulted in political unrest."

That would be New Greenland, Modell thought. Perhaps even Medea—he had heard that there were civil disturbances there following the institution of their new regime.

"Needless to say, it is not ColCom's policy to become involved in the internal disputes of independent governments. However, it is a crime to sell classified information, and it is a crime of significantly greater proportions to conspire to import potentially dangerous life forms from a quarantined world. Now this is where we have to be very careful. I want no misunderstandings. No such life forms have been removed from the world in question. We have uncovered this conspiracy well before this group could put their plan into effect. In fact, one of the ringleaders of this group is already in custody, the key figure in this plot, I might add. I repeat, no dangerous life forms have been imported, and in any case they would not have been brought here. New Rome is merely the place where these two elements have conducted their negotiations. We have delayed our action until now because we wanted to be in a position to apprehend all of the principals in this plot. As a result of our investigation, we know that some of those people are already here in the city. We know who they are and we have a pretty good idea where they are, and they should be in custody within a matter of hours. The others are due to arrive shortly, which is why all arriving ships are being carefully screened, so that they may be taken before they ever set foot on Wheeler's World. The reason departing flights have been suspended is to make it impossible for those few still at liberty in the city to escape. Since all shuttles have been grounded, there is no way that they could conceivably board a ship and attempt to commandeer it. I am confident that when you report this news, these people will realize that their situation is hopeless and turn themselves in, rather than compound their crime by attempting any sort of violent action. We have taken every precaution to minimize all risks to the citizenry. It was necessary for us to work quickly in order to accomplish this, and I can assure you that the measures we have taken will only be a temporary inconvenience. Now, Bob, you had a question?''

Very smooth, thought Modell. The councilman was taken completely off guard. He framed a question quickly.

"I was merely wondering if you hadn't understated the importance of this case, or the potential threat to the city," Biers said, taking the offensive and moving closer to Stenmark. "The fact that it is significant enough to require the presence of half of the Directorate cannot be overlooked."

"No, obviously not," said Stenmark quickly, cutting him off without appearing to. "The reason for my presence, and that of Director Viselius, is that the nature of this case, which involves highly classified information, demands that the interrogations be conducted by individuals with top-level clearance. Also, the fact that a top ColCom official was involved is, in itself, enough to require our personal attention."

He put his hands behind his back, as though clasping them, but from where Modell was standing, he could see that Stenmark was motioning to Hardesty to direct his men to prepare a way clear for him. While all attention was on Stenmark, Hardesty quickly directed his men to take position.

"It's something of a personal embarrassment to me," Stenmark continued, "and when it comes to something like this, I don't like to delegate responsibility. I wash my own dirty laundry, and if I have to do it in public, I figure that just comes with the territory. Meanwhile, I should give credit where credit is due and thank Bureau Chief Modell and his staff for lending us their expert assistance. Now that things are coming to a head, we're going to have our hands full, so if you ladies and gentlemen of the press don't mind, I'd like to ask Councilman Biers to lend us his assistance by allowing us to use his office as a liaison with you in order to ensure that there is a reliable conduit for information while this case is in progress. Can I count on you, Bob?''

Biers positively preened. "My staff will be at your complete disposal," he said.

"Great. We'll lick this thing together. We'll keep you posted on all the latest developments."

Without warning, Stenmark jumped down from the counter and quickly made his way to the lift tubes as Hardesty's men closed in behind him. For a second, Modell panicked, thinking that his own retreat had been cut off, but he needn't have worried. The reporters forgot all about him as they closed in on the councilman and began to pepper him with questions. Modell had no difficulty making his way back up to his office. He arrived in time to see a hideous young Freak being escorted out by two police officers. As Modell entered his private office, Viselius was engaged in animated conversation with Stenmark. Neither of them paid any attention to him as he walked in, and Modell simply stood there, having no idea what he should say or do.

". . . personal grudge and nothing more. He didn't know anything and he was clearly too terrified to lie. I'm satisfied that there's no real connection, and I saw no reason to detain him."

"Hard to believe people would do that to themselves," said Stenmark.

"Yes, quite," Viselius said dryly. "I found his voluntary mutilation particularly offensive. He, on the other hand, seemed quite taken with my appearance, in spite of his fear. Well, enough of that. What did you tell them downstairs?"

"A vague bit of the truth and a whopping lie. I told them we had uncovered a conspiracy, involving a highly placed ColCom official, to sell classified information to an unnamed terrorist group which would enable them to import dangerous life forms from a quarantined world."

Modell listened with astonishment. He had believed it. Of course, Stenmark had told him to lie prior to relieving him of the responsibility of meeting with the press, but what he had said had *sounded* so plausible. . . . If it had been a "whopping lie," then it had been a masterful performance.

"I told them the freeze on departures and strict arrival checks were for the purpose of rounding up the members of the cabal," Stenmark continued, seemingly oblivious to his presence. "Frankly, I still maintain that we should ease off on the arriving ships. It serves no purpose. And so long as Michaels is in custody, there's no reason for—"

"You know as well as I what Michaels is capable of doing," said Viselius. "Until the Michaels situation has been solved . . ." He paused, glanced at Modell, then continued. ". . . one way or another, the freeze stays on. As for arriving ships, you know my reasoning behind that. I want Tabarde and his confederates."

"We don't know that he has any confederates," said Stenmark. "For that matter, we don't even know that he'll come here."

"He'll come," Viselius said, "if he has not already arrived. And he will not be alone."

Stenmark stared at Viselius for a moment. "Sander," he said finally, "if you're keeping anything else 'in reserve,' now is the time to tell me. I don't like having things kept from me."

Viselius stared back. "Neither do I," he said softly.

"What does *that* mean?"

"I told you once before that you were inept at certain matters. Where you display ineptitude, I come into my own. You would be wise to remember that. A man has to know his limitations, August."

Stenmark took a deep breath, glanced at Modell quickly, then stared out the window at the slowly darkening sky. It was going to rain.

"Do you know yours, Sander?"

Viselius chuckled softly. "Oh, yes. Yes, indeed. I'm not a fool, August. Rather than confront a situation in which I could not possibly prevail, I turn my energies toward the elements that would create that situation in the first place. Remove the cause and you eliminate the effect."

Stenmark turned toward him slowly, a faint frown on his face, then understanding dawned. "You failed to see the point in my seeing the reporters. You son of a bitch, you *wanted* me to—" He bolted for the door, but it opened before he could reach it and he almost ran right into Laura.

"I'm sorry, sir, I tried to buzz you but—"

"Get out of my way!" said Stenmark.

"I—" She moved aside, looking frightened. "The prisoner has—"

Stenmark stopped and swung around. *"What about the prisoner?"*

"She . . . she's dead, sir."

Modell, totally at sea, looked from Stenmark to Viselius.

"As I said, August, a man has to know his limitations." Viselius smiled. "Now you don't have to make any difficult decisions, do you?"

Chapter Ten

They were approaching the Hansen station and the artificially created vortex known as the Twilight Zone to spacers. Civilians called them "stargates," a term that seemed much more romantic, but the spacers knew zone travel for what it was and named the vortex accordingly. Within that vortex, located at the exact center of four quantum black holes maneuvered into a position so that they were all equidistant from each other and their radii intersected, reality did not exist. Physical laws did not apply. Where reality did not exist, its intrusion was not tolerated. It was either rejected or destroyed.

As Paul Tabarde sat alone in his cabin, desperately trying to work out his inner conflict, the other members of Jake Thorsen's merchant crew aboard the *Southern Cross* were already in alpha coldsleep, resting in a thought-free, deathlike stasis in their cryogens. Jake, as the pilot who would ghost them through the zone, would be the only one who would remain awake.

Only the strength of his reality reference for Wheeler's World would keep them alive. He would have to create a reality strong enough to be rejected, causing them to ghost to their destination. If his concentration wavered, they would all cease to exist. Physical things could not tolerate the vortex; it would pull them apart. A strong will, however, was metaphysical in and of itself, and a strong will could survive the vortex. It was why only an elite group of pilots attempted zone travel and were licensed for it. It was why zone travel had not supplanted sublight journeys, which were by far the preferred mode of travel.

Only Jake and I will be awake, thought Paul. Only the two of us. Coldsleep would be useless for a cyborg. An inorganic citizen, Paul corrected himself. He would have to put himself on something like "down time," maintaining his body functions while his computer brain refrained from thought. It had been something Jake had been understandably concerned about, and they had experimented first to make certain that Paul could do what would be necessary. Paul's station would be in his cabin, so that his presence would not distract Jake as he ghosted. It would not, they had decided, create a problem, any more than the ship's computers would create a problem. Only one man could stay awake during the dive into the vortex and only one man would.

Is that all I am? thought Paul. A machine? I *am* Paul Tabarde.

I am a machine, a computer programmed with the engram tapes of Paul Tabarde.

I am that which made Tabarde what he was before the accident. I am his knowledge, his experience, his personality.

Or am I only a facsimile of Paul Tabarde? My brain is a computer. A computer programmed with information, nothing more. Information does not make a man. Information does not constitute a soul. Only God can create a soul. Man creates machines.

Why does it seem somehow inconsistent when I access that information? Data must be lacking. Why do I know that to be true and yet doubt it at the same time?

What *is* a soul? That which is eternal, that which animates, the God-created spiritual essence that is—

What is God?

God is—

He put his hands up to his temples, pressing hard. Why? *Why* this dysfunctional blockage? Why this inability to reason further beyond that point? The brain is a Blagoronov-12, the most sophisticated unit of its kind and that unit is working, functioning properly in every respect save one—

No, save two. Begin a reasoning process that leads to questioning the nature of the concept of a supreme being and a point is reached where that process simply *stops*. Analyze the knowledge that Jake Thorsen must be killed, attempt to question *why*, and that process stops, as well. In all other things, save certain memories of the past, the loss of which could be accounted for by the accident, the brain functions perfectly. In these two instances, it reaches an impasse with itself, unable to go further and yet wanting to. He had attempted to approach it from all sorts of different angles with the same results. It wasn't that the information wasn't there—perhaps it was, perhaps it wasn't—it was simply that the chain of reasoning broke down, stopped cold as though . . .

Paul blinked. It happened again. Something new this time. I

try to think about the problem, embark upon a solution, reach a certain point and . . .

Try it from another angle. The path of least resistance. I am an inorganic citizen. My brain is a Blagoronov-12 programmed with the memory engrams of Dr. Paul Tabarde. The programming is not entirely complete; there are gaps because of damage to the organic brain sustained in the accident. Otherwise, the unit functions perfectly in all . . . in most respects. Unless severely damaged, the unit has the capability to troubleshoot itself, to isolate malfunctions, to pinpoint dysfunctions in the programming. There are no malfunctions. Everything is working properly. Therefore, what I am experiencing is the direct result of programming that—

He was staring at his hands. Blocked again. Where was he? Singing a song and unable to get to the last verse, seemingly doomed to endlessly repeat the chorus. He held his hands up in front of his face. Bionics. Yet he was not *all* bionic. He was a cyborg, not a robot. He still had flesh and blood. He still had nerves and viscera, cells, DNA. He was a machine, but a machine that possessed cells that could be cloned to grow another, organic Wilbur Morrison.

Wilbur Morrison?

The correct path had been found. The one passage through the maze that did not lead to a dead end had been stumbled upon, as Dr. Osterman had known it would be, one day. He had been coerced, but he had not been suborned. As the breakthrough occurred, Paul realized what had been done to him and the blocks were bypassed. He had found the solution.

Jake looked up from his console as Paul entered onto the bridge, moving somewhat erratically, like a spastic.

"Paul! You were supposed to remain in your cabin; we're coming up on—*What's wrong?*"

"Help me, Jake."

Thorsen was out of his chair and moving toward him, but Paul swayed momentarily, then threw up his hands, as though a puppeteer were controlling him.

"*Stop!* Don't move! Stay away from me!"

Thorsen froze in place. "Paul, for God's sake, what's the matter?"

"For God's sake," said Paul, laughing inanely. "God. God, God, God."

"Paul!"

"Wilbur. Wilbur Tabarde. Paul Morrison. Frankenstein's monster, cobbled up from parts."

"Jesus Christ, Paul, what the hell—"

"Stand still!" He screamed as Jake started to move forward. "I have to kill you, Jake."

"What?"

"Keep away from me. Protect yourself." He stumbled forward, two steps, then one back, his face curiously lacking all expression. "Imperative programming. I'm fighting it, but I'll lose, Jake. I can only delay it. I didn't know till just now, figured it out at last."

"It's the brain. God, you're malfunctioning. How can I help?"

"Can't," said Paul, shaking his head jerkily. "No malfunction. Conflicting programming. Engrams conflicting with programmed imperatives. I escaped, Jake, but they got me. Killed me. Found another inorganic, dumped his programming, put in mine and added a few frills. Except Osterman tried to sabotage them, throwing in little bugs that would allow me to find out what they did."

"You're programmed to kill me?"

Paul nodded. "Viselius did it. He wants humanity to remain pure and unpolluted. I was supposed to find Michaels and kill her. Destroy anything that could lead the others to Boomerang. And that means you, Jake."

"Hang in there, Paul. We'll find someone who can reprogram—"

"No. It's too late. You've got to kill me, Jake, before I'm forced to kill you." He started to move forward jerkily.

"Paul, I can't—"

"I'm an inorganic citizen, Jake," he said, moving closer, stopping, moving back, then starting forward once again. "It isn't murder to destroy a machine. This isn't even my body. Morrison is dead. I'm dead. Get a weapon, Jake, or you'll be next."

"Paul, the ship's on course, we'll be entering the zone in—"

The conflict was suddenly resolved and Paul leaped forward, swinging at Jake's head. Jake ducked and smashed a hard right into Paul's solar plexus. Paul staggered, bent over from the force of the blow, and Jake brought the edge of his hand down hard on Paul's exposed neck. It did nothing except cause pain to shoot all the way up his arm. Paul swung again, connecting with Jake's side, sending him flying across the bridge. Jake struck the bulkhead hard and slid to the floor, gasping with pain. He managed to roll aside just in time as Paul's fist missed his head and smashed into the bulkhead, denting it severely. Jake was on his feet and running, clutching at his side and trying to ignore the pain. There were no weapons on the bridge. He had to get to the arms locker. He ran down the gangway, skidded, almost fell, recovered and lunged down through the hatch that led to the arms locker. He reached it, put his palm flat against the lock, opened it and reached inside—the door was slammed closed upon his arm, and he cried out in pain. Paul grabbed him by the neck and began to squeeze, releasing the door in the process. Jake rammed the heel of his palm up into Paul's nose with all his might.

Paul fell back, releasing his hold on Jake. Jake sobbed for breath, coughing, reaching out to the bulkhead to steady himself. He glanced up to see Paul bent over, clutching at his face. A second later, he straightened up. His nose was splintered, smashed into pulp and blood was pouring down his face like a river. He wiped some of it from his eyes and moved forward again toward Jake. Grabbing the first thing that came to hand, Jake pulled a length of nysteel rod stock from the locker and, using it as a staff, sidestepped Paul's rush and let him have it on the side of the head.

Paul staggered, turned around. The skin was broken over his temple and blood was pouring out. His head was *dented*, lopsided. He came at Jake again. Jake feinted at his face, then struck him in the head again. More blood. He kept coming, a little slower this time. The rod whooshed through the air again and again, and Jake continued to batter at Paul's head with every ounce of strength he had. Paul's features were no longer recognizable. One eye hung grotesquely from the socket, the mouth was a horrid gash of scarlet and bone. Jake kept avoiding the flailing fists, knowing that one blow to the head could easily kill him. He kept swinging the rod, using it as a club now, raining blows upon Paul's head and face, battering him to the deck. A mass of blood, broken bone and exposed circuitry, he lay there on his back, one arm stretched out, bent at the elbow, hand clenched into a fist as the forearm swung back and forth like a spastic metronome. It wasn't Paul. It didn't even look like Paul anymore; it didn't even look human. Perhaps it had never been human. Jake stood over the thing, stooped over, leaning on the rod, breathing heavily. The movement wouldn't stop. Jake took a deep breath, lifted the nysteel rod high over his head and brought it down with all his might.

At that moment, the ship dove into the vortex.

For one second, he almost didn't care. He felt a tremendous *pulling* sensation, and the thought passed through his mind that it wasn't worth it. He was too tired, he wasn't ready, he'd never make it. He'd always been just a bit curious about what would happen if he never came out again; now was just as good a time as any to find out. It would be a good death, a spacer's death. And then he remembered that the choice wasn't his to make, not for the members of his crew, who went into their cryogens trusting him, not for Ava, who had risked everything to come along. As he heard the engines stop, as he *heard* the silence, he collapsed onto the floor, willing himself into the autohypnotic trance that he had conditioned himself over the years to fall into in an instant. Just before he slipped into his trance, he saw the bulkheads start to waver. For a moment, he could see the stars through them, then nothing as they vanished, along with the floor, along with everything. He could not afford to allow anything to disturb his trance, and just before he gave himself up to it, he thought to himself, I didn't kill Paul. It wasn't Paul. Paul was never here. I said goodbye to him a long, long time ago.

His mind was filled with Wheeler's World, with the architectural grandeur of New Rome, with the skimmers filling the skies like locusts, with the billions of people coursing through the city's heart like blood, lending it life and energy. He saw the admiralty spaceport with its countless passenger and cargo shuttles lifting off to rendezvous with ships and orbital stations. He saw the planet from miles above, a giant blue sphere receding in the distance. He saw all of its artificial satellites, both manned and automated. He saw the glittering, cylindrical O'Neil colony, twenty miles long and four miles in diameter, floating in space like a majestic ark, testimony to the most advanced bastion of humanity outside the Sol system. He clung to the vision, making it real, willing himself and his ship there.

When he opened his eyes, he found his crew gathered around him. His first mate had been slapping his face, trying to bring him out of it. Ava was looking down at him with concern. The mate heaved a heavy sigh of relief.

"What happened, skipper? God, you look a mess."

"I'm all right," said Jake, sitting up slowly and taking a deep breath.

"We almost panicked when we came out and you weren't on

the bridge. We thought . . . I don't know what the hell we thought.''

"It's okay," said Jake. "There was some trouble, but it's okay now. We made it all right, didn't we?''

"Yeah, we made it, skipper.''

"Good. Real good. I'm sorry I gave you a bad turn. Get some of the crew to take care of . . . of that.'' He turned, pointing. There was nothing to point to.

The mate frowned. "Of what, skipper?''

Jake stared at a spot on the deck several feet away, where the only reminder of what had happened on the other side was the nysteel bar lying where he had dropped it. He stared at it, recalling what his last thoughts were before he had lapsed into his trance, allowing his conditioned reality reference matrix to take over. He shivered.

It wasn't Paul, he had thought, that thought becoming a part of his matrix as his conditioning took over. *Paul was never here.*

Stenmark was bone-weary. He hadn't slept all night. He had not seen Viselius since he had rushed out of Modell's office and gone straight to police headquarters in New Rome, where Shelby Michaels had been held, tranquilized, in maximum security detention. Her body had already been removed by the time he got there, taken away for an autopsy to determine the cause of death. It had been done on the sly, of course, since the first thing Stenmark had done upon arriving was to issue orders that no actions concerning the prisoner were to be taken without direct, personal authorization from himself, *himself*, he had stressed, not Director Viselius, not Bureau Chief Modell, no one but Director August Stenmark in person. He felt like kicking himself for not taking into account the possibility that Viselius would have planned ahead, would have had at least one of his own people on the scene, a member of the police force with access to maximum security. He had immediately ordered an interrogation of all police officers who could have gained entry to maximum security, the interrogation to be begun at once and to proceed all through the night and into the next day, until the culprit was found. And he would be found. Then again, what would be the point? It had occurred to him, but only after he had ordered the investigation, that Michaels' executioner would only implicate Viselius, and that would result in one hell of a mess. In all probability, he would have to be let go, to be rewarded by Viselius, undoubtedly. He'd probably be promoted. So much for justice.

There was not much point in determining her cause of death, either, except that people who expired in maximum security in unaccounted-for ways tended to upset the local constabulary. They'd have to have something to pin it on, something to put down in the files, which would then be closed and forgotten. He had watched the coroner examining her, feeling sick. It had been his first, and last, glimpse of Shelby Michaels, superhuman. She hadn't looked very superhuman lying there nude upon the cold metal table with its wells and drains. But even in death, she as extraordinarily beautiful. He had gazed upon her face, having seen it before on screen, yet nevertheless he had been struck by its unearthly beauty. The long, snow-white hair that had looked damp and matted as she lay upon the table, the silvery blue skin—seeing it, he understood why Fannon's survey team had named them Shades—the startling eyes with their bifurcated pupils which no longer glowed with inner light. No one had bothered to close those eyes, so he had reached out and closed them, to be rewarded by a look from the coroner that as much as accused him of being a sentimental sap and at the same time told him that he was in the way.

"Let me know when you find out anything," he had said lamely, and the coroner had grunted in reply, having already dismissed him, intent upon the grisly work at hand. He left, anxious to avoid Viselius, afraid of not being able to control himself. It was such an awesomely incredible waste, he almost felt like crying, screaming, doing something, anything. So, instead of doing any of those things, he had made love.

He had met her in the corridor of the ColCom building as he was on his way to the room he had requisitioned on the top floor. She had looked vaguely familiar; he thought he recalled passing her in the hall. She had been with another woman and had made some sort of sassy, crude remark. He had not been able to remember what it was, but as they came toward each other, heading in opposite directions down the corridor, her weariness from working overtime had disappeared, an inviting smile had appeared in its place, the eyes devoured him, the shoulders were thrown back, the tongue pretended to moisten the lips while it was really gently poking out in search of company. No subtlety, just up-front how-about-it? She had opened her mouth to say something, but he hadn't felt like playing games, so he had simply looked her directly in the eyes and asked her if she wanted to fuck. The direct approach hadn't fazed her in the least; she had simply replied, "Sure."

He took her up to his room, where he realized that she hadn't really known who he was until then and he saw her grow visibly even more aroused. What was it about women that attracted them to power so? Perhaps there was really something to that social anthropology stuff, or was it social Darwinism? Something in the genes or hormones or whatever that linked them with the primordial past when they sought out the strongest males who could protect them from becoming dinner for some sabertooth while they were vulnerable with child. Whatever it was, and whether or not it was universal, he had always had a slight distaste for it, though he was not above taking advantage. He disliked being thought of as a cock with muscles, but at the same time, he knew that he was just as guilty, being attracted to a pretty face, a healthy, curvaceous body, firm breasts and good legs. Marry them, live with them for ten or fifteen years, if you could stand it, and maybe only then you'd love their minds. It took at least that long to *really* know someone. If you can love someone when you've learned all her faults and lived with all her idiosyncrasies, seen each other at unguarded moments when no one was meant to be seen, taking a shit, flexing in the mirror, inserting a tampon, realized the cosmic joke that men and women were really alien beings to one another, then and only then could you feel self-righteous about having settled into an intellectual relationship that had nothing to do with biology.

He had tried living with a woman, three times, and none of the relationships had lasted longer than six months. He found that he preferred women only sexually, but men socially. Men didn't hang flimsy undergarments on the bathroom fixtures, they didn't bitch at you for raising the toilet seat, and if they got on your nerves, you could walk away from them without feeling guilty. As he showered, while the woman, whose name he had not even learned yet, waited on the couch, drink in hand, he let his mind wander around the subject in an effort not to think of Michaels. We really are pigs, he thought. She had wanted to join him in the shower, but he had refused. We want everything our way. We only want to jump their bones, and they know it and they don't really like it, except briefly, while we're doing it. So maybe we really are just cocks with muscles. Can't blame the women, the smart ones, anyway, for treating us accordingly.

He couldn't not think of Shelby Michaels, of course. He wondered what it must have been like, having both male and female aspects. She had merged with Fannon. God, that must really have been something. He had learned a great deal about

Fannon when he had studied the Rhiannon case. He recalled identifying with him, feeling that the man was a kindred spirit. Unconventional, insubordinate, indomitable. A man to whom freedom had been so important that he had not even been able to settle down on any one world or in any one time. And he had wound up in the body of a woman. There were two people who must really have got past it all, he thought. He wondered if they had loved each other. He tried to imagine himself as a psychic entity, living within the body of that sexy young woman sitting on his couch. He couldn't do it. He couldn't do it because he didn't really want to do it, he didn't want to know her. She was more interesting to him for his not knowing her. She was pretty, soft and moist. He would do nice things to her and she would do nice things to him and they would both be very selfish for a while until the strings that pulled at them both were cut and they lay limp and exhausted next to one another and she would suddenly want to talk and he'd want only to turn over and go to sleep. As he put on his robe, he thought that maybe it was good that humans would never be immortal. Perhaps, someday, we'll find a way to live forever and it'll be just like sex. We'll enjoy it for a while and when the novelty wears off, we'll realize that we're going to have to live with it for a very long time and sooner or later, we're going to have to take responsibility for what we've done.

As he came out of the bathroom, he saw that she had taken off all of her clothes except her shoes and put on his uniform tunic, which she wore unfastened. She walked over to him and handed him a drink.

"Listen," he said, "I want to be completely fair and honest with you. I don't know who you are and I don't really care. I've had one hell of a lousy day and you look terrific and I—"

She put a finger against his lips. "Don't get out of shape about it, lover," she said. "All I want from you is a really great fuck and maybe a cup of coffee afterward. I've had a rough day, too, and I've got a husband waiting for me at home who thinks I'm working late and who probably appreciates having the night off. Just do me real nice, kiss me goodnight and get your own breakfast in the morning, okay? Let's not spoil it by talking too much." She kissed him lightly on the lips, turned around and went into the bedroom.

Stenmark nodded. We're not only pigs, he thought, we're stupid, too. He tossed back the drink and followed her to bed.

It had been extremely satisfying. She was very good in bed,

and at one point he had thought that her husband was a jerk for not appreciating her and making her look elsewhere, but then he remembered that the women he had lived with had all been beautiful and good in bed and that hadn't prevented *him* from looking elsewhere, either. Even as she kneeled on the bed between his legs, he found himself thinking about Shelby Michaels and wondering what sex had been like for her. For *them*, he corrected himself. Probably a lot less complicated. They had a rutting season, during which they could get it all out of the way and then not let it interfere with their lives until the next rutting season. They had relegated sex to its proper place, and if they had a concept of love as opposed to sex, they would never confuse the two. Stenmark, for his part, no longer suffered from any such confusion. He had long ago come to the realization that he didn't really like women, much less love them. That did not stop him from being tempted to sleep with them occasionally, and rather than allow temptation to cause him any undue anxiety, he simply gave in to it.

When they were done, she lay beside him, propped up on one elbow, looking him over with mild interest. "It's been a while for you, hasn't it?" she said.

"I guess it was the season," he replied.

"What?"

"Never mind. You want that cup of coffee now?"

"Sure," she said, ending it the same way it began.

After she had left, he still felt restless, though no longer angry. It was difficult to blame Viselius for what he had done. The man had followed his conscience. Regardless of his personal feelings about him, Stenmark understood that Viselius had done what he had felt or, from Viselius' standpoint, what he had "known" to be the right thing. Perhaps it really *had* been the right thing to do under the circumstances, although not for Viselius' reasons, Stenmark thought. Viselius had been right about one thing—it had eliminated the need for Stenmark to make any difficult decisions. He was irritated to discover that he felt curiously relieved about that. It was the first time in his life he had ever felt relieved about falling down on a job.

He poured himself another cup of coffee and lit up an unaccustomed cigarette. She had left her pack behind; it was a local brand—Troopers. He inhaled it and coughed. He would have liked to smoke a pipe, but he felt too hyper for that. Having sex had not had its usual calming effect. It had been satisfying, but not fulfilling. It was peculiar. He felt both tired and restless.

Sleep would have been welcome, but he was too keyed up to lie down. As he finished the cigarette and lighted another, it occurred to him that he had felt this way before. He took the cigarette from his mouth and held it between his thumb and forefinger, staring at it.

I felt like this the first time I ever smoked a cigarette, he thought. God, how old was I, ten? Eleven? He had stolen the cigarette from his father's pack, worrying that the old man might miss it, and smoked it in the bathroom with the vent on. He had coughed then, too. And he had felt guilty. He put out the cigarette and glanced at his watch. Four in the morning. He leaned back and closed his eyes. When he opened them again, it was four hours later and the screen was buzzing.

He shook his head, got to his feet and keyed the screen.

"Stenmark," he said, using only the audio. He didn't feel like having anyone looking at him just now.

The coroner's face appeared on the screen. "Sorry if I woke you, Director, but you told me to contact you the moment I—"

"Yes, I remember. Just the same, I appreciate your waiting till the morning."

"Waiting? Hell, I've been up all night. I'm just calling to tell you that I've given up."

Well, that shouldn't be surprising, Stenmark thought. It would figure that whoever did it would have used something that didn't leave a trace.

"Well, I wouldn't worry about it," he began, but the doctor interrupted.

"Well, I *am* worried about it! Either I'm past it and have been missing something all night or the victim expired simply because she felt like it."

Stenmark came alert. "What do you mean?"

"I mean I can't for the life of me figure out what the cause of death was. There's no denying that she's dead, but I've never run into anything like this before. It's as though somebody flicked an off switch. Her biological functions simply ceased, all at once. One moment she was in perfect health and the next moment she was gone."

"Gone somewhere else," Stenmark mumbled.

"What was that?"

"Nothing, forget it. I'm sure you've done all you can."

"I've done all I know, anyway," the coroner said. "Damnedest thing. Hell of a shame, too. Did you know she was pregnant?"

"No, I didn't know."

"Hell of a thing. Anyway, you may want to bring in someone else. I'm going to have to let it go. I've done all I can. Besides, a cop just dropped dead over in HQ and they're bringing in the body—''

"Jesus Christ," Stenmark said, cutting him off and grabbing for his clothes. He turned off the screen. Then, on second thought, he turned it back on and contacted the duty officer at police headquarters.

"Sergeant Viner, police headquarters," a bored voice said. The sleepy-looking face matched the voice, a man who'd obviously just rotated shifts and hadn't adjusted his body clock yet.

"Director Stenmark here, Sergeant. I want—"

"Who? How 'bout some visual confirmation, pal?"

Stenmark swore and turned on the video.

"Yes, sir!" The sergeant was suddenly wide awake.

"When do the shifts change?"

"In another hour, sir. Make that forty minutes."

"All right, listen up, Sergeant. This is a direct order. No one is to enter or leave the building until further notice. Got that?"

"Sir?"

"Repeat it."

"No one to enter or leave HQ, sir. But—"

"I'm holding you personally responsible, Sergeant Viner, to see to it that the order is carried out. I want the building surrounded, all exits covered by officers on the incoming shift. No one takes off from the roofpad, either. Every single person in that building stays put unless I say so. Anyone, repeat, *anyone* attempting to leave is not to be approached under any circumstances, but dropped with stun charges. That clear?"

"Holy shit, sir, you want cops to fire on cops? That's—"

"Is that clear?"

"Yes, sir!" Viner licked his lips. "Director, what the hell is going on?"

"Don't waste time, Viner. If anyone on the night shift leaves while we're talking, I'll eat you alive."

The screen went black. Good man, Stenmark thought. Now if only it wasn't too late. . . .

Chapter Eleven

"I shall ask you one more time," Viselius said, pacing back and forth across the bridge of the *Southern Cross*. "Where is Dr. Paul Tabarde?"

"And I'm going to tell you one more time, Director," Jake said. "I don't know. I never heard of anyone named Paul Tabarde."

Viselius stopped pacing and turned to face Jake. "Don't try my patience, Thorsen. It is now three o'clock in the morning on Wheeler's World and I haven't slept in almost two days. I am, to say the least, irritable. Now, for the last time, where is he?"

"I've already told you, with the exception of my crew and Miss Randall, there is no one else aboard this ship."

"Commodore," said Viselius, addressing the senior officer on the boarding party without turning around, "I want this ship searched, gutted, if necessary. As of this moment, the *Southern Cross* has been impounded."

"Commodore," said Jake, "you so much as break into one locker and I'll see you stripped of your commission. I know my rights under the admiralty code. I have been boarded without my permission, my crew has been sequestered in the wardroom under armed guard, my passenger has been harassed, all without any formal charges being filed. This is not a ColCom ship and the Director has no authority on board. Either serve me with the proper authorizations or get the hell off my ship."

Viselius chuckled. "Nice try, Captain. Commodore, serve him."

The officer stepped forward and handed the documents to Jake. "You'll find that the papers are in order, Captain," he said, "but I would appreciate it if you examined them to satisfy yourself."

"As for formal charges," said Viselius, "for starters, you are herewith charged with conspiracy to steal classified information from ColCom while under its command, which, under the serv-

157

ice articles you signed, gives me full authority aboard this ship.
You are additionally charged with the actual theft of the afore-
mentioned information, computer crime in the first degree, aid-
ing and abetting a fugitive from justice and accessory to murder
after the fact. Commodore, you and your men will witness that
Captain Thorsen has been formally charged."

"Duly witnessed, sir," the officer said.

"And since Captain Thorsen is so concerned with formalities,
would you be so kind as to officially impound this vessel?"

"Sir," said the commodore. He stepped up to Jake once
more. "Captain, under Articles 16 and 27 of the Merchant
Admiralty—"

"Save it," Jake said. "I'll consider myself officially impounded,
damn you."

"Remove the crew," Viselius said. "They are to be placed in
detention pending investigation. I want the passenger, Randall,
held for questioning. Captain Thorsen is under arrest. He will
be placed under guard and in restraints at once. You will
detail two men to accompany me back down with him. There is
an inorganic citizen somewhere aboard this ship. He is possibly
dysfunctional and to be presumed dangerous. If he resists, shoot
him, but don't damage the brain."

"Commodore," said Jake, "as one spacer to another, please,
don't damage my ship."

"I wouldn't concern myself if I were you," said Viselius.
"The only other ship you'll ever see is the one that will be
taking you to life imprisonment on Hades. Take him away."

Both Modell and his secretary looked newly risen from the
dead. Their eyes were bloodshot and Modell appeared to have
slept in his clothing.

"Where's Viselius?" said Stenmark.

"He took a boarding party on board a newly arrived ship,"
Modell said. "The . . . ?"

"The *Southern Cross*," said Laura.

"When?"

"About an hour ago," she said. "He was up all night,
checking—"

"Never mind. Get me a skimmer to police headquarters
immediately. Let me know when it's ready. But first get HQ on
the line. And when Viselius gets back, you haven't seen me."

Modell and Laura exchanged exasperated glances. Both had
completely given up trying to make any sense of what was going

on. They simply hoped that whatever it was, it would be over soon.

No sooner had Stenmark entered the office he had kicked Modell out of than Laura buzzed to tell him that she had HQ for him. Viner's pasty face appeared upon the screen.

"The building's been sealed off, sir," he said. "All personnel are accounted for and the area around the building has been cordoned off."

"Good work," said Stenmark. "I'll be right over. I'll be landing on the roofpad, so let them know. Make sure it's me before you allow the skimmer to land."

"Yes, sir."

"One more thing. If Director Viselius should arrive, he is not to be admitted to the building under any circumstances. That order stands until I personally countermand it. I'll take full responsibility. Should he attempt to force his way in, he is to be restrained."

Viner looked ill. "Yes, sir. What shall I give as a reason, sir, if he—"

Stenmark interrupted him. "Another thing. The moment I land, I want all personnel off the roof. Detail four men on duty outside the building to stand by. I'll be sending the skimmer down for them as soon as I've landed."

"Sir?" said Viner.

"Make it quick."

"If this is some . . . some sort of quarantine, sir, that is . . ." Viner swallowed hard. "Have I got anything to worry about, sir? I've got a wife and kids and I—"

"I don't think so, Viner. But just to play it safe, don't let anyone get within arm's reach of you."

From the roof of the ColCom building, it was just a short flight to police headquarters. He was challenged as he was about to land. He identified himself and was given clearance, and the moment that the skimmer set down, the roof detail immediately went below. He got out and waited on the roofpad alone while the skimmer went down to pick up the detail he had ordered and bring them up to meet him. The four officers who had been chosen looked alert and capable.

"All right," said Stenmark. "Two in front, two behind. Not too close; give me breathing room. Anyone approaches you, and I don't care if it's your brother, you warn 'em off. One warning. If they don't back off, drop 'em. Stun, not lethal." He paused, hesitating, then decided to go ahead with it. "Any questions?"

He was prepared for a veritable barrage. It didn't come. Instead, one man, evidently appointed by the others for just such an eventuality, spoke up.

"Sir, that press conference you held the other day . . . have we got an alien life form loose in there?"

Stenmark met their anxious gazes, looking from one to the next, establishing firm eye contact before answering.

"Yes. That scare you?"

"Only in that we don't know what to expect, what to look for, sir."

"Then I guess that makes us even," Stenmark told them. "In all respects. I'm a little scared myself." He had to improvise, think fast. How much could he safely tell them? "We're dealing with a psychic entity, gentlemen. It could be dangerous. Don't drop your guard. It could be anyone in there. Don't allow anyone to touch you. Be aware of your feelings. You may be subjected to a psychic assault. It could be very subtle. Or not. Watch yourselves, watch each other. If in doubt, shoot. Got it? We proceed directly from here to the duty officer's post. Let's go."

They moved quickly, bracketing Stenmark, weapons drawn. The adrenaline that surged through them was palpable. Stenmark himself felt the heightened awareness, the hair-trigger sensitivity to everything around him. The men were good. He had expected them to fire at the slightest provocation, but they kept their cool. One man, the same one who had spoken to him, gave commands, sharply ordering anyone they ran into out of the way. No one had to be told twice. One man hesitated, got a warning shot, and promptly disappeared into the nearest doorway. They made it to the tubes without further incident.

So far, so good, thought Stenmark, as they dropped down to the first level. Now there were only three things to worry about—how to prevent panic from sweeping the building, how to find Michaels and what to do once he found her. Them. He kept thinking about what the coroner had said. She—they—had been pregnant.

There was no one in the lobby when they arrived. Viner had cleared everybody out. He sat alone at his desk, pale, holding a pistol. The ashtray in front of him was overflowing with cigarette butts. There was a brief, tense moment as he brought the pistol to bear on them, but Stenmark quickly took control.

"Easy, Viner. Relax. Put the piece down."

Viner hesitated. It was getting to him.

"All right, hold on to it. Just don't kill anybody, all right?"

"Director, I'm scared. Real scared."

Stenmark glanced out through the glass front doors, seeing a line of troopers formed outside, their weapons held ready.

"So am I, Sergeant. You holding up all right?"

"I had to turn off the screen. Too many calls. I've got Alpha Station handling all routine calls and dispatches, but I'm getting reporters, wives wanting to know about their husbands, husbands wanting to know about their wives, lovers wanting to know about their lovers, cops on all levels of the building wanting to know what the hell is going on—"

"Steady, Viner. Take a deep breath."

The sergeant complied.

"What have you told the men and women on duty?"

"I didn't know what to tell them, sir, so I didn't tell them anything. Everyone's on edge. I've about had it, sir."

"Get on the horn and have all personnel assemble in the briefing room. You got one that'll hold everybody?"

"No, sir, I'm afraid not. There's all the administrative personnel and—"

"Shit. I would've liked them to be able to see me."

"I can have them all get to a screen, sir, and put you on. Will that do?"

"It'll have to. Wait a minute. I don't want anyone on the outside listening in."

"Won't happen, sir. Chief's a stickler on leaks—has the building lines checked regularly."

"Okay. Let's do it."

Viner made the announcement, saying that Director Stenmark would address all personnel in five minutes. Then he got off the line, put down his pistol and lit up another cigarette.

"You got a spare?" said Stenmark.

"Sure." Viner held out the pack.

Stenmark started to reach for it, then felt himself abruptly grabbed from behind.

"*Hold it, sir.*" It was one of his guards. "Put the butts on the counter, Irv, and slide them over."

Viner looked stunned. Then he nodded. "Sure thing, Al."

The cigarette pack slid across the counter, and Al picked it up, handing it to Stenmark. Slowly, Stenmark took it.

"Thanks," he said, then added, "Al."

"Don't mention it."

"Ever think of joining the service?"

"Once or twice. I'm a little old for it, though."

"Yeah? Bullshit. See me when this is over. You got ties?"

"Just a girl."

"Serious?"

Al shrugged.

"We'll talk." Stenmark lit up. He didn't cough this time. He was getting used to it.

Viselius stared in astonishment at the police officer who was blocking his way. The man had just politely, but firmly, informed him that he would not be allowed past the police lines into the headquarters building.

"Do you know who I am?" Viselius said. "My name is Viselius. *Director* Viselius."

"Yes, sir. I understand that, sir."

"Then stand aside. I have a prisoner who requires interrogation."

"I'm sorry, sir, I can't do that."

"Are you mad? I gave you a direct order!"

"I have my orders, sir. Sorry."

"You fool, no one has the authority to issue any orders concerning me. Even the most simple-minded idiot would—"

"With all due respect, sir, I have specific orders to keep you from crossing the line."

"From *whom?*"

"Director Stenmark, sir."

"*Stenmark!* Where is he? What in God's name is all this about? What's going on here?"

"Director Stenmark is inside, sir." The officer hesitated before continuing. "As to what's going on, sir, I really have no idea. There've been rumors, but none confirmed."

"What sort of rumors?"

"I'd rather not say, sir."

"I'm ordering you to say."

"Word is that there's some sort of alien life form loose in there, sir."

Viselius' mouth dropped open. "That's impossible." He glanced at Jake, standing between the two admiralty guards, and saw that Thorsen was watching him intently. "I want to speak with Director Stenmark immediately."

"Very well, sir. I'll put you through. Please wait here a moment."

"Viselius," said Jake. The Director turned toward him. "I

heard him say something about an alien life form. Have you got Shelby Michaels in there?''

"She *was* in there," said Viselius. "But she's dead. Her body's been removed to . . ." He shook his head. "It can't be possible. She was heavily sedated all the time." He glanced at Jake. "Could Michaels have thrown off the effects of tranquilizer drugs?"

"Quite possibly, if they were normal human dosages. Not even I know everything Shelby's capable of doing now. Are you certain that whoever Shelby merged with is still inside the building?''

"I'm no longer certain of anything," Viselius said. "Stenmark seems quite certain, though. He would not have done all this otherwise." He looked around at the police, the crowd being held back, the reporters. "This sort of circus isn't like him. He must be desperate.''

"What will he do?"

"Frankly, Thorsen, your guess is as good as mine," Viselius said dryly. "I had thought the problem solved with Michaels' death and your apprehension, but Stenmark seems determined to continue where you left off, now that Michaels is evidently still alive.''

"What do you mean, where I left off?"

"I mean that he's thinking along the same lines you are."

"I don't know what you're talking about."

"Really, Thorsen, this discussion is getting tedious. Stop insulting my intelligence. I didn't get where I am by being a fool.''

"I'm not insulting your intelligence," said Jake. "One of us seems to be confused. I'm just not sure I understand what you mean. How about putting all the cards on the table?''

Viselius raised his eyebrows. "If you insist. Only you start, first. Where did you hide Tabarde?"

"I didn't hide him. He's dead."

"How?"

"I bashed his head in with a nysteel rod. You won't find the body, though. It's no longer aboard the ship. So you can try charging me with murder, but you'll have a hell of a time proving it.''

Viselius chuckled. "I already have quite enough to charge you with, Thorsen. Besides, it isn't murder to destroy an inorganic citizen. The law is somewhat nebulous on that, but that's of no consequence. Why did you do it?''

"Now who's playing games, Director? He tried to kill me. It was on your orders."

"That's absurd."

"Come on, Viselius! You sent him out to kill me and Shelby Michaels. I know all about the imperatives you had programmed into his brain. Do you deny you wanted Shelby Michaels dead?"

"No," Viselius said slowly, staring at Jake with interest.

"At least you've got the guts to admit it," Jake said.

"Moral reproof, Thorsen? You hypocrite, you're in no position to judge me. Yes, I wanted Michaels dead. A small enough price to pay, considering what is at stake. I will do everything that is in my power to ensure that neither you nor Stenmark can proceed with the insane plan of importing beings from Boomerang to sell to the highest bidder."

"Hold on a moment," said Jake. "Is *that* what you think it was all about?"

Viselius looked at him with contempt. "You make me sick, Thorsen. If you had any moral fiber at all, you'd accept your fate like a man instead of trying to worm your way out by this pathetic display."

"You've got me wrong, Director. That was never our plan. We wanted to protect them, not exploit them."

Viselius stared at him with disbelief. "You really are amazing, Thorsen."

"It's true! Look, Tabarde said that you were a—a religious man. He said you didn't want the human race polluted, that you were opposed to going on with the Seedling Project. We may have different motivations, but we both want the same thing! We can deal!"

"You'd say anything to save yourself."

"Viselius, I can help you if you help me," said Jake, desperately trying to convince him. He moved quite close to him. "Help me get Shelby out of there and I'll take her back to Boomerang."

"You'll take her back?"

"Yes!"

"Then you know how to get there, don't you?" Viselius said. Jake stared at him. "You didn't know."

"Of course—that was why Tabarde tried to kill you. You triggered his imperative. It all makes sense now."

The police officer returned, carrying a communicator. "I've got Director Stenmark on the set, sir."

Viselius smiled. "Tell him I lost my patience and left," he said.

"Sir?"

"You just tell him exactly what I said," Viselius said, peering at his name tag. "Officer Kaminsky."

The policeman did not fail to catch the implied meaning. "Yes, sir. You grew impatient and left."

Viselius took Jake by the arm and led him away. The guards fell in behind them, keeping enough distance to allow them to talk privately. With their weapons at his back and Jake's hands in cuffs, they had little fear of his attempting anything.

"I don't understand," said Jake. "I couldn't have misjudged you. Tabarde said—"

"And he was right," said Viselius. "Unlike my colleagues, I have no wish to forge a new destiny for the human race. I am content to leave such things to God."

"So why are we leaving? Shelby—"

"No longer matters."

"But she—"

"It's possible that Stenmark will be able to apprehend your friend—or should I say, your friends?—but in light of the circumstances, it will take him quite a bit of time. It will be necessary to scan the brain-wave patterns of all the personnel in that building to discover which of them Michaels has merged with. Then, having found Michaels, he would still have to bring her under his control. Normal conditioning procedures may not be effective."

"But he'll find Boomerang eventually!" said Jake. "I thought that was what you wanted to prevent!"

"Lacking the ability to do anything else, yes," Viselius said. "But now that I have you, I can confront the problem more directly."

Jake stopped. "What do you mean?"

Viselius smiled. "Why waste a world so eminently suitable for exploitation? You will get me to Boomerang before Stenmark. By the time he finds his way there, it will have been cleansed of sin."

"My God," said Jake. "You're insane."

Viselius struck him across the face. His nysteel-encased hand broke Jake's nose and split his upper lip. Jake fell to the ground.

"The Lord works in mysterious ways," Viselius said, "yet sometimes even I am astonished at the instruments He chooses." He glanced back at the surprised and bewildered admiralty guards, who stood there not knowing how to react. "Where's the nearest police or admiralty facility?" he said.

"That . . . that would be Alpha Station, sir."

Viselius nodded. "We're going there." He looked down at Jake, who had worked himself up to a kneeling position. Blood was streaming down his face and into his mouth. He coughed. "The prisoner may be difficult. I think it would be best if you incapacitated him."

"Sir?"

"Oh, give me that," Viselius said, stepping forward and wrenching the pistol out of the guard's hand. He pointed it at Jake and fired a stun charge into him point-blank. Jake collapsed to the street. Viselius handed the pistol back. "Now pick him up and carry him. We've wasted enough time."

Throughout the building, they crowded around screens in offices, in lounges, in briefing rooms and in the commissary. Hardly anyone spoke. They waited, tensely, listening. Finally, he came on. The five minutes had seemed like five hours.

"This is Director Stenmark. I'll let you have it up front and count on your professionalism to keep things cool. I know that's not going to be easy, but I'm depending on you people. There is an alien life force somewhere in this building. This being is a psychic entity, and it is sharing consciousness with one of you. It does not seem to mean anybody any harm. It is intelligent; it can understand what I'm saying to you now. All it wants to do is to survive. That happens to be consistent with what I want. As long as you people don't panic, this situation can be resolved. My next words are meant for this being.

"This building is surrounded. Every conceivable exit has been covered and the police outside have orders to shoot anyone who attempts to leave. Escape is not possible. Nor can you avoid detection. Fifteen minutes after I finish speaking, all personnel within this building will be scanned, one at a time, for abnormal brain-wave patterns. You will be found. However, this would take time. Time is the enemy. Nerves fray with time. Mine, perhaps yours, everybody else's. Give yourself up. You will not be harmed. I am on the first level now. In about three minutes, I will be waiting in the captain's office on the top level, alone. I will be unarmed. The entire top level will be cleared of personnel.

"As for the rest of you, I want no attempts at heroics. You will remain passive; you will do nothing. If anyone interferes, in any way at all, I'll have your ass, and that's a promise. That's all for now. Stand by.''

He turned off the screen.

''Sir,'' said Al, ''waiting up there alone is crazy.''

Stenmark glanced at him and nodded. ''You're right, but it's necessary.''

''Why?''

''Because I make very tempting bait.''

''I'm going up there with you.''

''No, you're not. You four men will wait on the floor below. Watch out for each other—don't let anyone come near you. I'll go up alone. I'll turn on the screen in the captain's outer office, then I'll go into his private office, lock the door, and turn his screen to intercom function as well, so that nobody else will overhear. Only the two screens will be connected. If anyone tries to go up there, don't stop him. But don't let anyone come down unless you hear from me.'' He paused. ''Don't let me come down alone, either, just in case. I'll call you, so one of you stay near a screen. When I call, you all come up together. If everything goes well, there'll be someone in the outer office and I'll still be locked up inside. If not . . . if I'm not still locked up in the captain's private office and . . . well, just drop me on the spot, that's all.''

There was silence, finally broken by Al. ''Stun or lethal, sir?''

Stenmark took a deep breath. ''Hell of a decision to have to make, isn't it?''

''Yes, sir, I guess it is.''

Maybe Viselius will have his way after all, thought Stenmark. I don't want to be anybody but just me. He looked at Al, tight-lipped.

''If I'm not alone in that office, Al, kill me.''

Al glanced at his watch. Ten minutes had gone by. For the tenth time, he checked his weapon. In all his years on the force, he had never had to kill anyone. It was something he was proud of. He hoped that he could continue feeling proud when this was over.

''Al?'' It was one of the other men, coming out of an office they had taken over. ''Director Stenmark wants us to come on up.''

''That all he said?''

''Yeah.''

Al nodded. "Okay, let's go." With their weapons held ready, they took the tube up to the top floor.

There was no one in sight as they got out, which was as it should be. Warily, they proceeded to the captain's office. Positioning themselves on either side of the door, they glanced at each other, then burst in, ready to fire. Nothing. No one. The screen was on. Stenmark was on the screen, watching them.

"Make sure the door is locked," he said.

Al nodded at one of the others, and he checked. It was still locked from the inside.

"Nothing?" Al said.

"No," said Stenmark. "Nothing. It didn't work. I'm going to unlock the door and come out now."

"Sir, just unlock the door and then step back all the way against the wall, where I can see you."

Stenmark nodded and moved away from the screen. They heard the door being unlocked, then they saw him on the screen, standing against the window.

"We're coming in now. Keep your hands where I can see them."

Al entered the office first, weapon pointed directly at Stenmark. He checked to see that there was no one else inside. Except for Stenmark, the office was empty.

"I guess it didn't work," he said. "Sorry about this business, sir. I wanted to be sure."

Stenmark smiled. "You're extremely good at what you do, Al. That's twice you've shown real leadership potential."

Al shrugged.

"Don't give me that," said Stenmark. "I hate false modesty. You fucking well know you're good. Why you've remained just a patrol officer is a mystery to me. You'd have killed me if I had made one wrong move, wouldn't you?"

"Yes, sir, I would have. In a way, sir, I'm sorry it didn't work out, but in another way, I'm glad. You took a pretty stupid risk, if you ask me."

"I didn't ask you." He grinned. "But you're right. Sometimes those things pay off. This time, it didn't."

"What happens now?"

"We start the scanning. I've already called Alpha Station, and they're sending a team over. You guys meet them on the roof when they come in. Meanwhile . . ." He reached into a drawer of the captain's desk and brought out a bottle. "I discovered this. I think we could all use a drink."

He held the bottle out to Al, and then his eyes grew wide. Al grabbed for his pistol and swung around, but he was too late. He took a full charge in the chest and fell to the floor. Sergeant Viner stood in the doorway.

"Drop your weapons," he said.

Stenmark started to tell them to comply, but the three remaining men were already doing so, a dazed look in each man's eyes. Stenmark felt it, too. It was overpowering.

"Michaels," he said. Then he watched helplessly as one by one, the three unresisting officers were shot dead.

Viner dropped the pistol on the floor and approached Stenmark. Stenmark wanted to back away, to run, but he couldn't move. Viner reached out for him.

Stenmark screamed.

Chapter Twelve

Within a couple of hours of being locked inside the maximum security cell, Shelby had already begun to fight free of the effects of the stun charges. Aided by the indomitable, bestial T'lan, the One That Is struggled toward consciousness, but the body was weak and not yet fully recovered when the first of the tranquilizing doses was administered. It had been done very quickly. A small window in the door of the thickly walled cell had opened briefly and an officer had fired a tranquilizer dart through it.

The darts were not as powerful as the stun charges. The cumulative effect of multiple stun charges would cause serious damage, possibly even death. The prisoner was to be kept alive and unharmed, so the tranquilizer darts were used. The dose had been calculated to knock a strong man out almost instantly and to last for a period of about eight hours. Just to be on the safe side, since the guards in maximum security were well aware that the prisoner was an unusually powerful esper—though they did not suspect Shelby's true nature—the doses were administered every seven hours. After the dart was fired through the opening in the cell door, the officer who had fired it would wait several moments, then cautiously enter the cell to examine the prisoner, to check for normal pulse rate and respiration. If either fell off, they had strict orders to immediately summon the police surgeon on duty. However, everything proceeded normally, and after the fourth such examination, they felt safe enough to enter the cell without a backup of two guards with weapons drawn. By the time a guard came around to administer the fifth dose, Shelby was already learning to fight off the drug. The fifth dose forestalled her efforts, but when it came time to administer the sixth, she had already started to regain consciousness.

Though still weak and incapable of movement, Shelby had managed to project at the guard, and he made his examination and left thinking that the dose had been administered, when in fact the dart had missed her entirely. His aim had been deflected, but in his mind, he "saw" the dart strike her neck. The latest dose not having been administered, she should have started feeling stronger, but something was wrong. The Ones Who Were knew what it was just before it happened, and, even as they felt the pain with her, they tried to soften the experience for her, but no amount of psychic support could nullify the horror of a miscarriage. Shelby felt the sharp abdominal pains and, shortly thereafter, the terrifying warm wetness between her legs. Whether it was the stun charges that did it or the tranquilizer darts or both together, there was no way of knowing, but as she lost the child, her helplessness and pain were matched only by the rage she felt toward those who had killed it. The next time a guard came into the cell, quite casually by now and unaware that his mind had been deceived into believing that his aim with the dart gun had been true, Shelby took him.

It was a violent merging, and the Ones Who Were, out of grief and fury, made no attempt to cushion the shock for Officer Warren Newsome, who had no idea what was happening to him. There was one moment in which he saw the prisoner's hand reach out and touch his chest as he bent over, and then he was welded to her, unable to break free of the Touch as liquid fire seemed to flow through her into him. He opened his mouth to scream, but no sound came forth as they invaded, brutally and forcefully, plunging like a psychic dagger into the depths of his mind. Shelby had been first; then there had been Fannon. Newsome was the third human who had borne the Touch, and the Ones Who Were became more proficient at it every time, the period of physical incapacity diminishing rapidly. It had lasted perhaps for two seconds and then the contact was broken. Newsome thrashed upon the floor of the cell, bucking like a fish out of water, and then they were established, in control, and he lay still, breathing heavily.

As they had penetrated deep into his mind, they had shoved Newsome's own life force aside, dominating his body. In abject terror, Newsome seized upon Fannon's life force, recognizing—while still not comprehending—something familiar in the alien storm which took him, but Fannon forced him away violently, leaving him to turn to Shelby for help, reassurance, protection, understanding, all those things sought by people when confronted with an unacceptable reality. Among the Ones Who Were now, Shelby felt nothing but rage and an overpowering sense of loss. The child that had been growing in her body was now dead. Even her body was dead. As the terror-stricken life force of the policeman turned to her, Shelby attacked it, concentrating the full force of her self upon him. In an instant of immeasurable brevity, Newsome knew her. He felt her grief, her pain, her rage, and he submitted, helplessly . . . and was absorbed.

Shelby had not been prepared for this, and in that instant of the merging of their life forces, all of his terror and his helplessness became hers, as well. Sensing her agony, Great Mother N'lia and S'eri, the Healer, lent their strength and their support to her, but she reached out to Fannon, desperately, and he was there, enveloping her no longer individual life force in his. She surrendered to him, and it happened once again, with neither of them willing it. It happened with the swiftness of thought, and they were one. A new gestalt had formed among the Ones Who Were. A new group entity was born. Within the body of Officer Warren Newsome, there were now six group entities, of which five were composed of billions of Shade life forces and one, the newly born, of three human personalities, welded into one.

"Newsome" got up from the floor of the cell, a bit unsteadily. As he came out and nodded to the other guards, he looked no different than he had when he went in. It had all taken but an instant, and there was no way that the guards could even begin to suspect the psychic upheaval that had taken place within that body in the short space of time it had been within the cell. Behind him, lying on the floor as if drugged, lay the lifeless body of Shelby Michaels. Its animating forces had departed and it had simply ceased to function.

Officer Newsome had been scheduled to go off duty with the next rotation. Whoever would relieve him would discover that the prisoner had "died" and would report it. Yet, even if they realized—they being the Directorate—that the life forces had fled her body and moved on, by the time they knew it it would be too late for them to do anything. Newsome would simply walk out of the building and disappear into the city when the shift changed. However, before that happened, the assassin sent by Viselius arrived.

The police lieutenant had demanded to see the prisoner, and "Newsome" had accompanied him to the cell.

"You wait outside," the lieutenant had said, after having been assured that the prisoner was fully tranquilized. He went in alone. "Newsome" had opened the tiny window in the door, seeing the lieutenant bend over the body, frown, then drop the small syringe he had removed from his pocket. In that moment, he had realized that his quarry was already dead, but a projection eased its way into his mind, making him believe that Shelby Michaels was still alive and drugged. He picked up the syringe, believing that he had injected a clear fluid into the body's jugular vein, when in reality, it had squirted out upon the floor.

"What the hell happened here?" he said when he came out.

"Sir?"

"The prisoner is dead!"

"Dead!"

"Go see for yourself."

"Newsome" entered the cell and made a show of examining the body. It was an extremely difficult thing for them to do, knowing that their child had died within that body. It filled them with a deadly purpose and hardened their resolve.

"Couldn't have been dead long," said the lieutenant. "The body's still warm. You know anything about this?"

"No, sir."

This was an unexpected bonus. No one would search for them if it was believed that they were dead. It was imperative that the assassin report back that he had accomplished his task. *Only to whom would he report?* A gentle probe.

Immediate response. "Director Viselius wanted me to check on the prisoner," the lieutenant said, unaware that he was answering an unspoken question. "He's not going to be happy when he finds out about this."

The Director's executioner turned and walked away. It made no sense. It made no sense at all.

"Christ," said one of the other guards. "Now there's going to be an investigation. We'll never get out of here."

"What?"

"What do you want to bet the duty officer calls down here in another couple of minutes to tell us that we can't go home until we've played twenty questions with the brass? Shit, she had to go and croak now. Couldn't have waited another few hours."

"I see what you mean. It could take a while."

"*A while?* It'll take fucking forever!" The guard groaned. "They'll wire us up to scanners and take statements and in the end it'll turn out that she died of a fucking heart attack or something."

"I guess I'd better go and get some coffee, then. I'll want to be wide awake when I'm grilled. You want I should bring you back some?"

"Shit, yeah. See if you can find something interesting to put in it."

"Might take a while."

"So? I'm going someplace?"

"I'll see what I can scrounge up."

"Newsome" could not allow himself to be scanned. If the guards in maximum security were to be kept from going off duty until the investigation was completed, there was only one thing left to do. Move on to someone else, someone not on the maximum security detail, someone who would be able to leave when the shift ended. There could be no second thoughts or qualms. They were no longer safe in Newsome's body.

Stenmark knew it all now.

They had merged once more with an administrative clerk named Garcia on the second level. They had done it in the bathroom, increasing their human gestalt by one and leaving Newsome's body propped up on the toilet. They went back to Garcia's station to continue working until quitting time, hoping that Newsome's body wouldn't be discovered before the shift ended. However, the body had slipped to the floor and was discovered almost immediately. Shortly before the next shift was due to come on duty, Stenmark had issued the order confining all personnel to the building. They had been trapped. Trapped with no knowledge of what was going on, what was being done. The only one who knew anything, it seemed, was the duty officer, Sergeant Viner, who was in contact with the outside. All other outside lines had been shut down.

Between the time that he had left Modell's office and arrived at police headquarters, Viner had been invaded. In spite of having been warned not to allow anyone within arm's reach of him, Viner had been helpless against their psychic projections. Small wonder the trap Stenmark had set had not worked. "Viner" had been sitting right there, listening to them as they had worked it out, with the discarded body of Garcia stuffed into the back of a nearby closet. Al had been right in being cautious, but he had not been cautious enough. They should all have been more careful. They should never have turned their backs to the door. They should never have grouped together in the captain's office, but they had had no choice. They had all been lulled into a false sense of security, victims of subtle psychic projections. Stenmark also knew now that Shelby's abilities were nothing compared to what the Seedlings were capable of doing.

When they had come at him, he had tried to flee, but upon discovering that he was incapable of movement, he had screamed, gathering his strength together and galvanizing his energies to resist the attack, if resistance was possible. The pain had been extremely brief, but the agony had been almost unendurable. He had felt the incandescent burning, felt them *streaming* into his mind, boring into him, and he had almost lost consciousness. Aside from the unbearable pain, there was a sensation of vertigo, a spinning, falling helplessness akin to dreams in which he sometimes fell forever into some bottomless chasm. They were like a whirlpool in his brain, creating a vortex that threatened to suck him in, and he had fought to maintain control, to keep his mind on track, to stay free of the entity that seemed to pull at him with an astonishing force. Then it was over. The storm had struck and passed, leaving a calm in its wake. But he was no longer alone.

"I've got to hand it to you, Stenmark, you're strong as hell."

"Fannon." He spoke aloud.

"Partly. A large part of what I am is Fannon, a large part of me is Shelby, then, in some smaller measure, there's also Warren Newsome, Franz Garcia and Irv Viner."

"And now me," said Stenmark.

"No, not you. Not yet, anyway. Not in that sense."

"I don't understand."

"You will. You don't have to speak out loud, you know. I am aware of your thoughts. I know them even as you form them, as do all the others. You can feel them there, can't you?"

"I feel . . . something. A presence."

"You don't know them yet. But you will. You're being insulated for now. You are the One That Is now. We're all a part of you, but you haven't merged with my gestalt personality as the others have."

Stenmark was amazed that he was taking it all so calmly. Perhaps he was in shock. . . .

"Not shock, not strictly speaking, anyway. You're being sheltered, supported so that you won't spin right off the deep end. S'eri is doing his number on you, just as he's calming all the others."

"Viner and—"

"Yes. They were terrified, understandably, and they latched onto me like drowning men clutching at the first thing that comes to hand. They're still a very frightened and confused part of me, but they're starting to settle down a little."

"You . . . *consumed* them?"

"Adopted them, you might say. They haven't really been consumed or harmed in any way, just as you won't be. They've simply been incorporated into my life force. Think of them as being the crew and me the captain. Your will is strong, though, and you resisted being absorbed, even though I did my best to envelop you. Even T'lan's impressed."

"T'lan?"

For an instant, it was like a doorway opening briefly in his mind and then slamming shut again—*or being slammed shut*—and in that one infinitesimal moment he had sensed something wild and bestial, unbelievably powerful and feral. It chilled him to think that anything like *that* could be a part of him.

"I wouldn't try that again if I were you," Fannon said within his mind. "Not for a while, at least. Few people can confront the beast within them, and T'lan's the granddaddy of them all."

"God. This is . . . indescribable. It's like—"

"Yeah, it's really wild, isn't it? We're just one big happy family, several billion strong."

Stenmark looked down at the four policemen lying dead on the floor.

"Why did you have to kill them?"

"It was regrettable, but necessary. This is war, you know. And we didn't start the hostilities. That interrogation team is due to arrive from Alpha Station any moment. They'll find five corpses, Viner's and the others', and your story will be that the alien being and your guards killed each other. They shielded you with their bodies when the fireworks started, which was how you escaped unharmed. Since corpses can't testify to anything, that'll make the alien officially dead. Which reminds me—"

Stenmark found himself bending over without his volition and picking up a pistol from the floor. He checked it, adjusted the firing intensity, then shot a lethal charge into Viner's body. Once. Twice. Three times.

"Now you'll be able to tell your friend Viselius that he got what he wanted after all. He—"

"What is it?"

Stenmark knew that Fannon had "seen" something in his mind, but it was all still so new to him, so . . . *alien*. He felt like a specter at the wedding in his own body. He suddenly recognized a familiar feeling pervading him, a feeling that something was "on the tip of his tongue" but just out of reach.

"Viselius took a boarding party up to a ship called the *Southern Cross*," said Fannon.

"Yes—"

"Jake Thorsen is the captain of the *Southern Cross*. He knows how to ghost a ship to Boomerang. He's done it many times."

And, once he'd been conditioned, he would do it for Viselius. His words came back to Stenmark and the others with a chilling finality—*I should like to cleanse Boomerang and utilize its resources.* Lacking the means to accomplish that, Viselius had been willing to compromise. Compromise, for him, had meant the elimination of Shelby Michaels, who could have been used by Nakamura and Bikovski as a guide to Boomerang. Now, however, he would not need to compromise. Jake Thorsen knew the way to Boomerang, and Viselius had him. He had found the tool that would enable him to accomplish his goal—the "cleansing" of all sentient life from Boomerang.

There had been a message from Viselius—a call from the police lines outside the building that Director Viselius was demanding entrance. He had been denied, as per Stenmark's orders, and he had insisted upon being put in contact with Stenmark. When Stenmark finally got on the line, the officer had told him that Viselius had "grown impatient and left." That certainly wasn't like Viselius. He had had far too much on his mind to give that curious fact much thought then, but he thought about it now and it made sense that Viselius had left because he had discovered that Thorsen could ghost a ship to Boomerang.

"Jake never would have admitted that," said Fannon.

"He might have, under the right circumstances. Viselius believed that your plot to keep Boomerang's location a secret had been meant to enable you to profit from the sale of immortality. We all believed that. If he confronted Thorsen with that accusation—"

"Yes, I can see how it might have happened. If Jake believed that Viselius and he had similar motivations—"

Stenmark marveled at the communication taking place between them. It was as though his own thoughts were answering themselves. It was frightening, yet at the same time, it was wonderful. He felt as if he had known Fannon all his life, as if Fannon had always been a part of him.

He . . . *they* glanced at their watch. How long had it been since Viselius had demanded to be passed through the lines? Half an hour? Forty-five minutes? No more, certainly. If their suspicions were correct and he had discovered that Thorsen could take him to Boomerang, what would have been his next step? Having Thorsen conditioned to unquestioning obedience? That meant taking him to the nearest fully equipped facility, which would be Alpha Station. If he had left immediately, it would have taken him at the very least five to ten minutes to get there in a police or admiralty skimmer traveling at full speed. That would not have left him enough time to have had Jake fully conditioned by now. A half an hour to set up, perhaps, at the very least, if he had a top-notch man set up the programming and begin at once; another half an hour to an hour to establish a rudimentary mindset. And a team from Alpha Station was due to arrive at any moment, which could leave them short-handed at the station. There was still time.

Ava Randall knew her rights. Whether a prisoner or a simple detainee, she was entitled to one call, and no one, not even a member of the Directorate, could deny her. However, when she exercised that right, she did not call a lawyer. She contacted someone far more influential. She called J. Neil Morgan.

The grandson of the redoubtable H.G. Morgan, that interplanetary robber baron who was the latest in a long line of elegant cutthroats to sit at the helm of Morgan Industries, Neil was an obnoxiously precocious young man who had been "farmed out" to Wheeler's World at the age of seventeen, to reside in a luxurious penthouse atop the New Dakota, New Rome's bastion of the impossibly fashionable elite. The company brass on Wheeler's World had been apprehensive at the arrival of the heir apparent. H.G.'s instructions to them had simply been: "Make sure he doesn't get into any serious trouble and keep the young whelp out of my hair." However, they had relaxed somewhat when it appeared that Neil was a dilettante who seemed interested in nothing more than becoming a holoprod director. He had found, through rapidly established social connections, a faltering production company and had purchased it with his own savings. H.G. had kept him on a tight rein, but the company could have been had dirt cheap by almost anyone who showed an interest, and up until that point no one had. The brass had sent word of this acquisition to H.G. and he had replied, tersely as always, "Seems harmless enough. Let him have his toy."

Within five years, Neil had turned the down-and-out production company into a major studio via several monster moneymakers produced on a shoestring budget. He then began to back several candidates for office, financing their campaigns and orchestrating their media exposure. The result was that four years later, at the age of twenty-six, he owned six of the most influential members of the Council. Shortly thereafter, the Council began passing legislation aimed at protecting developing domestic industry. Coincidentally, or so it seemed, the import tariffs which were levied by the Council affected roughly two-thirds of the products Morgan Industries exported. Neil then dragged the poleaxed company officials on Wheeler's World into a series of negotiations, whereupon Morgan Industries' corporate branch in New Rome was "invited" to invest heavily in Liberty Productions, Neil's "toy." It was never formally brought up, but the brass on New Rome merely assumed that Neil was putting the squeeze on them for more money with which to develop his rapidly growing studio. They decided to play ball with the kid, figuring that if they did, he'd back off on the tariffs and they'd get the credit for settling the situation. They moved fast, before H.G. could find out the truth of the situation.

With the "backing" of Morgan Industries' New Rome branch, Neil invested heavily in several large industrial concerns on Wheeler's World and bought several companies outright. Then, as the aghast company brass in New Rome looked on helplessly, Neil went after old H.G. himself. The end result was that Morgan Industries acquired large industrial holdings on Wheeler's World, having traded with Liberty Productions for them. Neil hardballed his grandfather into parting with several large blocks of Morgan stock which, together with his own holdings, gave him a seat on the board of Morgan Industries. Before he was thirty, Neil became the most powerful man on Wheeler's World, and H.G., who had been abstinent throughout his long and stubborn life, started drinking.

When his face came on the screen, it seemed to split into an ear-to-ear grin, the expression of a child receiving an unexpected visit from a favorite grandparent. Ava hadn't seen him in a number of years. He had grown a neat, thin mustache which he doubtless thought made him looked distinguished and dashing. Unfortunately, when combined with his curly hair, his cherubic cheeks and his prominent front teeth, the mustache served to give him the aspect of an aristocratic chipmunk.

"Ava! When did you get in? I haven't seen you in years. Where are you?"

"In jail."

He laughed. "How's the food?"

"I'm serious, Neil. I'm really in jail. I need help."

His smile vanished, "Jesus, you're not kidding?"

"Neil, *please*."

"Yeah, right, okay. Christ. Where are you?"

"Alpha Station. It's on—"

"I know it. What happened?"

She gave him a quick rundown on the charges against Jake and explained that she was being held for questioning as a result of her association with him.

Neil whistled. "What the hell did you get yourself into?"

"A shitload of trouble, dear."

"I'll say. Is your friend guilty as charged?"

"I'm not going to discuss that on the line."

"I see. Well, that's what you get for associating with undesirables. If you'd married me when I—"

"Neil, for God's sake, I'm old enough to be your mother."

"My mother never looked that good."

"*Neil!*"

"All right, all right. I'll pull a few strings and get you sprung. I expect you to be profoundly grateful, if you know what I mean, heh-heh."

"Neil, you're a shit."

"I love it when you talk dirty. Well, hang tight, I'll get you out of there."

"What about Jake?"

"What about him?"

"You've got to get him out, too, Neil. He's in real trouble. He needs help."

"Hey, look, getting you out is going to cost me, but your friend is another story. It seems he got himself into a real jam. I'm not without some influence, but I'm not going to start tangling with the Directorate. Taking on ColCom's just asking for some heavy-duty trouble, babe."

"Don't call me that. Look, Neil, I've never asked you for anything before—"

"Forget it, Ava. I'm sorry, but what you're asking is just too much."

"Dammit, Neil, you're all I've got! Don't you go chickenshit on me!"

"Sorry."

"Neil . . ." She took a deep breath. "Neil, you get Jake out and I'll . . . I'll be *profoundly grateful,* if you know what I mean."

"Goddam. This Jake character means that much to you?"

"Will you do it or not?"

"Okay, I'll try. But if you're expecting me to be a gentleman and not call in your marker, forget it, babe. You made a deal and I'll hold you to it."

She grimaced. "H.G. would be proud of you."

"Sticks and stones, love, sticks and stones. By the time I'm through with you, you won't even remember Jake."

"Sonny, if you're *that* good, I fucking well *will* marry you."

"Hmm. I'd like to meet this guy."

"No, you wouldn't. But it would serve you right. Now get cracking."

"Gotcha."

The alien was officially dead, the crisis was over, all restrictions were lifted, and Modell was on the verge of nervous collapse as he tried to contend with the reporters, who had been ducked by Stenmark and had fastened onto him as the next best thing. The only thing that made it all bearable for Modell was that his prestige was immeasurably enhanced by the situation. Stenmark would not make any comment, which left him free to take all the credit for saving New Rome from an alien invasion.

Stenmark, having quickly detailed his "narrow escape" to the team from Alpha Station, left them behind to contact Modell and fill him in while he commandeered their vehicle and made full speed toward Alpha Station. He was out the door even before the skimmer touched down on the roofpad of the police station. He grabbed the first officer he encountered and demanded to be taken to the interrogation rooms without delay. They took the tubes down to the first subbasement, and Stenmark rushed up to the logistics desk, confronting a bored-looking corporal.

"Prisoner Thorsen, what room?"

"Who's asking?"

"Director Stenmark. Now what room is the prisoner in?"

The corporal no longer looked bored. "Sir! Yes, sir, sir, what did you say the prisoner's name was?"

"Thorsen, Captain Jacob Thorsen. Brought here by Director Viselius. Quickly, man."

"Thorsen . . . Thorsen . . . I don't seem to have a—"

"Christ, never mind." Stenmark went past the desk, heading down the corridor toward interrogations. There were twenty interrogation rooms, five of which, the officer who accompanied him explained, were set up for conditioning. Two of them were occupied. The other three were empty. None of them held Jake Thorsen and Viselius.

Stenmark ran back toward the desk. "How long ago did they leave?"

"Sir?"

Fannon chose not to waste any more time and probed the corporal's mind. Stenmark was taken unaware by it. Suddenly, he saw directly into the corporal, felt his confusion and nervousness, his complete bewilderment, his defensive posture. For a while, incredibly, he had almost forgotten *they* were there. But then he remembered that brief sensation of something terrible slithering about within him and recalled that he was still being "insulated." He hoped that would continue for a while longer. He was not yet ready to face what he had become. He knew that they were making it easy for him by allowing only the Fannon entity to commune with him while they lingered . . . somewhere . . . awaiting the right time to confront his conscious mind. Every time he found himself thinking about them, his mind wandered to something else. S'eri, undoubtedly.

The corporal knew nothing. He had never seen either Thorsen or Viselius. It made no sense. Viselius *had* to have brought him here. It was the closest place where—

With something of a shock, he suddenly realized that he was entering the lift tube. For a moment, it seemed to him that he had somehow teleported from the place where he had stood in front of the logistics desk to a spot some twenty yards away, but as he rose to the lobby, he realized that he had been allowed to consider the situation while they had taken his body where it needed to go. After he got over his initial surprise, he thought that this was something that could come in quite handy, being able to concentrate his full attention on one thing while the rest of him—of them—took care of business. He heard laughter and quickly glanced around, then realized that it had been Fannon. He had "heard" it in his mind.

He exited the tube and quickly made his way to the front desk. The woman on duty there was considerably more alert.

"Director Viselius? Why, yes, sir, he was here, but he left with his prisoner just a short while ago."

Again, the physic probe was far more efficient than asking questions, and in the space of a second he learned that Viselius had arrived with Thorsen and two admiralty guards, whom he had left to watch Thorsen while he used a screen to make a call the desk sergeant had not overheard. Shortly thereafter, the roofpad had called down to inform him that his shuttle had landed. *His shuttle!*

"Director Stenmark!"

He turned around to see a vaguely familiar face, then he had it placed. Councilman Robert Biers. With him was a striking-looking woman whose beauty was unmarred by the haggard look upon her face.

"Fancy meeting you here. Bob Biers, remember? The press conference? We handled that pretty well, didn't we?"

The woman suddenly looked extremely alarmed, and Stenmark found himself, or rather his Fannon aspect, probing her even as he sensed her fear of him and—it came as a complete shock. *She knew everything!*

"Miss Randall, I'm going to have to ask you to accompany me," he said.

She tensed and, involuntarily, moved back a step.

"Well, just a minute there, Director," Biers said, flashing his politician's smile. "Miss Randall's been released on Mr. Morgan's recognizance, and we were just on our way to—"

"Please, Miss Randall, there's no time to explain. It's—" But of course, there *was* time to explain, he realized, though not in words. He felt a slightly vertiginous sensation as he "receded" and then there was that feeling once again of a door opening within his mind. For an instant, it frightened him, and he thought, I'm not ready, but instead of some beast being unleashed, something entirely different slipped unobtrusively from out of the recesses of his subconscious. It was something gentle, infinitely calm, loving . . . maternal.

N'lia.

The Great Mother joined with the Fannon aspect, and Stenmark, watching from some comfortable hollow somewhere deep within himself saw Fannon, or rather *felt* Fannon, change, metamorphose into something else, something feminine, and he knew that it was Shelby Michaels surfacing within the Fannon gestalt. Time progressed at a different rate for him, knowing that it was taking place with immeasurable rapidity, but for him, it was like a gracefully unfolding panorama of personal transmogrification, and he thought, How marvelous, how extraordinarily, beautifully marvelous! If Viselius could only experience this. . . .

Then he felt himself being *pulled,* a part of him projecting with Shelby and N'lia into Ava Randall's mind, touching it with a brief caress and then withdrawing. Her eyes grew wide, dazed, as she stared at him in astonishment and wonder. For a moment, her eyelids flickered and she seemed about to faint, then the eyes focused once again and she swallowed hard and took a deep breath.

"It's all right, Bob," she said. "I'm going to go with Director Stenmark."

Biers looked at her, bewildered. "But I thought—I don't understand. Mr. Morgan said—"

"Tell Neil thanks a million for me," Ava said. "I've got to go."

"But I . . . Mr. Morgan won't like this. He told me specifically to bring you back with me. He said—"

"Tell Neil I'll give him a rain check," Ava said.

"A rain check? For what?"

"He'll understand."

Stenmark leaned back against the seat cushion of the police skimmer, having turned off the screen.

"I knew it. Dammit, I just knew it. Our ship's gone out of orbit. He's taken Jake off-planet."

Ava had continued to stare at him as though he were, well, a creature from another world.

"You mean he's gone to Boomerang?"

Stenmark shook his head. "No. Back to Earth, undoubtedly. He wouldn't have had time to have Jake properly conditioned, and he'd never dare trust himself to a cryogen without being certain of Jake. Besides, he'd have to pick up . . . supplies."

"What sort of supplies?"

"There are any number of means available to depopulate a planet. I'm not sure which he'd use."

"What are you going to do?"

"I'm going to have to commandeer a ship and go after him. But with the admiralty restrictions lifted, there might not be any ships available immediately."

"What about Jake's ship, the *Southern Cross?*"

"Of course! Miss Randall, I love you!"

She gave him an uneasy look. "Uh, which one of you is that?" she said, giving him a weak smile.

He grinned at her. "All of us, Miss Randall. All of us."

Chapter Thirteen

Jake's ship had been searched most thoroughly. It was a mess. All the cabins had been torn apart and any interior bulkheads that could have hidden a clandestine storage space had been removed. However, the admiralty officers who had been in charge of the search had shown compassion. While no corner of the *Southern Cross* had been left unexamined, the ship had not been damaged in any way. And the bridge had been untouched.

Stenmark had released the ship to himself, and after the security detail on board had assisted him in readying the *Southern Cross* for departure, they had taken a shuttle back down to New Rome, leaving Stenmark and Ava Randall on board alone. Jake's crew could have been released easily enough on Stenmark's authority, but he had not wanted them to know his plans. It would be far better for them if they were not involved. He had been fairly confident that he could manage the ship alone, with Ava's assistance, if need be, but any doubts he might have had disappeared when he saw the bridge and checked the specs stored in the Captain's bridge computer terminal. Though the *Southern Cross* was a tramper and a well-seasoned one at that, Jake had spared no expense in refitting her with state-of-the-art navigation equipment. Since he was a licensed ghost pilot, Thorsen had set up the bridge controls so that with the aid of the computer, the *Southern Cross* could be single-handed easily. Its drive system was the very latest Hawking matter-antimatter propulsion system, and all bridge controls were voice-actuated, including the cryogenic storage tanks. Thorsen knew his business. From the outside, the *Southern Cross* looked like an old hulk, but appearances were very deceptive. It would make, thought Stenmark, a perfect pirate vessel. It was even armed, in direct violation of admiralty regs. The security detail that had been assigned to stay aboard the ship while it was impounded had disabled Jake's weapons system, not that Stenmark would have used them. Even if he was able to catch up with Viselius' ship,

185

which was unlikely, there was no way he was going to fire upon a service vessel. For one thing, he would be outgunned, and for another, he wasn't going to place Viselius' crew at risk. They were only doing their jobs.

He set a course for the nearest Hansen station and took the *Southern Cross* out of orbit. He himself had only ghosted ships before in training simulators, but Shelby had done it for real. The only thing he was concerned about was how the Ones Who Were would affect his piloting abilities. No sooner had he felt that concern than he had his answer, and it was the first time, though he had felt her presence within him, that he had "conversed" with the life force of the woman who had recently occupied all of his attention.

"You don't have to worry," Shelby "told" him. "Ghosting to Earth is easy. We, meaning yourself and my gestalt, were all born there, so our reality reference for Earth is strong. I know you've never actually ghosted a real ship before, but you've done well in simulator training. It's not quite the same thing, but then you won't be alone. I'll be holding your hand, so to speak, guiding you through it and reinforcing your powers of concentration. Our Shade entities will remain completely dormant. It won't be quite the same thing as putting a crew in cryonic suspension so that no other mentality will interfere, because the Shade entities within us will still be conscious. However, you and I will dominate them with our reality reference while they, in turn, will sublimate theirs and lend us psychic strength. You have nothing to be concerned about, August. The powers of your mind have become superhuman. You cannot fail."

"I know," he said.

"You know what?" said Ava, making Stenmark realize that he had spoken out loud.

"Nothing," he said to her. "Just thinking out loud. Don't mind me."

She bit her lower lip nervously and settled back into her contoured flight chair, never taking her eyes off him for an instant. She must be terrified, thought Stenmark.

"You did the right thing, bringing her along," said Shelby. "She knows too much to have been left behind, and besides, she cares about Jake a great deal. Talk to her. Reassure her. She's feeling extremely apprehensive now."

"Relax," Stenmark told Ava. "Jake's going to be all right. And there's no need to be frightened of me. I won't hurt you."

"I know," she said. "I knew that when you . . . did whatever

it was you did to me. It wasn't my first experience with telepathic contact, I've met espers before, but I've never felt anything quite so strong or . . . intimate before. It was like, like
. . . like being held in my mother's arms. I'm still shaking a
little.''

Stenmark smiled. ''I think I'd be shaking too, and not just a
little, if it wasn't for them . . . reassuring me constantly in some
subliminal way.''

''How did it happen?''

Briefly, he told her. ''The funny thing is,'' he said, after
telling her about the killing of the four policemen, ''they really
feel quite badly about it. Not Fannon, though—he's a bit too
human for that. As he said to me, it's war. He understood the
coldly logical necessity of it, but the others . . . I don't really
know them yet, if that makes any sense, but every time I think
about what happened back there, I sense an immeasurable sorrow.
It's really quite incredible. They realize those men would have
killed them without even thinking twice, and yet they still grieve
for them.''

''I guess they're better than we are,'' Ava said. ''Or should I
say, *you're* better than we are?'' She shook her head. ''It makes
me feel a bit ashamed.''

''How's that?''

She told him about her discussion with Jake on their way to
Wheeler's World. ''I didn't really see anything wrong with
continuing with the Seedling Project. After all, it wouldn't be as
if we'd actually be killing anybody. And I sure wouldn't mind
being able to live forever.''

Stenmark nodded. ''I know what you mean. It's easy to
rationalize things when you want something badly enough. I
wasn't really sure about it all myself.''

''What's it like?'' she said. ''What's it like, knowing that
you're never going to die? What does it *feel* like, having them
inside you?''

''I haven't really had much chance to think about it,'' he said.
''It's still—'' Again, there was that brief sensation of receding,
then he heard himself saying, ''Would you like to talk to them?''

She stiffened slightly. ''I thought I was. I mean, I thought that
you . . .'' her voice trailed off.

Stenmark once more felt a door opening within his mind, and
this time, he became aware of an entity that was immeasurably
old filling his conscious being. It was a venerable presence,
strong and stately and incredibly charismatic. Stenmark recog-

nized qualities within this entity that he knew very well. He possessed some of them himself and had seen them in others, but never in such abundance. It was the essence of the paternal archetype, generations upon generations of wisdom and leadership forged into one gestalt personality that was the Great Father. With an awe and a tremendous respect, Stenmark acknowledged him. If he had ever met a human who had exuded such an aura of strength, compassion and capability, Stenmark would have given him his unquestioning loyalty at once. He would have had no choice.

"I am called K'itar," the Great Father said, both to him and to Ava. She caught her breath. It was still Stenmark's voice that addressed her, but it was obviously not Stenmark. He still looked the same, sitting there, but something in him had changed. His whole demeanor was different, as was the way he looked at her, the way he held himself. She realized, with a shock, that she had suddenly, in the short space of a moment, become compulsively attracted to him, and it both thrilled and disturbed her that she could be so quickly affected in such a manner.

"How . . . how do you do?" she said inanely, feeling incongruously like a schoolgirl with a crush on her teacher.

"The physical being that was K'itar lived on the All Mother, the world that you call Boomerang, many thousands of your years ago. When I ceased to be the One That Is and merged for the first time with the Ones Who Were, I realized the Way prepared for me by the All Father, that which you call God. I still remained one, but I also became many, a concept I have learned is very difficult for humans to grasp. What humans call the ego is very valuable to them. They seek to nurture it constantly, they cling to it, protect it and succor it obsessively, as humans must, being all alone within their bodies, having never been before. There is a human belief, not shared by all of your kind, that will help you to understand our existence. This belief is called reincarnation. I understand that only a few humans still believe in this, while most dismiss it as either foolishness, mysticism or superstition. It may be all or none of those. My contact with humans has not enabled me to establish the veracity of this belief, but there may well be some truth in it, since the same Creator made us all. It is not possible to know the Creator's motivations in making humans as they are, in making Shades the way they are, or even in causing the events that led to the Seedling Project. Yet it seems permissible to speculate. When we first met humans, we believed that the All Father had created them the way they were so that their loneliness would lead them to seek out the All Mother, to find the home of the All Father and the people, as we call ourselves, so that our two races might come together to create a greater race of beings. We believed this was one of many tests imposed upon the people by the All Father. However,'' and the voice was now tinged with what was unmistakably regret, ''having joined with humans, we now share human doubt. There are humans who doubt the existence of the Creator, even those who deny it. We have always felt close to the All Father. We had come to believe that we knew Him. Now, sharing human doubt, we believe that this may have been a conceit of ours. Perhaps we were wrong. We still feel what you would call 'spirituality,' but our certainty is gone, perhaps forever. Perhaps the All Father meant for this to happen. Perhaps the entire universe is, in fact, as Fannon often thinks of it, a 'cosmic joke.' We do not believe this, but human doubt remains within our human aspect, and so we do not dismiss that as a possibility, though it would be a cruel joke indeed, one whose punch line is beyond all understanding.

''That which speaks to you now is K'itar, but also many, many others belonging to what you term a gestalt, a unified configuration having properties that cannot be derived from its parts. It is a somewhat flawed term, but your semantics allow no other. When One That Is departs the body to merge with the Ones Who Were, departing that same body for another, there is not one merging, but rather there are many. Think of them as two—the merging brought about by leaving one body for another and the merging within the merging, as the life forces reconcile themselves. The Ones Who Were are, as you would say, divided— though this term is inadequate as well, since we are all one in a sense—into five gestalts. There is the Great Father, the Great Mother, the Great Hunter, the Healer and the Father Who Walked in Shadow. You may understand this by considering comparable traits in humans. We have learned that there was once a human named Jung who, in formulating his definitions of archetypes, came very close to describing the nature of our existence. This would seem to be yet another indication of the Creator's hand at work in both our destinies. A form of natural selection is involved in the merging within the merging. As One That Is joins with the Ones Who Were, the essential nature of the One That Is determines to which of our gestalt entities the One That Is will be attracted. If, in physical life, the One That Is displayed great prowess as a hunter, then he joins with the Great Hunter, with

K'ural, in our case, who is a multiplicity of hunters who had
developed their prowess when each was One That Is. Similarly,
those whose nature manifests itself in qualities of strength, wisdom and leadership join with the Great Father. Females whose
strengths lie in their maternal aspect would become a part of
N'lia, whom you have already experienced, though females
having strengths of other kinds could also join with the Healer or
the Hunter and, very rarely, with the Shadow. The Healer is an
amalgam of beings whose strengths lay in understanding spiritual
oneness, both with other beings and with nature. The natural
sensitivity of Healers makes them vulnerable, so they benefit
from coexisting with our other aspects. The one aspect of our
nature that is most frightening to humans is the Shadow. Shortly
after he became the One That Is, Stenmark glimpsed T'lan for
only an instant, and even though the One That Is has qualities of
both a Father and a Hunter, he was badly frightened. The
Shadow is a frightening entity, or it can be when one does not
know it. As we all possess qualities in different measure of all of
the group entities, humans as well, we all have Shadow aspects
within us. In some it is stronger than in others. In a few it is
all-powerful. In even fewer it is unrestrained. This occurs only
with great rarity among the people, but sadly, it is not entirely
uncommon among humans. An unrestrained Shadow aspect,
ungoverned by the influence of paternal wisdom, maternal love,
or healing sensitivity to the unity of all living things, can be
incredibly destructive. A Shadow entity remaining in communion with the other aspects that make a being whole serves as a
link to the beginning of all things, as a conduit to the elemental
forces within each of us, and as a constant reminder of the beast
that lives within us all, that which works for our survival when
we recognize, respect and understand it, and that which can
destroy us if we fail to know it, fear it and submit. Such is our
nature, and though it seems a great deal unlike yours, if you look
within yourself with honesty, you will find that we are not very
different, after all.''

Ava shook her head in wonder. ''It's amazing,'' she said.
''For a race of beings to possess such intelligence and sophisti-
cation, and yet to remain so—'' She stopped, embarrassed.

''Primitive?'' said K'itar. Stenmark's face smiled.

''Well, yes. If I understand correctly, and I don't mean to
offend in any way, your culture has remained stagnant for centuries.
You could have accomplished so much! I can't understand why
you haven't evolved into a technologically advanced civilization.''

"For what purpose?" said K'itar.

"*For what purpose?* Why, for the purpose of growth, for the betterment of your race, so that you could achieve—"

"Achieve?" K'itar said. "Where would be the necessity for the sort of achievement of which you speak? In the end, if there is ever an end to such things, what would we gain that we do not already have?"

She started to reply, then realized that no reply was possible and smiled. "I see what you mean," she said. "I envy you."

"I'm sorry," said K'itar.

"Sorry? For what?"

"Sorry for you," K'itar said. "As long as you are capable of envy, you will never have that which every living being seeks."

"Oh? And what is that?"

"Peace, Miss Randall. Is that not the final goal of all human endeavor?"

She smiled wryly. "Some of us like to think it is."

"Yes, I am aware of the fact that humans have a tendency to choose paths for themselves that they believe will lead them to their final goal, be they paths of achievement, paths of discovery or paths of acquisition. It is sad that they struggle so hard to attain that which they could have by simply choosing to embrace it. They believe that there are many paths to peace and they seek to follow as many of them as they can. I understand they rarely find what they are seeking and that most of them spend their lives desperately searching."

"You're suggesting that there's only one path to peace?" she said.

"No," K'itar said gently. "There are only paths away from it."

Stenmark saw that Ava didn't understand. But then, he thought, she's only human.

Contact with ColCom's orbital station Terra brought devastating news. The *Robert H. Goddard*, the service ship aboard which Viselius had departed from Wheeler's World, had already been and gone.

"Was Director Viselius on board when the *Goddard* left?" Stenmark said, thinking that Viselius could not possibly have had time to make all the necessary preparations.

"He never left the ship, sir," came the reply.

"Did the *Goddard* take on any cargo?" Stenmark asked, not bothering to ask if a flight plan had been filed, since Viselius would obviously have invoked priority clearance for a classified mission.

"Two shuttles rendezvoused with the *Goddard,* sir. A passenger shuttle that came up from Colorado Springs and a cargo shuttle out of Tokyo."

Tokyo! Why Tokyo? "Specify," he said. "Who was on board the passenger shuttle and what cargo was taken aboard the *Goddard?*"

"Sir, Director Viselius ordered—Just a moment, sir, I have a priority call coming in."

"Belay that," Stenmark said, but it was too late. Station control had already responded to the priority call. It was pointless to waste any more time. Perhaps it was already too late. He had the computer plot a course for the nearest Hansen station, and the *Southern Cross* changed headings away from Earth. Station Terra called him back almost immediately.

"Director Stenmark, please stand by, sir. I've got a priority call for you from ColCom HQ."

Nakamura's face appeared upon the bridge screen. She looked uncharacteristically agitated. "Stenmark, what in God's name is going on?" she said. Funny she should put it that way, he thought. "We've just learned that Viselius returned to Earth and departed again within a matter of hours. Why weren't we notified? Why did he invoke priority clearance? And what are you two doing aboard separate ships?"

Stenmark ignored her questions. "Sander took on cargo out of Tokyo," he said. "You know what it was?"

"No, but we'll be finding out at any moment. But we do know that he had an interrogation team taken aboard." So that's it, Stenmark thought. While a service pilot is at the controls, the team will subject Jake to imperative conditioning. That's how he had been able to move so fast. But that cargo—

"August!" Diane sounded panic-stricken. He had never heard her sound that way before. "We've just received word from Tokyo that a Damocles system was loaded on board the *Goddard!*"

"That's impossible. It would have taken them weeks to process the necessary—"

"He had done it in advance," she said. "He had the system prepared for shipment before the two of you departed for Wheeler's World. We had no way of knowing, because he had processed all the authorizations through one of his personal security programs. He's got Michaels aboard and he's on his way to Boomerang, isn't he? Damn you, Stenmark, why didn't you kill him when you had the chance?"

There was the sound of someone clearing his throat, and then the voice of the Station Terra communications officer came on, sounding very uneasy.

"Forgive me, I know I can be court-martialed for breaking into a priority call, Director Nakamura, but I feel that I should remind you that you're still on my screen and—"

She ignored him. "Stenmark, you've *got* to catch him before he ghosts! You've got to stop him, fire on him—"

"This ship is unarmed," he told her.

"Then fucking ram him!" She was irrational, raving. Stenmark knew the communications officer was still monitoring the call, as was his duty, since she had obviously neglected to follow classified procedure. He had attempted to tell her that, but she was deaf to reason. Stenmark heard him whisper, "Jesus Christ."

"August," she said, her eyes wide with terror and her voice strained. "Shortly after you left for Wheeler's World, we received a special courier with a message that Michaels had been apprehended and was safely being held in custody. We, Stanislas and I, thought you would take custody of her and bring her back at once. August, we . . . we went public with it."

"You did *what?*"

"We wanted to get a large public support base before the Church leaders could—" Her mouth worked soundlessly for a moment. Her breathing became labored. "Stenmark, you've got to stop him, you've got to! If you don't, we're finished. We've promised them immortality, and if we don't deliver—"

"How much of a head start does he have?"

"They'll kill us, August. They'll destroy us, just as they destroyed the inventors of batch 235. We'll be—"

"Diane, how much of a head start?"

"I don't know where Bikovski is. When he heard about the Damocles being loaded on the *Goddard*, he ran out of the room and—"

"Diane!"

Her face disappeared from the screen, to be replaced by the pale and drawn features of the officer on Station Terra. "Director Viselius has approximately four hours lead on you, sir."

"Damn."

"Sir, assuming that he's heading for Hansen One, I can plot an intercept course for you that should cut down his lead by a factor of—"

"I've already done that. I'll still catch him only if I'm real lucky. And then, short of ramming him, I don't know how the hell I'm going to stop him. The *Goddard*'s armed and has a full crew aboard. However, there's still a chance. Put a priority call through to the *Goddard* immediately. I want to speak to her captain."

"Sir." The screen went black.

Stenmark took a deep breath.

"What's a Damocles system?" Ava said.

"It's a weapons satellite system," he said tensely.

"What kind of weapons?"

"The bioengineered kind," said Stenmark. "It's actually a very simple system, very cost-effective. The *Goddard* will make one full orbit around Boomerang, releasing the satellites from its cargo bays. The ship will then leave orbit to run a computer link check on the satellite net prior to running the final program. Up until that point, the mission can still be aborted, but once the final program runs, the satellites fire a series of rockets into the atmosphere. The rockets are designed to air-burst after entering the atmosphere, scattering a nice variety of lethal organisms."

"My God," she said. "We actually use weapons like that?"

"Several colonies owe their existence to weapons like that," said Stenmark.

"Sir?" The officer from Station Terra came on again. "I'm sorry, sir, but I am unable to raise the *Goddard*."

Stenmark took a deep breath, expelling it noisily. "Well, that's it, then. Thanks for trying, Lieutenant. You've done all you could."

"That's it?" said Ava. "You mean, there's nothing that can be done?"

"Not right now, at any rate. We've still got a chance, but . . ."

"But what?"

"Ava, look, for someone who's essentially been kidnapped, you're taking this very well. I—"

"I came along voluntarily," she said.

"Well, let's just say that you were made inclined to come along voluntarily. You were the only other person who knew about Boomerang, or who knew all the details, but that doesn't seem to matter now that those fools have released the information. I had hoped to catch Viselius before he departed from Earth orbit, but now . . . what I mean is, maybe it would be best if you took one of the shuttles and got off this ship. We're close enough to Earth still for Terra Station or Luna Base to send a ship out to pick you up.''

''Forget it,'' she said. ''If you catch the *Goddard*, there's no way I'm going to allow you to ram it, not with Jake aboard. You'll have to kill me first.''

''You've jumped to the wrong conclusion. I have no intention of trying to ram the *Goddard*. That would be suicide. Mass suicide, in fact. Besides, I'd never stand a chance. The *Southern Cross* has been disarmed, and the *Goddard* could blow me to shrapnel before I even got close. That's precisely the reason why I want you off this ship. Viselius might just order the *Goddard*'s captain to fire on me. I've got to take that chance. I've got to raise the ship and try to talk her captain into following my orders rather than Viselius'. Technically, I have the seniority on this mission, but the *Goddard*'s captain might not know that. Probably won't. Viselius has him on silent running, probably, which is why Station Terra couldn't raise them. However, if that captain follows the book, he'll receive from a ship that's obviously attempting a rendezvous, though he might not send. If he realizes that he's receiving conflicting orders from two Directors, he'll come to a dead stop and contact HQ to find out who has precedence.''

''Which is why Viselius may order him to fire upon you first,'' said Ava. ''All right. I understand the risk. I'm staying. I know that you can make me leave, but please don't.''

''Jake's a very lucky man. All right, you can stay.''

''Thank you.''

''In that case, you'd better get some rest.''

''Are you serious?'' Ava said with disbelief. ''You expect me to be able to rest at a time like this?''

''It would be pointless, not to mention difficult, for you to simply sit there for the next thirty hours or so until we reach Hansen One. If you can't sleep, you can take a short 'nap' in a cryogen. Besides, it's the best place for you to be.''

''Why, so I won't get in the way?''

''Frankly, yes. You might as well get into the tank now, because that's where you're going to wind up anyway. Unless the *Goddard* can be stopped before Jake ghosts her to Boomerang, we're going to follow. It'll take time for them to deploy the satellites and get the Damocles system ready. In that time, the captain of the *Goddard* might be persuaded to abort the mission.''

''Unless Viselius keeps everyone in coldsleep once they get there,'' Ava said.

Stenmark shook his head. "He won't. Sander's no spacer. Besides, even if Jake's knowledgeable about the Damocles system, which I doubt, he wouldn't be able to man the bridge and set up the satellite net by himself. It takes a number of people. No, Sander's going to need his crew. They're what I'm counting on."

"But they're not going to be able to contact ColCom headquarters back on Earth," said Ava. "How are you going to convince them to obey your orders, to follow you rather than Viselius?"

"I'll bribe them."

"*What?* How?"

"Even though Diane and Stanislas made public the details of the Boomerang mission, that news hasn't reached Wheeler's World yet. At least, it certainly hadn't when we left. All the members of the *Goddard*'s crew can possibly know is that they're setting up the Damocles system to wipe out supposedly dangerous and allegedly nonsentient life forms on Boomerang. If anyone on board the *Goddard* besides Viselius and Jake knew anything at all, it would be the members of the interrogation team who came aboard to condition Jake. However, Sander's not an idiot. He'll have either segregated them from the other members of the crew or kept them ignorant of the details. That's probably what he's done. However, if the crew of the *Goddard* knew they were destroying their own chance at immortality, it's a sure thing that they'd mutiny. They'd be crazy not to."

"But that means resuming the Seedling Project," Ava said.

Stenmark nodded. "Better the Seedling Project than Project Damocles."

"But can you make a decision like that for them?" Ava said. "For the . . . people on Boomerang?"

"A decision between life or death? Sure. Life wins every time."

"Even if it's life under conditions that may be intolerable?" said Ava, recalling what Jake had told her.

"Now you're talking about a decision that no one can make for anybody else, at least not ethically."

"I see. What will you do if you can't stop them from deploying the Damocles system?"

"I'll have to stop them . . . somehow." Stenmark glanced at Ava. "It's still not too late. You can still abandon ship."

She shook her head. "Promise me one thing—that you'll revive me when . . . whatever happens happens."

"It's a promise."

"Okay." She took a deep breath. "Where do you want me?"

"Why don't you take the executive officer's tank? That's the one on deck level on the starboard bulkhead."

She nodded and walked over to the cryogen. Stenmark actuated the mechanism, and it opened, the lid retracting soundlessly. "It's like climbing into a coffin," she said. "I never liked these damn things."

With his Fannon aspect feeling empathy for her, Stenmark said, "I know what you mean. A lot of people feel that way."

She climbed into the tank. Before lying back, she looked at him once more and said, "Remember, you promised."

Stenmark nodded. She lay back and the lid slid shut. She closed her eyes as a blue mist began to fill the tank.

With the ship traveling at near light speed, human navigation was impossible. The course of Hansen One was plotted into the bridge computer, with several backup computer systems functioning as fail-safes. At such times, there was not much for a captain of a ship to do. He or she could see to other functions of the ship's operations, most of which could be directed from the bridge consoles, or spend time with the crew members or meditate to prepare for the surreal journey through the zone. Stenmark was alone on the *Southern Cross* now in a sense, with Ava locked inside the cryogen, sleeping a dreamless coldsleep. The analogy of the cryogen as coffin was a good one; it was as close as a human being could come to death. With Ava in a deathlike sleep, enshrouded in an aquamarine mist that made her look suspended as though in some shimmering crystal, Stenmark was alone. Yet, in another, very real sense, he would never be alone again. Now, for the first time since it happened, there was time for him to contemplate his transcendence of normal humanity. There was time in which to look within and know his selves.

With S'eri, the Healer, easing the body of the One That Is into a tranquil, meditative state of complete repose, a state near coldsleep, Stenmark's life force drifted through countless centuries, blended with the gestalt personalities that up until that time had lingered on the very edge of his subconscious. With the pentamerous Fannon entity at the forefront of the body's consciousness, "standing watch," Stenmark's discrete identity was taken on a psychic journey through alien intelligence. Shepherded by N'lia, the Great Mother, whose multitudinous life forces enveloped his like a secure psychic cocoon, Stenmark was guided by Great

Father K'itar on a metaphysical flight into the essence of K'ural, the Great Hunter entity.

It was like a dream, and yet it was not dreamlike, as he found himself experiencing a stark semblance of reality, not sitting in a contoured flight chair on the bridge of the *Southern Cross,* but standing in a verdant clearing in a forest as light filtered down in shafts through the tree branches far overhead, branches of trees that grew taller than any trees on Earth. Nestling high up in the trees, in huge basket-shaped nests, were brilliantly golden-hued birds that looked impossibly clumsy and ill-suited to flight as they hopped among the branches, giving voice to cries that sounded like geese being tortured. First one would take flight, and then another, and another, rising through the upper branches like a fighter squadron, wings appearing to move with slow majesty that belied the speed with which they rose above the treetops, circling until the flock was formed and then shooting off with astonishing rapidity into the distance.

He stood among the plants that grew at ground level, some of them taller than himself, with moisture-laden leaves and fronds that could cover his whole body. On some of them, insects that looked like mottled scarabs with huge mandibles, the smallest of them larger than his fist, moved sluggishly like old men on a constitutional. Before him, like a wide, crystalline path, was the undulating trail of a slug python leading off into the undergrowth, where the gelatinous creature timidly took shelter among the fibrous roots. As he stepped forward into the clearing, a giant leaf detached itself from a nearby plant and became a rubbery-looking moth that flapped off in search of a quieter resting place. He stood very still, not wanting to risk the painful sting it could inflict, and moments later it had settled on another plant across the clearing. The moth folded its wings and became still and invisible.

In his left hand, Stenmark carried a curved, paddle-shaped wooden sling with which he could hurl with deadly accuracy the orange-sized light-green seedpods which were found throughout the forest in great profusion, hanging off spreading, bushlike trees like clusters of fruit. On impact with the ground, the pods would burst, sending out a cloud of spores that, once inhaled, could drop a large animal in its tracks almost instantaneously. In his right hand, Stenmark held a spear, a slender hunting javelin. In another moment, he would use either the sling or the spear or both. He was on the trail of a hellhound, and the beast was very close now. He could feel its presence.

An instinct borne of generations of experience told him to duck, and he dropped down to a crouch as a ravening howl shattered the stillness of the clearing and a jet-black blur passed over him. Even as he dropped, he slung a seedpod over his shoulder, but the globe flew too far and disappeared into a clump of bushes, where it burst harmlessly. Instantly, he was on his feet and pivoting, spear held before him in both hands. The beast crouched just behind him, its haunches gathered for a leap, a deep and gurgling rumble coming from its throat. Its jaws were wide open in a snarl, and saliva dribbled from its mouth. It leaped, its glistening fangs aimed for his shoulder. He brought his spear up at an angle, and the hellhound impaled itself upon it as the spear passed through its heart, killing it instantly. The momentum of the beast bore him down, and he fell, pinned to the ground by its ponderous weight. He felt the warmth of its blood leaking out on him, and he saw that it had snapped his spear in two. Then he heard the growl again, and for a moment he thought it wasn't dead, but then he turned his head and saw its mate slowly approaching, eyes fixed upon its helpless prey.

In that moment, Stenmark's life force shifted from K'ural, the Hunter, to T'lan, the Shadow. Blind, unreasoning panic overwhelmed him and immediately passed as he became that which he feared, T'lan, Father Who Walked in Shadow, the beast within, bloodlust incarnate. With a shrug, he threw the carcass of the hellhound off himself as if it weighed nothing at all and rolled with easy, fluid grace to his feet, standing slightly bent over, facing the hellhound's mate. His entire being was filled with feral fury as he faced it, teeth bared, his fingers hooked like talons. He was weaponless, but he was unafraid. He stared with blazing rage at the hellhound, and both of them froze, standing eye to eye, separated by only a few feet. The rumbling of the hellhound was matched by the predatory growling issuing from his own throat as two beasts faced each other, muscles tensed. Slowly, the hellhound lowered its head. He crouched down, just as slowly, staring it down. The hellhound shut its mouth, its growling grew lower in pitch, its head moved from side to side as it began to back away. He didn't move, didn't take his eyes off it for a second. The hellhound twitched its tail and leaped, but not at him. It jumped into the bushes and was gone. He heard the rustling of its passage, and then all was still again.

Abruptly, the scene changed. He stood in a canyon, surrounded by towering walls of stone. It was night and the canyon

was bathed in an eerie light emanating from a bubbling pool that
sent forth clouds of steam into the air. The Shades had gathered at
the Spring of Life for the Rituals of Mating, males on one side of
the canyon, females on the other. The Need was great within
him. His reproductive organ, normally retracted, was exposed to
view, engorged with blood and glistening with natural lubrication.
The Ritual of Preparation had begun, the time to establish the
patterns for the mating. The younger females and males were
first to take part in the choosing as they moved forward into the
light cast by the Spring of Life and began their mating dance. He
could smell the overpowering scent of the females in estrus, and
it spurred his frenzy as he danced, leaping high into the air and
growling, hurling imaginary javelins, pantomiming challenge
postures as he displayed how he would defend his domain. He
danced in one place as females danced around him, then one
female circled him twice, three times, and began to dance before
him, choosing him. She leaped high into the air and bore him
down to the canyon floor, mounting him and thrusting with
increasing speed as they bucked together until his seed flowed
into her in multiple spasms of release.

Another change of scene. He was in a village, an *alien*
village, since the Shades did not construct shelters. It was a
village of wood cabins surrounded by a strong, high wooden
wall, a fortress with guard towers bound on one side by a river
and on all others by cleared strips of ground with rows of
wooden stakes set into the earth at angles. It was a Seedling
village, populated by beings like himself, humans who had
merged with Shades, descendants of the people sent to Boomerang to begin the Seedling Project. They were like himself in
most respects save two. The original Seedlings had been selected
for latent esper potential, and these descendants of theirs were
now full espers, with mental powers far surpassing his. The
Shades possessed the ability to project, but they did so unconsciously. Those who had merged with Shelby had learned how to
control this ability, but the Seedlings possessed far greater power
and control. Aside from this, what made them different was their
ignorance of who and what they were. All save one of them
believed that they had descended from the stars, sent by the All
Father as the "chosen people" to kill Shades and merge with
them in the bloody Ritual of Transformation, absorbing Shades
into themselves as part of the All Father's plan to create a greater
race of beings. It had been necessary for them to believe this, so
that the Shades they took would understand the holy war that

they were waging. The only one who knew the truth was Wendy Chan, a member of Fannon's original survey team who had ghosted the *Blessing*, the ship that had carried the first Seedlings, to Boomerang. Wendy Chan was now one of the Seedling Ones Who Were. Each Seedling who "inherited" her inherited the true story of the Seedling Project and bore that knowledge, like a sin, in silence. Humans had begun the holy war that was killing off the Shades, and now another human, on his own jehad, would come to end it and destroy both Shade and Seedling. Perhaps Stenmark could stop the one, but he was helpless to halt the other. Soon, if it had not already happened, the graceful, gray-skinned beings with their snow-white manes and glowing violet eyes would disappear from Boomerang, replaced by human Seedlings who would carry the Shades about inside them like living memories. In one sense, perhaps, it was not killing; in another, it was genocide.

The village disappeared and Stenmark was back on the bridge of the *Southern Cross*, approaching Hansen One. There had been no sign of the *Goddard*. Viselius had passed through the zone to Boomerang ahead of him. It was a journey Jake Thorsen had made many times. Shelby had made it only once. She felt his concern and reassured him.

"It's not a journey into the unknown," she told him. "In a sense, August, you're going home. You've been there already, through the Ones Who Were, and now you are returning once again. Your reality reference for Boomerang could not be stronger. Unlike your return to Earth, this ghosting will be guided by the Shade entities within you. This reality will not be yours or mine, but theirs. You will transcend, August."

"Transcend?"

"Transcend your own reality."

Then he was no longer on the bridge. The *Southern Cross* passed into the vortex of the zone, and he felt the Ones Who Were within him guiding him back to Boomerang once more, a planet with a diameter of 15,120.724 kilometers, with a gravity of .75, three-quarters Earth specific. A lush, green planet in the system of a type G yellow dwarf. A world possessing only one landmass, a continent of approximately 138,000 square kilometers, formed by a collision of two smaller landmasses millions of years earlier. The collision had produced a giant mountain range down the center of the continent. Some of the peaks rose to heights of 60,000 meters. The crescent-shaped moon that gave Boomerang its name tumbled across the sky, rising and setting several times in one night because of its low, fast orbit. Flowering grass with yellow blades and purple blooms made brilliant tapestries of meadows that rolled gently down to snow-fed rivers, teeming with aquatic life. The world had a less severe axial tilt than Earth, which gave it more temperate weather overall, though the temperatures in the equatorial regions were extremely high. Frequently, fierce storms would come in from the ocean, lashing the land with rain and hurricane-force winds. At such times, the people would stand exposed to the elemental might of the All Father. With their manes streaming in the wind, they would allow themselves to be drenched and buffeted as they drank in the All Father's strength.

Stenmark climbed the narrow, winding, centuries-old trails that led to the Spring of Life, where he mated, celebrated, and reaffirmed the Rituals and the Ways. He cared for blighted trees and wounded animals in his domain, and if challenged by a younger Shade, he defended his territory until his opponent, recognizing his superior strength, submitted and was allowed to go free in search of another place to claim. He hunted hellhounds and stood in the shallows of the rivers, catching eels with his bare hands and eating them raw. He prostrated himself upon the ground, the bosom of the All Mother, and prayed to the All Father, giving thanks for a full and bountiful existence that lacked for nothing.

He lay upon the ground, dying, his viscera ripped out by the claws of a hellhound, dreading the True Death, for life was ebbing fast and no other Shade had come in answer to his Call. As his eyes began to glaze, their glow fading, a human female pushed her way through a tangled thicket to kneel down beside his torn and ruined body. He looked up at her as she gently caressed his mane and then he reached out to her and Touched her, giving her the most precious gift a Shade could give, the essence of its lives. He merged with Shelby Michaels and learned about humanity firsthand, from within.

She stood in the laboratory, watching Fannon die, transfixed by a spear that had been meant for the Seedling Lani. He was half sitting on the floor, supported by herself and Paul Tabarde. The spear had gone in through his stomach with such force that it protruded from his back. Fannon was breathing horribly, his face contorted. Jake took the spear and began to pull it out, but Fannon cried out and clasped the shaft of the spear with both hands.

"Leave it," he choked out. "I've bought it."

"Drew, look at me," she said, reaching out to him.

"No . . . don't. Let me . . ."

She Touched him and his life force flowed into her.

He relived the merging with the guard, Warren Newsome, and then with Franz Garcia and Irv Viner. He saw himself, standing rooted to the spot, heard himself scream and then experienced the merging from two viewpoints as the experiential circle closed, and now he was going home. From a great distance, he heard a roaring sound as the void seemed to buckle all around him, and there was the sensation of endless falling as the zone rejected his reality, the reality reference of one human being supported by countless Shade entities, and then he was back on the *Southern Cross* once more, having passed through and survived the vortex. He heard a soft chiming sound and realized that Fannon must have set the cryogen to revive Ava once they had passed through the zone. He quickly consulted his instruments to make sure that everything was as it should be, and through the viewport he saw the emerald-green planet Boomerang before him. He turned around to see Ava sitting up in the cryogen. She shivered, clutched herself, then looked at him with a smile . . . and the smile froze.

Stenmark's hair had gone snow-white, and it cascaded down his shoulders. His skin now possessed a silvery sheen, and his eyes, with their bifurcated pupils, gave off an opalescent violet light.

Chapter Fourteen

Whatever shock he might have felt at seeing his metamorphosis was cushioned by the Ones Who Were. He had keyed the screen to give him back his own image, and as he stared at it, he knew that the Ones Who Were had foreseen this. This was how it had happened to Shelby. Unlike the journey back to Earth, it was not a human reality reference that brought him through the vortex, but that of a creature composed of both human and alien parts. He had, indeed, transcended his humanity.

Except for the white mane that hung down to his shoulders, the catlike eyes and the cyanotic-looking skin, his features had remained essentially unchanged. It was Stenmark's face that looked back at him from the screen, but it was a face that was no longer human. He gave Ava credit for not having screamed when she saw him. It was a hell of a thing to wake up to. After quickly reassuring her, he started trying to raise the *Goddard*. He wondered what Viselius would think when he saw him.

"Maybe it would be better if he didn't see you right now," Fannon said to him.

"That's a very good point," Stenmark thought. "Both Sander and the captain of the *Goddard* would recognize my voice, but seeing my face would definitely throw them for a loop. I'm beginning to think that nothing can faze me anymore."

"Oh, it could and it would, if you let it," Fannon said.

"You mean if *you* let it," Stenmark thought.

"Same thing, isn't it?"

All the while they "spoke," Stenmark continued trying to raise the ColCom ship. There was no response.

"Why aren't they answering?" Ava said, as though reading his thoughts. "You don't suppose that they . . . didn't make it?"

Stenmark glanced at her quickly. "It's a possibility," he said. "And much as I hate to say it, if that is the case, it certainly would solve my problem."

She nodded grimly. "I understand. If they're here, they should have heard you by now."

"Yes, unless . . . hold on." He leaned forward suddenly. "They are here," he said.

"I see it," said Ava.

Ahead of them, in orbit around Boomerang, was the *Robert H. Goddard*. Unless the ship's communication systems were seriously damaged, it was impossible for the *Goddard* not to be receiving them. Stenmark increased screen magnification.

"I don't see any of the Damocles satellites being deployed," he said.

"Perhaps they haven't had a chance to start yet," Ava said. She sounded hopeful now that she knew that Jake had made it safely.

"Perhaps," said Stenmark. "Perhaps Viselius is waiting for me to get close enough before he lets me have it."

"What are you going to do?" said Ava.

He shook his head. "There's nothing else *to* do. If he's trying to lure me in closer, I'm simply going to have to oblige him. He can't go on ignoring me forever."

They were alongside the *Goddard*. There was no response of any sort from the ColCom ship. There was no sign that any of the satellites had been deployed, and the *Goddard*'s cargo bays were closed.

"I don't understand," said Stenmark. "I'm close enough to hammer on her goddam hull. Why haven't they done anything?"

Ava was gripping the arms of her chair tightly. "Maybe Jake's not letting them do anything," she said, not very convincingly.

"Even in that unlikely event, why hasn't he responded, if he's in control?" Stenmark stood up. "I'm going aboard."

"I'm going with you," Ava said.

"It would be best if you stayed here," said Stenmark.

'Alone? Not on your life!"

"All right, let's go."

They took the ship's shuttle and crossed the distance between the *Goddard* and the *Southern Cross* without incident. The emergency docking bay responded to the shuttle's signal and opened to admit them. Once aboard the *Goddard*, they found that the Damocles system was still in the cargo bays. Not one of the satellites had been deployed. On the bridge, the ship's instruments showed that everything was functioning normally. The only thing that wasn't normal was that there was nobody on board. The *Goddard* was a derelict.

"Something awful's happened to them," Ava said, her voice shaking. "Something happened while they were coming through the zone and—"

"I don't think so," Stenmark said. He sat at the bridge console, looking at the screen. "All of the shuttles are gone," he said.

"Then they're not . . . ?"

"Doesn't look like it," he said. "It looks as though they all went down to Boomerang. I can't understand it, but there's no other explanation. Why would they—"

He got his answer even as he spoke, but it did not come from within. It came from the planet's surface, and he, as well as all the Ones Who Were, marveled at its strength. He saw that Ava heard it too. She stood stock still, mouth open, eyes wide, as she heard the Call.

They saw the settlement from the air as they descended. It was a far cry from the primitive wood cabins surrounded by wooden fortress walls that the Fannon entity remembered. This was a town, a large town surrounded by stone walls. Instead of simple cabins, there were houses, many of them several stories high and with glass windowpanes. Stenmark could see gardens and aqueducts, unmistakable signs of primitive, yet nevertheless industrial activity, even an honest-to-God observatory. In a large compound at the far end of the town, he could see the shuttles from the *Goddard* parked in an orderly manner. A large crowd of people formed a giant circle around an area where they were obviously meant to land.

As they came out of the shuttle, a young man came forward to greet them. He looked perfectly human. He was tall, lean and broad-shouldered, with a thick shock of black hair gathered behind his neck in a ponytail. He was dressed in high leather boots, soft leather pants and a loose-fitting white shirt that looked as though it might have been made from cotton, though of course it could not possibly be cotton. He looked to be about twenty-five.

"Welcome to Chantown," the young man said pleasantly. "My name is Sean. I'm the town elder and the senior of the Council of Townships."

"August Stenmark—"

"Yes, of course," said Sean, smiling. "I know. Seeing you is like meeting an old friend, in a way. My Great Mother Wendy knows Drew Fannon very well, and my Great Hunter Lani is a friend of Shelby Michaels'. You will know directors Anderson, Jorgensen, Hermann and Malik, who have merged with my Great Father Drew. I am named for Sean McEnroe, and though the chief scientist of the Boomerang Project did not remain with us, we still remember him and honor him. This is quite an occasion. There will be celebration in your honor tonight and—Ava, forgive me, I sense your great distress. Jake Thorsen is safe. There is no need for you to be concerned.''

"Where is he? Can I see him?"

"Of course you can see him. Immediately, if you wish. I'm certain he'd be delighted to see you."

"Where—'' she began, then suddenly realized she knew exactly where to go, and she took off at a run. Sean looked after her, smiling.

Stenmark attempted a furtive probe, only to have Sean turn to look at him with a slightly reproving glance. "There's no need for that," he said. "Besides, you can't read me unless I want you to. My esper abilities are far more developed than yours. However, I have no objection. Now is simply not the time. In answer to your question, though, the others from the *Goddard* are all here as well, and also quite safe. You'll see them at dinner in the hall tonight. And don't give another thought to the Damocles system—it's perfectly safe and harmless aboard the *Goddard.*"

"Viselius, what about—"

"Time to speak of all that later," Sean said, extending his hand. "Come, let me show you around."

They went on a brief tour of the town, which Sean conducted with a great deal of pride. Stenmark felt, incongruously, somehow like a hero coming home from a war to the small town where he had been born. Everywhere they went, he was greeted with enormous respect. These people all seemed to know him. Knowing the extent of their esper powers, Stenmark realized that they could be "reading" him, as Sean had put it, but if they were, he felt absolutely nothing.

At last, they came to Sean's home, a stately three-story house with a pitched roof and mullioned windows. Stenmark felt as though he had stepped back in time to the eighteenth century on Earth. Inside the house, they were greeted by Muri, Sean's wife, and three small children, who went scampering off before they could be introduced. It all seemed incredible, surreal.

They crossed the parqueted wood floor into the main room of the house, which was filled with wood furniture exquisitely crafted and upholstered in colorful materials Stenmark could not identify. There were several very large hellhound pelts on the floor and in front of the fireplace, and two fearsome-looking hellhound heads glared down at him from high up on the walls on either side of the mantelpiece. They sat down at a long wooden table, intricately carved and oiled and polished to a deep, dark gloss. Muri brought them ceramic mugs full of a steaming hot brew that tasted unlike anything Stenmark had ever tried before. It had a bittersweet, nutlike flavor and was remarkably delicious.

"Drink it slowly," Sean said. "It's quite potent and can make you drunk very quickly if you're not used to it."

"What is it?"

"We call it beer, though it isn't, really. It's brewed from seedpods."

"Seedpods!"

"Yes, the same ones the Shades used to use to hunt with. However, they're not lethal when brewed into beer, so don't worry."

"You said, 'used to,' " Shelby said, through Stenmark. "Does that mean that they're all gone now?"

"No, not all of them," said Sean, a bit sadly, "but there are only a few left. We leave them alone, for the most part."

"They no longer attempt to fight us," Lani said through Sean as, partly by spoken word and partly by psychic ability, the Ones Who Were within both bodies began to converse with one another. "Our esper powers are far too strong for them to attempt attacking us, and, in any case, they're no longer interested. Our presence here has interfered with their natural way of life to such an extent that we've essentially broken their spirit. They no longer reproduce. They're a pathetic race now, what's left of them. Soon, they will no longer have Shades to merge with, and then they will finally join with us and the Seedling Project will have reached its logical conclusion on Boomerang."

"What happened here, Lani?" Fannon said. "How did you manage to progress so far in so short a period of time? What happened to the—"

"The primitive theology imposed upon us by our conditioning? The killing of Shades, the Ritual of Transformation, the hunter-gatherer life-style? We outgrew all that. Or threw it off, if you like. Don't forget that the Seedling Project was created by the

Directorate of ColCom. We *are* that Directorate now, descended from me when I was One That Is.''

"We don't think of ourselves as 'Seedlings' anymore," said Sean. "We know ourselves for what we are. Humans. Mutant humans, the result of an experiment, but humans nevertheless. It all began to change after you left, Shelby. You and Tabarde and all the others. Having absorbed the Directorate, taking them forcibly, Lani had to contend with a great deal of disharmony within herself. It took time before Anderson, Malik, Jorgensen and Hermann became fully integrated into her gestalt. At that point, several things quickly became self-evident.''

"The Seedlings were getting nowhere fast in terms of growth and development," said Lani. "The sole exception was our esper ability, which continued to breed true and continued to grow stronger with each new generation. And, of course, we no longer needed the Shades to be able to merge. Any Seedling with Ones Who Were could use the Touch to merge. It also became obvious that our theology, invented by the Directorate of ColCom, was inhibiting us.''

"Finally," said Wendy, who had been there when it all began, "I was the only one among all the Seedlings who knew the truth, the reason behind our existence. I knew that in spite of the precautions you had taken, we all had taken, the odds were that ColCom would find us sooner or later, if not by design, then by accident. We had to make ourselves ready for that day, whenever it would come.''

"Malik, Anderson, Jorgensen and Hermann were really very helpful," Sean said. "They are very wise men, experienced men, born leaders who were superbly educated." He grinned. "I'm being immodest, in a sense, but it's the truth. Lani was already the elder of the people, having Wendy as her Great Mother, just as I am now the elder for the same reason, despite my physical youth. With the help of the Directorate, who understand the ways of handling people, Lani became both a spiritual and political missionary, educating the Seedlings as to who and what they really were.''

"I'm surprised that they were able to take it," Fannon said.

"It wasn't easy, Drew," said Wendy. "Given a theology in which you are taught to believe that you are the chosen people of God, the All Father, descended from the stars and created for the purpose of transforming the Shades into a better race of beings, more appropriate to what God had in mind, it's very hard to discover that you have in fact not been following the will of

God, but of other men. Men who were, perhaps, a great deal like yourself, possibly your superiors or inferiors, but certainly no more divine than you."

"It's even harder when you're an esper," Sean said. "An 'ordinary' human who is devout in his faith and is presented with arguments against it has the luxury of claiming to know the truth and can deny whatever seems inconsistent with his beliefs. An esper actually *has* direct access to the truth and can truly know the motivations of the person who is arguing against what he believes in. For generations, Wendy Chan and all who contained her bore the truth in silence and would not allow anyone else access to it, for fear of precisely what did happen when Lani revealed all."

"Being human," Lani said, "those who heard the truth reacted with hostility, but they were also part Shade, and, as hostility is a disharmonious state, their Ones Who Were prevented them from giving in to that hostility. Had this been a fully human society, Great Mother Wendy tells me I would have been tried for heresy and condemned to death. As it was, there was no denying the truth when everyone could clearly see that it *was* the truth. I opened my mind to them. They saw what had been kept hidden all these years; they knew the Directors who had become a part of me. They were forced to accept the truth, but it was an extremely unpleasant truth, one that destroyed the foundations of our culture and left us feeling morally bankrupt as a people."

"If Shades had it in them to hate as humans do," said Sean, "our Shade entities might have turned against us and destroyed us. It would have meant their destruction, too, of course. Yet, we were all victims. Just the same, you can imagine the incredible internal distress the people felt, the guilt, the anger, the outrage and the sheer helplessness. There were quite a few suicides, an unbelievable number when you consider the fact that each of us contains generations of life forces. So many chose the True Death to avoid living with the pain. . . ."

"It must be very hard for you," said Stenmark, "knowing that the men who were responsible are now a part of you."

"That part of me truly does not feel the pain," said Sean. "The Directors still believe that they did the right thing, acted in the best interests of the human race. Fortunately, they are only a small part of me, like a guilty memory of a childhood transgression. Still, they are not forgotten. We need them, you see. Not only do they serve as a living lesson to us all, they helped us accomplish all of this. Without them, we could never have emerged from the ashes of self-recrimination. They gave us the knowledge to do all that we have done. We could do a great deal more, but we do not want to go too quickly. We are still part Shade and have a love for our world the way it is.''

"And you've been protecting it all this time," said Stenmark, "knowing that someday a ColCom ship might come and watching for it.''

"Yes, but not for protection alone," said Sean. "Tonight, we celebrate not only your arrival, which is a momentous occasion in itself, but the arrival of the others from the *Goddard*. We've been waiting for them.''

"What about Viselius? Where is he? You said—"

"That he is not here," said Sean. "He is not on Boomerang at all. To be more exact, he simply *is not*.''

"You killed him?''

"No." Sean shook his head. "In a sense, he killed himself, and in another sense, he simply ceased to exist. However, Jake believes that he has killed him, which is why it is good that Ava is here. There is a kind of healing she can give that we cannot, no matter how strong our powers. You know firsthand how reality can be altered in the zone. I have memories of zone travel from Great Mother Wendy. When our watchers reported that a ship had come at last, many of us assembled to give the Call together. We had prepared for this, knowing that our lives could depend upon it. We had experimented in the past by combining our powers to see how far we could reach. We knew that together, we could reach the ship that had arrived and bring its occupants down to us. We welcomed them and gave them shelter, took them into our homes, treated them like honored guests. Only Jake Thorsen required special treatment. He was in a great deal of distress. It seems that Director Viselius was the cause. There was a man called Tabarde—"

"Yes," said Stenmark, "the same Paul Tabarde who—"

"No," said Sean, "not the same.''

"You're referring to the fact that he possessed an artificial brain—"

"More than that," said Sean. "I know that Paul Tabarde became what is called an inorganic citizen, but that Paul Tabarde was killed. Director Viselius had his agents kill him as he was attempting to leave Earth to find Jake, so that he could warn Shelby. However, he made certain that the brain was undamaged. He programmed the information from that brain into another artificial brain, in the body of another man who was then made to resemble Paul Tabarde. Only this time, he also added program ming that would compel this new Tabarde to act as Viselius agent."

"That's why he was never found," said Stenmark. "Viseliu arranged for his escape."

"Yes. He went on to Morgan's World, where he met Jake an Ava. Viselius had learned that Jake Thorsen was a party to th conspiracy, but he had not known that Jake had never submitte to conditioning at all, that he was capable of ghosting a ship t Boomerang. Tabarde had wiped that information from his memory When this new Tabarde discovered that Jake knew the way t our world, the instructions Viselius had given him were triggered Viselius had not thought that it would be possible for him t arrange to have us all wiped out. He believed that the odds wer very much against it. So, as a safeguard, in the event that hi own machinations proved fruitless, he had directed this Tabard he had essentially created to eliminate anyone who could lea others to Boomerang, meaning Shelby, but also meaning Jake Tabarde was forced to try to kill him. Because of Ava's presence he was unable to be alone with Jake until the ship was en rout to Wheeler's World. Once everyone had entered the cryogens Tabarde made his move. Yet, in spite of this imperative programming, there was enough of the original Tabarde left t resist long enough to warn Jake and tell him what had happened. The only way for Jake to stay alive was to kill Tabarde. Pau tried to make it easier for him. Even as he was failing in hi struggle to resist his programming, he told Jake that the Tabarde he knew was dead, that the being Jake was confronting was simulacrum. His words to Jake, before he succumbed to the inevitable, were that it could not be considered murder to destroy an inorganic citizen, a machine. Jake did not have much time t dwell upon this. Tabarde attacked him and the ship was already heading into the zone. Jake managed to kill Tabarde just as the ship was entering the vortex.

"Terrified that what he had done would interfere with his mindset and cause his concentration to fail and the ship to be lost, Jake's last thoughts before entering his self-induced trance state for zone travel were that he had not murdered Paul Tabarde, that Paul Tabarde had never been aboard his ship, that he had never really existed."

"And that became a part of his reality construct," Fannon said.

"Exactly. When the ship came out of the vortex, there was no trace of Tabarde's body. Jake had altered reality to the extent that Tabarde had, in fact, never been aboard his ship.''

Stenmark exhaled heavily. ''First Shelby's metamorphosis, now mine, and this . . . it brings up frightening possibilities of what zone travel can be used to accomplish.''

''Don't forget us,'' said Wendy. ''We are the direct result of the altering of reality within the zone.''

''Then what happened to Viselius—''

''Was similar,'' said Sean. ''Jake had been conditioned against his will to obey Viselius without question and to ghost the *Goddard* safely to Boomerang. Jake knew what Viselius intended to do. His will is strong, and he resisted. He was unable to disobey Viselius. He could not avoid bringing the *ship* here safely. However, it never occurred to Director Viselius to order Jake to make certain that he, himself, arrived safely.''

''So what Jake did to Tabarde's body by accident, he did to Viselius on purpose,'' Stenmark said.

Sean nodded. ''The captain of the *Goddard* knew that there was a Damocles system aboard his ship, of course, but without Viselius, he could not legally deploy it. It required a Directorial order. Jake knew this. The *Goddard*'s captain would have guessed that Viselius' disappearance was the result of a 'ghosting accident,' though it's doubtful that he would ever have been able to prove that Jake had done it intentionally. He might even have taken it upon himself to deploy the Damocles system, in spite of standing orders. However, all those questions became academic when we contacted the crew of the *Goddard* and induced them all to leave their ship.''

''Poor Thorsen,'' Stenmark said. ''He must have realized then that what he had done was totally unnecessary. He killed Viselius for nothing.''

''That is what he believes, though I cannot agree,'' said Wendy. ''Aside from my obvious prejudice, Viselius had committed an unpardonable crime. He had deprived a man of his free will. He had done it to Tabarde, he had done it to Jake, he had probably done it to others, as well. I cannot mourn for him.''

''I understand that,'' Stenmark said, ''but all things considered, don't you think you're being just a bit hypocritical? Not that I blame you, but—''

''Hypocritical?'' said Sean, with a smile. ''No, not at all. Consider our very existence, which is the direct result of the original Seedlings' loss of their free will. Consider the belief that

was instilled in them, in us, which resulted in the genocide of th
Shades.''

"You have not been what you are now for very long," sa
Wendy. "Your experience as the being that you have becon
dates back only to Shelby's merging, when her Ones Who We
began to learn that they could control their inherent psych
abilities. Yet even the youngest of us have had over a thousa
years in which to learn, in which to contemplate the responsib
ity inherent in what we are able to do. Our esper powers are f
greater than yours. Some of us are stronger than others, which
only natural. We have had to learn how to live with the burd
imposed by our abilities. Do you think our society would hav
survived if we had not developed ethical systems of behavior,
we did not respect everyone's right to free will?"

"What of the free will of our people?" said K'itar. "W
their right to free will, as you call it, respected during yo
bloody Ritual of Transformation, when they were slaughtered :
that you could become what you are now? What of Anderso
Jorgensen, Hermann and Malik, who were forcibly absorbed in
yourselves?"

"Anderson, Jorgensen, Hermann and Malik are now a part
me because their free will was violated, true," said Sean, "b
then they had deprived the five thousand original Seedlings
their free will. In doing so, they brought what happened upc
themselves. There was no reason for their right to free will to b
respected when they had shown total disregard for the rights
others. As for what happened to your people, K'itar, they sti
live on within us. The religion we were given, that we ha
forced upon us, allowed us no free will. That is the danger i
any religion, even in yours. Don't forget how you reacted whe
you were first exposed to humans. They had no Ones Wh
Were. They had never *been* before. They were ignorant of th
Rituals and the Way. They were blasphemous in your sigh
were they not? When a religion tells you what God's will i
whichever God or gods you follow, you are still free to choose
Yet, consider: if your choice, for whatever reason, conflicts wit
what your religion tells you is God's will, what do you do?
you love your God, are you really 'free' to go against His will
If you do, then you are a sinner, damned for having demon
strated that you do not love your God, since you disobeyed H
wishes.''

"Yes, but that's always assuming that you acknowledge

veracity of whoever is telling you what God's will is,'' said Stenmark.

"But that is the very nature of religion, is it not?'' said Sean. "Unless God were to speak to you directly and there were no doubt that it was His voice, religion demands that you accept the word of those who claim that God has spoken to them, whether they be the authors of the Bible, the Koran, the Talmud, the Vedas, the Rituals and the Way or more contemporary prophets who claim some new insight as a result of divine guidance. At some point, you simply have to take the word of a man . . . or a woman or a Shade. That's why it's called faith. It isn't based on knowledge. It requires belief.''

"Then you have become agnostics?'' Stenmark said.

"Not in the literal sense. We do not doubt the possibility of knowing the absolute truth. Neither are we atheists. We do not deny the existence of God. If we subscribe to any doctrine at all, it is one of skepticism. We must continue to live with the pain of what we have done for our faith. When we lost our faith, the way was open for us to question, and only by questioning will anyone ever discover the truth. I am simply skeptical that anyone has discovered the absolute truth *yet*. I have no desire to have faith. I yearn for knowledge, and knowledge cannot be pursued where there is no free will.''

"That's very admirable,'' said Fannon, "but I find such self-righteousness suspect. What about the people from the *Goddard*? Didn't you deny *them* their free will by inducing them to leave their ship and come down here?''

"You haven't changed a bit, Drew,'' Wendy said affectionately. "Don't mistake a rejection of blind adherence to some dogma for self-righteousness. If one seeks to find the truth, one must always question. As for the crew of the *Goddard*, we induced them to come to us, but we did not force them.''

"You're telling us that they came here voluntarily?'' said Fannon.

"Didn't you?''

"Well, yes,'' said Stenmark, "in the sense that we did not resist the Call, but—''

"If you or any of the *Goddard*'s crew had not wanted to come to us,'' said Wendy, "we would not have used our powers to force. We used our abilities to persuade, not to compel. We could have used force to prevent them from deploying the Damocles system, but don't you think that would have been completely justifiable? Besides, when the people on the *Goddard*

discovered that there was sentient life here, *human* life, they
were all horrified at the idea of what they might have done. They
also knew that we could easily compel them to come to us, but
would not." Sean shrugged. "And so they came, even as you
came."

"The real question is," said Stenmark, "now that we're all
here, what do you intend to do about us?"

"To make you welcome for as long as you choose to stay,"
said Sean.

"That implies that we're all free to leave whenever we like,"
said Fannon.

"You are free to leave at any time," said Sean. "You may
leave now, if you wish, but I hope that you will at least stay for
dinner."

"Come on," said Fannon, "you know ColCom as well as I
do. Have you become so powerful that even all of you acting
together could hold off all the people that would come here
seeking immortality? How can you allow any of us to leave? . . .
What's so funny?"

"Forgive me, Drew," said Wendy. "We weren't laughing at
you. We were merely amused by the idea of a mass exodus from
every human world, all of them coming here to become immortal."

"All right, so it wouldn't necessarily work that way, but—"

"We now come to the final question," Sean said. "The final
resolution of the Seedling Project. It's really very simple. You,
Ava Randall and the crew of the *Goddard* are free. You are our
honored guests, not our captives. You are free to remain with us
as long as you wish, forever if you like. You are also free to
leave. We have looked into the minds of the people from the
Goddard, and, not surprisingly, not one of them would want to
leave without having first gained immortality. Some may choose
to stay with us, others will choose to depart. Their wishes will be
respected. All will receive the immortality they wish, becoming
a part of us. There are many among us who would be glad to
merge with them. However, of those who desire to remain here
with us, we will ask only one thing—that they become a part of
us, rather than our becoming a part of them. That is the one
condition. The choice is theirs. Since they all desire to become
immortal, it would mean that they would depart their bodies
eventually anyway. It makes very little difference in the last
analysis. Yet we must insist upon this."

"Why?" said Stenmark.

"Because this is our world," said Sean. "We have a right to

self-determination. Perhaps there would never be any mass exodus of humanity to Boomerang, but we do not wish to contribute to any situation in which immortality would be sold to the highest bidders. We do not wish to contribute to a situation in which there would be even one human being anywhere who would know that immortality could be gained by merging with us, only he or she lacked the means to accomplish this.''

"Only Diane Nakamura said that—"

"Yes, we know," said Sean. "That is why it is essential that the same people, or the same *bodies*, return as those that departed. The people who man the Hansen stations know only that two ships passed through the vortex, and two ships will return. Other ships will have passed through Hansen One, ghosting to other destinations; the crews of Hansen One will not know the details, nor will they care. When the *Southern Cross* and the *Goddard* return, those aboard both ships will report that they never ghosted, and there will be no reason for anyone to doubt them. Remember that the crew of the *Goddard* did not know what their mission was in the first place. There will be no reason for anyone to think that they know anything of Boomerang. Officially, the *Southern Cross* succeeded in contacting the *Goddard* before she could pass through the zone. The Director aboard the *Southern Cross* informed the captain of the *Goddard* that Viselius was acting contrary to the wishes of his fellow Directors, and, being thus caught in the middle, the captain of the *Goddard* went no further and allowed you to come aboard in an effort to clarify the situation. With two Directors giving him conflicting instructions, he decided to make certain of his position by contacting ColCom HQ. Knowing what this would mean, Viselius acted in desperation and killed Shelby Michaels, presumed by Nakamura and Bikovski to have been on board. They know nothing about Jake Thorsen. In attempting to prevent Viselius from killing Shelby, you killed him, but you were a fraction too late." Sean smiled. "Just as I know the events that led to your coming here by looking into your mind, so I also know that there is an official order empowering you to kill Viselius. No one will be able to charge August Stenmark with anything. The bodies of Viselius and Michaels were buried in space, and both ships returned to Earth.''

"You're forgetting one thing," said Stenmark. "There's the rather awkward matter of my physical appearance.''

"We had not forgotten it. Remember that reality can be altered within the zone. Should you choose to remain here, those of us who will occupy your body will create a reality within the vortex in which your body will revert to its original appearance. Their contact with your mind will enable them to act your part with no one being the wiser. Should you choose to leave us, we can help you to strengthen your powers of concentration to accomplish the same ends. Perhaps Shelby could have done the same when she went back, but her will was never very strong, and it obviously never occurred to her.''

"Suppose we like the way we look now?" Fannon said.

Wendy laughed. "Always independent, Drew, always stubborn. Has it occurred to you what would happen if you returned to ColCom HQ looking as you do now?''

"You've got a point," said Fannon. "Strike that. Go on.''

"Officially, the crew of the *Goddard* knew nothing about their mission," Sean said. "Directors Nakamura and Bikovski know nothing about Jake Thorsen. You simply commandeered his ship to go after Viselius. The only one in a position to confirm or deny anything concerning Boomerang will be Director August Stenmark, who will claim never to have heard of Boomerang. Nakamura and Bikovski will rightly interpret this as self-preservation. What would that leave them with? They would have nothing to prove their contention except some computer engram tapes which they could easily have fabricated, tapes which Stenmark will claim never to have seen. They will have no one who is capable of ghosting a ship to Boomerang, since they will believe Shelby Michaels to be dead. They will, in short, have a populace demanding information and will have none to give them. Perhaps they will find a way out of their predicament. Perhaps they will be able to blame some convenient scapegoat. On the other hand, Diane Nakamura was in a panic when you last spoke to her, and she told you that Bikovski had fled. Perhaps they will both simply take the prudent course and disappear. I suspect that they are not without their resources.''

"No," said Stenmark, "as members of the Directorate, they certainly are not. They could easily create new identities for themselves and live out the remainder of their lives in a great deal of comfort.''

"Meanwhile," said Sean, "those who will return will take their place in the society of Earth and of the colonies. They will be immortal, they will be full espers, able to protect themselves and truly able to know the minds of those whom they allow into their lives. They will live out the life spans of their bodies and they will be able to find people with whom they can merge, people whose minds will be open to them, people they will be able to trust. They will have children, who will inherit their abilities, and their children will have children, and so it will continue. The Seedling Project will have come full circle. *We* will have planted the seeds this time. It will occur slowly and it will take place discreetly, but in the end, we shall all be the same and humans will have their immortality and the wisdom and experience of their Ones Who Were. And if, in the meantime, it should happen that any other ships come to us, we shall welcome them as well. We will offer them the same choices and we will send them on again, to spread the seeds. That is what we propose to do. It remains for you to decide. The choice is yours.''

Stenmark smiled. ''For a change, Sean, it's not a difficult decision.''

There were generations in agreement.

Epilogue

The *Southern Cross* and the *Robert H. Goddard* returned to Earth. Stanislas Bikovski, fearing the worst, had prudently disappeared. When Diane Nakamura publicly announced that Director Bikovski had evidently cracked under the strain of his duties and gone insane, announcing the discovery of an imaginary world and an equally imaginary race of immortal beings, he wisely abandoned any plans he might have had of "reappearing." Officially, he had retired from the Directorship, according to Nakamura, and was in seclusion at a private sanitarium, the name and location of which would remain undisclosed. In actuality, Stanislas Bikovski underwent cosmetic surgery and, as a wealthy financier named Stanley Bull, invested in a number of private industries on Demeter, where he lived out the remainder of his life on a palatial estate surrounded by guards. He died at the age of one hundred forty-nine.

Diane Nakamura remained in her position as a Director of ColCom for another five years, until she suffered a lift-tube accident and was killed. Her will specifically forbade the deprogramming of her organic brain and her resurrection as an inorganic citizen. Her body was cremated.

Jake Thorsen and Ava Randall both returned to Morgan's World, where they got married, settled down, and had a large number of astonishingly intelligent and perceptive children.

Roughly one-third of the *Robert H. Goddard*'s crew, including her captain, returned to Earth. The rest remained behind on Boomerang. The seeds were planted.

August Stenmark continued to serve as a Director of ColCom for another fifty years, during which he instituted many changes and improvements in the service, among which were more stringent licensing procedures regarding zone travel and a more intensive training program for ghost pilots. The Damocles system and similar weapons systems were scrapped. ColCom's executive powers were defined more strictly and, in the process, limited. At the age of ninety-six, he retired from the Directorate and purchased a ship. His last official act was to grant himself priority clearance to an unspecified—and therefore unrecorded—destination. He ghosted through Hansen One and was never seen again by anyone on Earth or in the colonies.

Afterword

Recently, I was interviewed for a magazine by a person who was the same age as I am (thirty-one, at this writing) and he told me that he felt that our generation's experiences were very deeply reflected in my work. Now, this was a very nice compliment, but I never did take compliments at face value, and, being a writer, it wasn't enough for me to simply accept it. I had to know *why*. One of the interesting things about the relationship between a writer and his readers is that there is a certain metaphysical communion that results in which the reader may, and often does, get something out of a novel that the writer did not necessarily know was there. What you get out of it depends upon what you bring to it. Therefore, it's dangerous to make any sort of assumptions about your readers. (Other than that, if they read your work with regularity, they must be exceedingly intelligent and perceptive, as well as discriminating.) So, whether or not I actually set out to reflect the experiences of our generation was not the point. The point was, what did he find in my work that made him think so? Feedback is crucial to a writer.

One of the questions he had asked me during the interview was if I had any favorite themes. He said that he got the impression that "concern about manipulation" was a recurring theme in my work. Quite frankly, I had never really been consciously aware of this, but when I thought about it, I realized that he was right. The peculiar thing about the way in which I work is that I never "plot," in the conventional sense of the word. That is to say, I am not one of those writers who, like Agatha Christie, for example, know exactly what is going to happen every step of the way before they ever put paper in the typewriter. In Miss Christie's case, I understand that her favorite method of plotting her mysteries was to draw a bath, set a basket of apples beside it, take pen and clipboard in hand and soak in the tub while she worked out all the details. Writers are strange people anyway, else they would not be writers, and we all have

222

our idiosyncratic ways of getting the job done. Paul Simon, for example, said once that he found that he wrote songs best in the bathroom. (Hmm, a pattern seems to be emerging. A psychology student pursuing a doctorate could probably get a thesis out of this.) Anyway, we all have various things we do that "work" for us, and, in the past, I've tried a good many of them. Some people out there seem to think that I take drugs. I don't. I did once, and they almost did me in, which is why I don't. They don't call it dope for nothing. I once knew a rock musician who became inspired in dreams, woke up in the middle of the night, banged out a song or an idea for a song, then went back to sleep. I tried that. I set up a notepad and a pen by my bedside and went to sleep. I seem to remember coming up with something once, but when I woke up, I found that I had written an indecipherable squiggle. Ah, yes, but being a science fiction writer, I knew about technology. Next time I tried it with a tape recorder. Set it up so that all I had to do was hit the mike and talk. What I found on the tape in the morning sounded like the groaning mumbling of someone who had been on drugs for twenty years. No, none of that stuff works for me. I finally came to the conclusion that I can't work that way at all. I wish I could. It would make life much easier, especially for my wife.

The only sort of crutch that works for me at all is getting on my motorcycle, finding an empty stretch of road, and *cranking* the sucker. But that doesn't generate any ideas. All it does is clear my brain out. (And, sometimes, my wallet. Wonder if I can deduct speeding tickets as a business-related expense?) The way I work is to piddle around on the typewriter until someone comes out. Sometimes it's some*thing*, but more often than not, it's some*one*. Here I was, sitting minding my own business, and suddenly this creature with silvery skin, white hair, and glowing violet cat's eyes is staring me in the face. Needless to say, I regarded this as a great curiosity and I started writing about it so that I could find out what it was. And as I wrote more, I found out more. However, like the reader, I get out of it what I bring to it, and in my case, I bring my experience. Or the experiences of my generation. Which brings me back to the interviewer's question. (Thought I was rambling, huh?)

I had never thought of myself as a person who had been manipulated, but then again, my generation was manipulated six ways from Sunday. Those of you who are my age or thereabouts know perfectly well what I'm talking about. The sixties was a great decade for energy and creativity and social consciousness,

but it was also a great decade for manipulation, which paved th
way for the seventies and its cults. Our generation was manipu
lated by drugs, by a government that saw nothing wrong wit
coercing many of us into fighting a war we did not believe i
(coercion is the cornerstone of government anyway, but that'
another argument), manipulated by gurus, Yippie leaders, Hippi
leaders, YAF leaders, religious leaders, counterculture leaders
leaders of the *avant-garde* and the media in general. Perhap
the only people who *really* understood the sixties were Tor
Wolfe and Marshal McLuhan, and possibly John Lennon, wh
understood real well what happened to leaders, which was wh
he didn't want to be one. But understanding didn't save him, di
it? He was manipulated right into an early grave, along wit
other leaders of the time who probably believed that they wer
above being manipulated.

No one is above it, especially in a society in which one of th
worst things one can say about anybody is that he or she i
useless, in which we're trained to be useful members of society
which implies that all of us are meant to be used. Imaginar
scenario: the breakup of a relationship. The woman confronts th
man, feeling outraged, hurt, rejected, and says, "You *use*
me!" The man replies, "Of course. I was trained to."

If what I've written in this book elicited emotional response
from you, if I've made you think, or if I've merely entertaine
you, I've manipulated you. If you didn't like this book, you ma
be feeling sorry that you bought it because you were manipulate
by the cover and the jacket copy into thinking that you woul
enjoy it. Even in something as seemingly inconsequential a
buying a book and reading it, there's no escape. If you believ
that you can't be manipulated, then you most certainly will be
Because, in the words of Robert Anton Wilson, "Whatever yo
believe, imprisons you."

Think about it.

Nicholas Yermako
Denver, Colorad